Annie opened a sm

"I surveyed a few residents," she began. "I believe their spirits can be improved by something as simple as home face-lifts, like the one I've started. Fresh paint. Maybe new drapes. Possibly some rosebushes and weeded yards. Those things take sweat equity."

"And money. Paint isn't free. Cosmetic changes won't break the stranglehold gangs have on local teens. If you want to do something meaningful, get me the names of the gang leaders."

Annie and Sky faced off across the table. "Maybe the gang leaders will give up and move on if we create the kind of community where families want to live. Restore hope."

"Perhaps that's true in prosperous neighborhoods. Did any of the residents you talked to tell you how many hours a day they spend riding buses back and forth into Louisville to work at minimum-wage jobs that barely put food on their tables? Those privileged few who actually *found* new jobs?"

"I haven't totally gained their trust yet," Annie admitted. "But I plan to. I thought I'd distribute flyers inviting residents to a meeting where I can lay out my ideas in greater detail."

"Good luck."

"I *had* hoped I could enlist your support."

He clattered down the steps and strode down the walkway without so much as a backward glance.

Dear Reader,

A lot of writers say that a story will come to life fully formed in their minds. For me, more often the characters appear first and then I need to find them a home. *Annie's Neighborhood* was different. The houses in her neighborhood came first.

Whenever I travel, I do so with a tour book of the state in hand. On a trip to Kentucky I wanted to see the home of the Kentucky Derby. We'd just missed the race, but the immediate area was still decked out in new paint and roses. On leaving Churchill Downs, we wound through a warren of streets lined with older Victorian houses. The once-vibrant neighborhood looked faded. Homes needed paint. Retaining walls were cracked and overgrown with vines. Lovely stained-glass dormer windows looked dull, and wrought-iron fencing was rusted. The greater city of Louisville, built by immigrants who worked in manufacturing, was a city in transition. A news article said some areas were battling an infiltration of gangs. But even as we left the state I kept thinking about those homes, about how beautiful they could be. Maybe they are now.

My story of course is a total work of fiction, and Annie's a character who rattled around in my head for quite a while. She had a murky background and needed roots. She needed my faded homes.

And because I write love stories, independent though Annie is, she needed a family. Who better than a once-burned, jaded cop? Sky Cordova is in the middle of a custody fight with his ex. He's also trying to keep the peace in a dying community populated by apathetic homeowners cowed by defiant gangs. And then Annie Emerson shows up! She's testament to the fact that big changes begin with small ones—when it comes to houses *and* hearts.

And that's how this story was born. I'm glad Harlequin Heartwarming provided it with a home. I love to hear from readers. Contact me via email at rdfox@cox.net, or by writing to me at 7739 E. Broadway Blvd. #101, Tucson, AZ 85710-3941.

Sincerely,

Roz

HARLEQUIN HEARTWARMING

Roz Denny Fox

Annie's Neighborhood

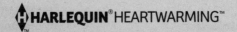

Recycling programs
for this product may
not exist in your area.

ISBN-13: 978-0-373-36631-6

ANNIE'S NEIGHBORHOOD

HARLEQUIN®

www.Harlequin.com

Printed in U.S.A.

ROZ DENNY FOX

Roz saw her first book, *Red Hot Pepper*, published by Harlequin in February 1990. She's written for several Harlequin series, as well as online serials and special projects. Besides being a writer, Roz has worked as a medical secretary and as an administrative assistant in both an elementary school and a community college. Part of her love for writing came from moving around with her husband during his tenure in the marine corps and as a telephone engineer. The richness of settings and the diversity of friendships she experienced continue to make their way into her stories. Roz enjoys corresponding with readers either via email, rdfox@cox.net, or by mail (7739 E. Broadway Blvd. #101, Tucson, AZ 85710-3941). You can also check her website, www.Korynna.com/RozFox.

Books by Roz Denny Fox

HARLEQUIN HEARTWARMING

HEARTS ENTWINED
THE WESTERN DARE
THE BOSS NEXT DOOR
THE HOPE DRESS

HARLEQUIN EVERLASTING

A SECRET TO TELL YOU

HARLEQUIN AMERICAN ROMANCE

1036–TOO MANY BROTHERS
1087–THE SECRET WEDDING DRESS
1185–THE PERFECT TREE
       "Noelle and the Wise Man"
1404–THE MAVERICK RETURNS

HARLEQUIN SUPERROMANCE

1128–THE SECRET DAUGHTER
1148–MARRIED IN HASTE
1184–A COWBOY AT HEART
1220–DADDY'S LITTLE MATCHMAKER
1254–SHE WALKS THE LINE
1290–A MOM FOR MATTHEW
1320–MORE TO TEXAS THAN COWBOYS
1368–ANGELS OF THE BIG SKY
1388–ON ANGEL WINGS
1412–REAL COWBOYS
1459–LOOKING FOR SOPHIE
1509–MORE THAN A MEMORY
1518–A TEXAS-MADE FAMILY
1586–THE BABY ALBUM

I'd like to take this opportunity to thank Executive Editor Paula Eykelhof, my editor of many years, as well as Victoria Curran, Heartwarming senior editor, and Marsha Zinberg, Executive Editor of Special Projects, for the time and work they devote to acquiring and publishing good stories so many readers enjoy.

CHAPTER ONE

ANNIE EMERSON WAS the lone occupant in the family car traveling behind the hearse that carried her grandmother to her final resting place. She stared numbly out a tinted side window. At the church, old friends of Ida Vance had said that at eighty-eight she'd lived a full, happy, productive life. But Gran Ida, as everyone called her, was Annie's only known relative, and Annie wasn't prepared to say goodbye.

She felt like a stranger in Briar Run, a small town bordering Louisville, Kentucky, where she'd grown up, and where Gran Ida had lived for nearly seventy years. Soon her grandmother would rest beside the man she'd loved and honored all those years, even though John Vance had died in World War II.

As the car crawled along, Annie reflected on the little she really knew about the woman who'd raised her from infancy. Ida didn't dwell on the past. In fact, it wasn't until after Annie had sought and accepted a scholarship to UCLA—

half a country away in California—that Ida
deigned to share a bit of Annie's own history.
Gran got out an old photo album and showed
Annie pictures of her grandfather, John, who'd
come home to Kentucky on leave before World
War II turned really ugly. He had bought the
Victorian home, then left again to fight and die
before Ida discovered she was pregnant with a
daughter from whom, sadly, she'd be estranged
for many years. *That daughter had been Annie's
mother, but she still knew next to nothing about
Mary Louise Emerson.* Because Annie had bad-
gered her, Gran admitted that the girl who'd run
away at sixteen with an itinerant musician had
reappeared at her door one rainy night seventeen years later, ill, pregnant and penniless; she
swore she was married and her last name was
Emerson. Later, weakened by a difficult birth,
Mary Louise died without providing proof of
any marriage.

That had all taken place thirty-four years
ago—her entire lifetime, Annie thought, wiping away tears of grief. For the past fourteen
years she'd lived and worked in L.A. The truth
was that she'd fled Briar Run because the boy
she'd dated for two years and was sure she loved
and loved her in return had let his parents break
them up over Annie's iffy parentage. That cre-

ated a grievance, which stuck with her long after Gran Ida informed her Brock Barnard and his family had moved away. The hurt went so deep, Annie hadn't been able to come back to Briar Run even for short visits until two weeks ago, when it became clear that Gran desperately needed her.

During those intervening years she had earned a master's in social work, and had taken a job in L.A. Her hours as a caseworker in a depressed area were horrendous. Her original aim had been to help young women like her mother. In the back of her mind, she'd foolishly imagined finding her father—which never happened. Letting an unknown, uncaring dad and Brock Barnard's rejection drive her decisions for so long made no sense. And now, too late, Annie wrestled with guilt for avoiding Briar Run all this time.

And why hadn't she insisted Gran come and live with her? Maybe she could have gotten her the kind of medical care that might have prolonged her life. Gran loved her yearly visits to the coast, and Annie always sent her plane tickets. But Gran never stayed for more than a month. For the remainder of the year they spoke on the phone every Sunday evening. That felt like a cop-out now. *She should have noticed signs of heart trouble during Gran Ida's last visit.* She'd chalked up Gran's occasional memory lapses to old age. Annie truly hadn't suspected something might be seriously wrong. Not until a neighbor called to say Ida had trouble finding her way home from the grocery store. Or she'd put a kettle of water on the stove and let it burn dry. Annie had immediately phoned Gran's doctor. He'd said bluntly that Annie needed to come to Kentucky and arrange assisted living for Ida, whose arteries were hardening—arteriosclerotic heart disease, he'd called it.

Taking any time off meant Annie had to dump her caseload on her overburdened coworkers—which took her a while. Then, after she got here, Gran flatly refused to discuss moving to a senior center anywhere, certainly not one in California. In fact, these past two weeks Gran had talked and acted as if Annie'd come home to stay.

The car stopped behind the hearse, next to a grassy knoll where a blue canopy stood. Annie's mind blanked when the funeral director opened her door, helped her out and led her to where Ida's pastor waited at the head of an open grave. Copious tears clogged her throat. Few people had come to the graveside service. Annie acknowledged Ida's next-door neighbors, the Gilroys and the Spurlocks. There was a well-dressed older gentleman she recalled seeing at church, but she didn't know him.

After the minister wound down a short eulogy, too short in Annie's estimation, mourners murmured condolences and drifted away. Annie hadn't planned a reception. First, she didn't think she could face one. Also, even Gran Ida had said a lot of their old friends and neighbors had moved away.

Annie bent to place a long-stemmed white rose on Gran Ida's casket. Gran Ida loved flowers, roses in particular.

The well-dressed stranger approached as Annie straightened. He gave her a business card, saying, "I'm Oliver Manchester, Ms. Emerson. I handle your grandmother's legal affairs. We should meet at your earliest convenience to go over Ida's will, you being her only heir," he said.

Annie had been so grief-stricken by Gran's death, she hadn't thought beyond arranging a funeral. She read the man's card and tried to compose her response. "I, ah, left my rental car at the funeral home. If you're free at one o'clock," she said after a glance at her watch, "I can stop by. I'm anxious to get everything sorted out because I need to get back to my job in L.A. as soon as possible. I only arranged for a four-week leave."

"One o'clock is good. Our meeting shouldn't take long. I must admit, though, I was under the impression that you weren't returning to California. When Ida phoned me to say you were coming, she indicated you'd be staying on to help revive the neighborhood."

Annie frowned. Her grandmother had said something similar to her several times. She hadn't argued, and now there seemed no point in making excuses to Mr. Manchester. She tucked his business card in her purse without further comment, and watched him walk to a dark blue sedan. As he drove away, Annie belatedly wished she'd asked if her grandmother had many outstanding bills. Oh, well, it didn't matter; she was prepared to settle them. For a number of years she'd sent Gran Ida regular checks to cover rising food and living costs. Considering how badly the once-pristine home needed painting, Annie wished she'd sent more. What she really wished was that she'd made time to visit. Once again her heart constricted with guilt. If Gran had ever said she needed her, Annie would've come. Now all that might have enticed her to stay was gone.

IT WAS TEN after one when Annie jockeyed her subcompact rental car into an on-street parking spot outside Oliver Manchester's office. Climbing out, she paused to lock the door, and tightened her grip on her purse; she'd noticed that all the offices and shops had iron grates installed over their doors and windows.

She racked her brain, but couldn't recall Gran's ever mentioning the town's business district going downhill.

At the barred door, Annie read a typed sign instructing callers to push a buzzer for admission. Strangely this reminded her of the area where she worked—in the tough, run-down neighborhoods of south L.A.

A woman opened the door and unlocked the outer grate after Annie supplied her name. "Mr. Manchester's expecting you," she said. "Would you care for coffee, or perhaps a cold soda, before you go into your meeting?" She smiled at Annie as she relocked the grate.

"No, thank you. Mr. Manchester told me he didn't expect this to take long."

Nodding, the woman opened a door and announced Annie's arrival. She stood aside, letting her enter a private office. The attorney's office was posh in the manner of old-time Southern aristocrats. The dark green pile carpet was deep. Leather chairs and an oversize mahogany desk befitted a well-to-do lawyer. Oil paintings graced his walls, and crystal decanters sparkled on a corner bar. It was easy to see why Manchester wanted to protect his belongings with bars.

He came around his desk to pull out a chair for Annie. "I've gathered all of Ida's files," he said, retaking his seat. He opened a manila folder and indicated a spreadsheet on his computer screen.

Annie blanched. Surely Gran Ida couldn't be so much in arrears that it required a spreadsheet.

"I'm sure you know Ida worked as a lead seamstress for a local lingerie factory until it went out of business."

"Yes." Annie's voice reflected a modicum of pride. "During my senior year of high school, Gran was honored as the company's longest-serving employee. Her award was a brand-new sewing machine we put to good use sewing my college wardrobe."

"Ida could have retired well before then. She was fifty-six when you came into her life, and she felt the need to prove to Family Services that she was able to care for you."

"For which I'm grateful." Annie smiled.

The lawyer cleared his throat. "Ida bequeathed

you the house, of course. It's a bit of an albatross, I'm afraid, given how this community has declined in the three years since the glove factory, our last major employer, shut down."

Annie opened her purse. "Mr. Manchester, I don't make a huge salary as a social worker. Neither do I have time to spend everything I earn. I'm ready to cover any bills Gran Ida left unpaid. Should they add up to more than I expect, I'll take out a loan. If you'll provide me with a full accounting of her debts, I'll begin paying them today."

Leaning back, the man lowered his glasses and stared at Annie. "You mean you aren't aware that in addition to her home, Ida has left you annuities and tax-free municipal bonds totaling nearly a million dollars?"

Annie's jaw dropped and her purse slipped off her lap to hit the carpet with a dull thud. She swallowed a lump that rose in her throat and bent quickly to hide a rush of tears. When she straightened, she had to dash them away, all the while shaking her head in denial.

"I can see you had no idea," Manchester said, turning to print what was on his computer screen.

"N-no," Annie stammered. "How...how can that be?" she asked, fumbling out a tissue. "Gran's salary was modest. And she's been retired for years."

"Ida made her first will when John died. She funded her first annuity with his military death benefit. Saving was important to her. The only time she skipped funding what she called her nest egg was after Mary Louise ran off with that guitar player. Ida dipped into it to find her daughter. A private investigator she hired did locate Mary Louise living in a tent on the west coast. She made plain that she hated Kentucky, and told the P.I. she had no intention of ever returning. It almost broke Ida's heart, but she rallied, cut Mary Louise out of her will and resumed her investments." The lawyer passed Annie a sheaf of papers. "Ida eventually forgave your mother, because you turned out to be the gift that gave her life purpose."

"I knew some of that. Not that Gran Ida tracked down…my mother." Annie looked blindly at rows of figures that blurred. Figures showing, among other things, that Gran had also invested every penny Annie had sent her over the years. "I never felt we lived frugally," Annie murmured. "Gran Ida was lavish with her love and she convinced me I could do anything I set my mind to, although she didn't really want me going away to college. Letting me go was generous—I understand that better now. Forgive me, Mr. Manchester, but this is too much for me to take in right now. I need to go back to the house, think about all of this, and I'll contact you again in a day or so."

He stood at once. "By all means. If it matters, I do know Ida's greatest hope was that you'd live here and use your many skills to help families in Briar Run rebuild this community she loved so much. I realize that's a tall order," he added.

"I have a job. Gran is gone, and anyway, I'm not sure what she thought I could do..." Annie's voice trailed off.

"Well, I don't blame you. I'm retiring in a few months, and will be moving to Florida. This fund Ida built up will allow you to enjoy a very comfortable life, Annie."

Something in his comment annoyed her. Was he suggesting she do nothing and live off her grandmother's largess? The very notion grated all the way back to Ida's house. *Her house now.* She pulled into the drive, stopped and rubbed at her temples, where a headache was starting. As she left the car, she realized there was a flurry of activity at the homes on either side of Gran's. The Spurlocks, a young, newly married couple, and the Gilroys, longtime retired friends of Ida's, had work vehicles parked in their driveways. Locksmiths, according to signs on a panel truck, and a glass company apparently replacing broken windows on her neighbors' homes.

The women saw her, and hurried over. That was when Annie saw her front door standing agape. By then her shoes had crunched broken glass on the porch. "What happened?" she asked Peggy Gilroy, who was first to reach the steps.

"Break-ins," Peggy announced. "When we were at Ida's funeral. I'm glad you got home while the workmen are still here. You'll need to arrange repairs before dark, Annie. We scared the intruders off when we pulled in. I should have told you not to list Ida's funeral service in the paper. That was like an open invitation to gang members."

"We have gangs? I knew Louisville had problems, but Gran Ida never said a word about Briar Run. I suppose she didn't want to worry me." Annie glanced from one to the other of the women, and both nodded. Annie then turned to their husbands, who remained with the workmen. "Did you report this to the police for all of us?"

The two women facing her exchanged worried frowns. "It might not be the best avenue," Peggy said quickly. "The gang is run by bad elements out of Louisville. They've gained a foothold here over the past year. Our shrinking police force has enough trouble dealing with serious crime—worse things than broken windows and a few stolen electronics. Just do the repairs and lie low, Annie, so we don't attract the gangs' attention."

"Are you *kidding?* Three houses vandalized and the local cops can't be bothered to do anything about it? I think not." She hauled out her cell phone and punched in 9-1-1. As Peggy and Missy hurried away, still looking concerned, Annie paced back and forth on her porch, kicking at broken glass. She waved one hand in the air as she impressed on the dispatcher that they needed police intervention ASAP. Then she peered inside at all the things strewn around, but decided it was best not to touch anything.

THIRTY-FIVE-YEAR-OLD police chief Skylar Cordova took a call from his dispatcher about a series of daytime home break-ins. He stifled a weary sigh, took down the addresses, then asked the dispatcher to contact Lieutenant Koot Talmage, his second-in-command, to meet him at the scene. Talmage was a good, competent cop, even if he'd told Sky that he was only waiting it out until his retirement at the end of the year.

This wasn't Sky's first job choice. He'd been an army reservist called up from his big-city police job in Baltimore to serve his country. By the time he'd finished two tours in Iraq and one in Afghanistan, with months between tours spent at a variety of military bases, his old job, out of necessity, had been filled, although his captain had tried to save it. Since Corrine, Sky's wife, divorced him while he was gone and subsequently married a bigwig Kentucky racehorse breeder, this job put Sky as close to his five-year-old son, Zachary, as he'd been able to manage.

He'd been chief of Briar Run less than a year, but it hadn't taken him very long to see that his force couldn't handle the escalating crime being directed from outside his legal reach in Louisville. Reciprocal help was a joke; it meant when Louisville cops had time, and they were up to their eyeballs, too.

Out of self-interest, Sky had feelers out, hoping to turn up a job in a larger town, with a force that offered a bigger staff. However, in this slow economy police departments everywhere were cutting back, not expanding, as was the case here. His already minuscule force had been cut in half again in the last budgetary process, implemented by Aaron Loomis, the new city manager who'd been appointed by the governor to pull Briar Run out of debt.

Sky pulled up to a trio of homes that had seen better days. In fact, this whole street, like many in the neighborhood—including his, a few blocks away—looked as tired as he felt.

Koot drove in and parked behind him as Sky picked up his clipboard of report sheets. Shoving his sunglasses off the bridge of his nose into shaggy hair he hadn't found time to get cut, Sky waited for his friend and coworker to join him.

The older man came up, blotting sweat from his cocoa-brown face. "Enid called me from dispatch. She said three homes in a row were vandalized while the occupants attended a funeral. Whose work do you reckon it is?"

"I don't know. I just got here and haven't interviewed anyone yet." Sky started to say more, but broke off as a woman separated herself from a foursome watching workmen install a window. She came toward them, undoing her hair from a band that had confined it. Sky's attention stalled on thick, black waves unraveling around her shoulders, hair that shone almost blue in the sunlight. She was tall, but not quite as tall as his five feet eleven, even though she wore heels. A no-nonsense navy suit didn't hide her womanly shape. He couldn't help staring as she approached. The closer she got, the more Sky was mesmerized by her flawless skin and smoke-gray eyes fringed by jet dark lashes. Obviously natural lashes. In this job he often dealt with women who achieved that look with stuff that came in a tube and tended to smear when they cried. Women he encountered in the course of a workday were always crying, it seemed.

The woman stopped a few feet short of the men. "I'm Annie Emerson," she said straightaway. "I called to report the fact that three homes were broken into and vandalized while we all attended my grandmother's funeral."

"I'm sorry for your loss," Sky muttered, unable to quit staring at her long enough to write her name on the report sheet, until Koot jabbed him none too gently in the ribs. "Ah, yes. We, uh, got the call. I'm Chief Sky Cordova. This is Lieutenant Talmage."

Annie lifted an eyebrow. His hasty condolence fell a bit flat. She knew his job probably had him mouthing the words on a regular basis, but his perfunctory tone got under her skin. "I didn't expect such high-ranking officials to show up. Mrs. Gilroy—" Annie pointed to the older of the two other women at the scene "—felt you'd be too busy to come at all."

"Our department is small, and we're stretched thin," Koot explained. "We can see your exterior vandalism. Can you tell us what's missing from inside? And did anyone see the perpetrators or their car, or get any kind of useful description?"

Annie hesitated. "As I said, I was at my grandmother's funeral, and the others left before me, arriving home first. The center house belongs to my grandmother, Ida Vance," Annie said, then with trembling lips corrected and stammered, "N-no, that's not true. It's my home now."

Sky glanced up from the sheet on which he was scribbling. "Is it Miss or Mrs. Emerson?"

"Ms.," she said. Was he trying to learn her marital status? Why? None of his business in any case. "You should speak to Peggy and George Gilroy or Mike and Missy Spurlock. I didn't go in because I didn't want to disturb any evidence. I assume my neighbors came home straight from the cemetery." Annie chewed on her lip. "That would've been a little before one o'clock. Instead of calling the police, they contacted repairmen." Gazing directly at Sky, Annie added, "I gathered they thought contacting you was pointless."

Sky bristled, immediately going on the defensive. "At the moment, I and three officers cover all of Briar Run. Our open cases consist of two rapes, an unsolved drive-by shooting and a couple of gang-related drug deals," he said, waving his pen. "Petty crimes do sometimes get wait-listed."

The woman facing him didn't so much as flinch, which made Sky wonder about her. He thought most females would. "You call a bold, daytime break-in of three homes, with wanton destruction of property, a *petty crime?*"

Koot grabbed Sky's arm and tugged him toward the two couples who stood by the houses. "I'll dust these places for fingerprints as soon as we collect a list of missing items, Chief."

Sky nodded, still gritting his teeth.

George Gilroy leaned on his cane, and looked uncomfortable when the two cops joined him. After a bit of probing, he admitted, "We lost a TV, a DVD player and a pearl necklace Peggy had left out on her dresser. The thieves grabbed the easy stuff."

Peggy piped up. "But other things got broken. Some dishes seemed to be randomly swept off our sideboard."

"Ms. Emerson guessed you got home around one," Sky said. "It's three now. Were the perpetrators gone when you arrived?"

"Hi, I'm Mike Spurlock." The younger man barged into the group. "The thieves must've heard us drive in, or else they had a lookout posted. I noticed our broken windows and told

Missy to stay in the car. I entered the house through a side door, and saw our back door swinging as if they'd just run out. After I made sure there was no one inside, I had my wife come in to make a note of what all they took."

"Our new flat-screen TV is gone, along with some wedding gifts I hadn't even taken out of their boxes," Missy said tearfully. "A vase, a duplicate coffeemaker I intended to return. We're starting out our married life and don't own much yet." Missy Spurlock curled into her husband's embrace.

Sky, who was scribbling everything down, turned to Annie. "What was taken from your place?"

"I told you I didn't go inside. And even if I went from room to room, I might not know what's missing."

"Why not?"

"I'm visiting, or I have been for two weeks. This is the home where I grew up, but I, ah, have been living in California until I came to see about my grandmother's health."

Sky tapped his pen impatiently on the clipboard again. "You can't say what's gone, yet you were most adamant about wanting us to solve this case. The truth is, Ms. Emerson, odds are everything stolen today has already been hocked and the money divvied up."

"It sounds as if you know who did this. So, can't you round them up for questioning?"

Pretty as she was, her barbs got Sky's back up. "It's an all-too-familiar pattern," he admitted. "If I were a betting man, which I'm not, my money would go on poor, dumb, local kids acting as puppets controlled by drug-dealer puppeteers from Louisville. Oh, I'd like to knock some sense into these kids—tell them they're lucky to have folks, whether or not the family has trouble making ends meet. They have a roof over their heads and food in their bellies, which is a lot more than kids I've seen in war-torn countries where families subsist on nothing. You, Ms. Emerson, would be wise to cut your losses here and hightail it back to your safe haven in California."

"Well, thank you for the three-minute lecture, Chief Cordova. I applaud you for serving our country, as you apparently did. May I point out that your current job is to serve the taxpayers of Briar Run? If these are local kids going down the wrong path, it seems to me part of your job should be to show them a better one… by example."

Koot Talmage, who'd returned from dusting

around Annie's door and windows, listened to their conversation—along with her neighbors. Talmage nudged his boss. "Why don't you head out, Chief? I'll wind up here, go to the office and type these reports. We can keep an ear to the ground. I doubt it'll yield anything helpful, but the word will go out about who we suspect."

Sky shook off Koot's hand. He continued to glare at the woman whose intelligent gray eyes remained locked on him. Sky had to say he found Annie Emerson irritating, although definitely attractive. He hadn't taken such a long look at any woman in quite a while. Not since Corrine's defection led to the outright lies she continued to tell the family court about him. Ms. Emerson's dig, as well as Koot's blasé attitude, and yes, also his own hostile one, woke a sleeping noble-mindedness in Sky—something he thought he'd lost. An innate sense of justice that first made him serve his fellow man in law enforcement and then in the military resurfaced now. It surprised him that the glimmer still existed inside him and burned hot enough to spark a response, considering the carnage he'd witnessed and lived through during two wars. Yet there it was.

"I suggest, Ms. Emerson, that you make a list of missing goods and get it to us. Rest assured,

I *will* find the culprit or culprits, retrieve your stolen property and bring the perpetrators to justice," he promised, glancing at the other couples before he spun on his boot heel and strode back to his car.

Koot, slower to react, muttered goodbye and rushed to catch up to his rapidly retreating boss. "Chief, have you lost your ever-lovin' mind? Why on earth would you give our word that we'll solve a crime that's virtually impossible to solve?"

"Because the lady's right. It's our job." Sky opened his car and tossed the clipboard inside. Following it, he slammed his car door and drove off. He didn't tell Koot he intended to dig into this case on his own, in his spare time. Anything he could find would give him a legitimate reason to go back and check on Annie Emerson. He was bothered by a look she had about her that suggested she might take matters into her own hands—making her a lamb in this den of jackals. She ought to return to California for her own good. *And his.* He'd growled at her for no good reason other than he found her attractive and that bugged him.

Perhaps if he went back when he was in a calmer frame of mind, he could convince her that this community wasn't safe for a woman like her, especially a woman who planned to live alone in that big, old ramshackle house. Presuming she lived alone. She hadn't said so, but then he hadn't asked, either. That bugged him, too. Although, of course—as she'd likely point out—it was none of his business.

ARMS CROSSED, ANNIE stared after the arrogant cop's car until it disappeared around the corner.

George Gilroy watched her. "I believe you hit a sore spot with Chief Cordova, Annie. He's right, in one sense. This town's gone to the dogs. Peggy and I could sell and move. Our son wants us to come to Dallas, but this is home. We have good memories of raising our boy here—well, he's over forty now—and moving to a big city at our age is kind of frightening," he lamented with a sad shake of his head.

Annie commiserated with the couple who'd been good friends to Gran Ida and to her. Peggy Gilroy, younger than her husband by ten or so years, had taught Annie how to cook, and often looked after her until Gran Ida got home from work.

Still in a bad mood, Annie negotiated with the locksmith and the glass company for her repairs. While they did them, she wandered along the sidewalk, studying the homes that had once looked so much nicer. All needed paint. Yards were weedy and several houses had tattered drapes in the windows. Annie remembered that Gran had mentioned neighbors losing their jobs when the glove factory closed.

Walking back home, Annie saw a battered bike at one house, and a rusted wagon outside another. It struck her that her old neighborhood had become similar to the ones she served in L.A. Maybe Gran Ida was right to suggest she stay and try to help. Gran was gone, but Annie's roots were sunk deep in this neighborhood.

As Mr. Manchester had pointed out, Gran Ida was well past middle age when she'd taken on raising a baby alone. He'd said Gran had fended off Family Services in order to keep Annie. She imagined the trials and tribulations an older woman would have had to navigate. At fifty-six, Gran had stood at a crossroad, her choices either to give her errant daughter's newborn up for adoption, or devote her later years to nurturing an energetic child. Gran Ida had chosen Annie.

Back at the Victorian, Annie paid the workmen and went inside to meander through the rooms. She ran a hand over a scarred table where she'd done her homework, and where Gran set up a sewing machine to teach her to sew. Gran read to her by the light of the fire-place on wintry nights when Annie was frightened by ice storms that knocked out their power. She must have done that after coming home exhausted from tedious sewing all day on delicate lingerie fabrics.

Going into the vintage kitchen, Annie filled the teakettle, and while water heated, she considered Gran's legacy—a stately old house with worn contents, but a flush bank account…and dreams. Big dreams. Glancing out the window, as lights came on in houses along the street, Annie felt she, too, stood at a crossroad. She could abandon this house after donating its contents and use Gran's money to enhance her life in L.A. Or, as Gran Ida had frequently stressed in her final days, Annie could stay and try to restore the neighborhood. Try to return it to the happy place it had once been.

CHAPTER TWO

IT TOOK SKY over a week to track down some of the goods stolen from the trio of families on Rose Arbor Street. By tracing serial numbers, he found the two TVs at an obscure pawn shop across the border in Indiana. The broker brought out a cherrywood chest filled with silverware for twelve, which he said he'd also taken from the man who'd pawned the TV—a regular-looking guy claiming to be down on his luck. That was always the standard story. Sky didn't have any silver on his list, but he redeemed the ticket in case it belonged to one of the couples.

As he left the pawn shop with the merchandise, he admitted it felt good to have made progress via old-fashioned legwork. It had been quite a while since he'd felt like this—good about his job. Maybe he'd let too much slide lately. Granted, he didn't recognize the pawnbroker's description of the guy who'd pawned these things, but Sky assumed the actual thieves were local kids who turned over the wares to gang leaders. The leaders were known to stay in the background during robberies or other crimes. It burned him to have a gang like that operating under his nose. *Any gang.* The one called the *Stingers* needed to be stopped. It was a particularly notorious one that had come to his attention numerous times.

Drumming his fingers on the steering wheel, Sky pondered the steps his small department could take to start rooting out these sleazy leaders. It shouldn't have been possible for three families to be burgled so openly in the middle of an otherwise normal day.

Entering his neighborhood, he started to wonder if Annie Emerson had packed up and gone back to California. He'd avoided her street since the break-ins for reasons he didn't care to examine. Now, thinking she might have been a one-time blip on his radar, he felt a small sting of regret. If he was honest about it, their brief encounter had been scintillating—and intriguing. Yet he deliberately hadn't looked her up since then, because he'd closed off that part of his life. He hadn't let himself feel anything for a woman since his marriage fell apart—through what he believed was little fault of his. It represented a failure all the same.

Sky turned at the traffic light at the corner of

Rose Arbor and Dusty Rose. Ah, Annie Emerson hadn't gone anywhere. Approaching her old Victorian, he saw her at the front of the house as she sanded peeling paint from the lower siding. He parked, got out of his cruiser, and as he headed up the walkway to speak to her, he realized her noisy electric sander blocked the sound of his footsteps. Reaching out, he tapped her shoulder to announce his presence.

Annie yelped and flung the sander down.

It struck Sky on the shin. In the corner of his mind that wasn't registering pain, he was thankful the sander had an automatic shutoff, or it would've have done serious damage to his leg. With that thought whirling in his head, he wasn't aware that his grip on Ms. Emerson's shoulder had tightened, and he wasn't at all prepared when, without turning, she grabbed his wrist, jabbed her pointy elbow into his solar plexus and sent him flying. Even as he flipped through the air, Sky had no idea what had happened until he found himself lying flat on his back, staring into the blinding sun without his sunglasses. Then his world blurred as the toe of Annie's sneaker on his throat cut off his blood supply. The pretty face he remembered swam before him. Today, her arresting gray eyes were obscured by the bill of a Dodgers baseball cap.

In martial arts fighting stance, Annie peered down into the stunned blue eyes of the police chief. "For heaven's sake, what were you thinking, sneaking up behind me like that?" she demanded, yanking out earbuds attached to an iPod tucked into her shirt pocket.

Hearing him gasp for air, she lifted her sneaker from his neck. As he continued to blink up in confusion, she extended a hand to help him to his feet.

Sky ignored her offer. Shaking his head to clear the cobwebs, he eased up on one elbow until he finally fit together the series of events that had landed him in this predicament. Chagrinned, he cast a stealthy glance up and down the street to see who might have witnessed his ignominious takedown at the hands of a woman. *Thank goodness no one else was around.* Only then did he allow himself to feel grudgingly impressed.

It took a moment before he vaulted up and dusted off the seat of his pants. Fleeting admiration already gone, and needing to counter his embarrassment, Sky shouted back at her. "What were *you* thinking, leaving yourself exposed to anyone who might be up to no good? You know young toughs roam these streets looking for easy marks, which you were. Between the blasting music and sander noise, you were totally zoned out."

"Brother! Talk about arrogance." Annie settled both fists on her hips.

"What would you have done if I'd been a thug? A thug with backup. I'm talking about gangs, lady. You were a sitting duck!"

Annie pointed a thumb at herself. "For your information, I've spent eight years doing social work on some pretty mean streets in L.A. Not to brag, but I hold a one-stripe red belt in tae kwon do. I figure I can take care of myself."

"Big deal," Sky snapped, snatching self-righteousness from the air that sizzled between them. "Martial arts moves aren't an effective defense against a group of hoodlums packing heat."

"You're right," Annie said. Backing down at once, she bent to retrieve her fallen sander. "I'm sure you didn't intend to scare me half to death, and I'm just as sure you didn't drop by to get involved in a shouting match. To what do I owe this visit, Chief?"

Needing to buy time for his reeling nerves to settle, Sky bent and scooped up his sunglasses out of a patch of weeds, where they'd flown during his somersault. Her sudden graceful capitulation surprised him—and provoked him at the same time. He studied her obliquely through the dark lenses, and found himself liking the fact that she was a woman of contradictions as well as the fact that she could admit to being wrong. That reaction immediately flip-flopped and her apologetic demeanor suddenly annoyed him. Because seeing her contrite left him wanting to untuck all that gorgeous black hair under the Dodgers baseball cap.

"I came by to see your neighbors," he said gruffly. "This morning I managed to run down their stolen televisions. The other items they lost I doubt we'll ever recover. It's fortunate that George and Mike had paperwork on their TVs, which gave me serial numbers. Other run-of-the-mill household articles rarely provide cops with a workable trail."

Annie nodded. "I'm so glad you got their TVs back. Neither family can afford to replace them. George is on disability, and Mike works on commission. He and Missy are still paying off their wedding. I asked if either family has theft insurance. Both carry basic fire coverage, and that's all."

"What about you?" Sky asked abruptly. "To my knowledge you never gave us any information on what you lost."

"Gran's TV was old. She was a lifelong

reader, so she didn't have any other electronics. The intruders did dump everything on her bookshelves. Gran also pieced and sewed quilts her church group passed on to a family crisis center. She was passionate about making a new kid-sized quilt for every child who ended up with their mom in an abuse shelter. But from what I could tell, her sewing supplies are intact. One thing that might be missing is her good silver. Truthfully I can't say. I hadn't seen it since I got here. But knowing Gran, she might have given it away. Although it meant a lot to her since it belonged to her mother."

"Huh, you may be in luck," Sky said, moved by the way her whole demeanor softened when she spoke of her grandmother. "The same guy who pawned the TVs left a chest of silverware. I have it in the car. I picked it up on the off chance it belonged to one of you three. If you can identify the set, the pawnbroker is out a bundle of cash." He shook his head. "Who would've thought old silverware would be worth so much?"

"Wow, getting it back when I wasn't even sure it had been stolen would be lucky." Annie set her sander on the porch and prepared to follow him. "Solid sterling is costly in today's market. Gran had a full service for twelve people. The pattern is La Perle. Some pieces are stamped with the maker's name. If I recall, it's Reed and Barton. Gran Ida didn't own a lot of nice things. But in keeping with her Southern heritage, she always set a formal table for holidays."

"Hmm. My mom's not Southern. She's a born and bred New Yorker, and she whipped us into shape for big family gatherings, too. I hope the silver is yours. If not, I'll have to drive back to the pawn shop across the border."

"Is that what the gang does? Shuffle what they pilfer out of state?" Annie matched his longer stride, seeming interested in hearing his answers.

"Unfortunately, they run an efficient underground," Sky said as they reached his cruiser. He faced her home as he popped open the trunk of his car. "So I guess you're doing a facelift, hoping to sell the house for a higher price," he said, jerking a thumb toward the Victorian. "Not that you asked for my advice. However, it's free. Renovating isn't worth your time and money. Our housing market stinks. It wasn't great when I moved here a little over a year ago. I shouldn't have bought, and wish I'd rented instead. Only I needed to prove to… Oh, never mind," he muttered, drawing her attention to the contents in the trunk.

Annie's brain skipped from his question to his comment about the house and on to his abruptly cut-off revelation that might have revealed something personal. "Oh, that *is* Gran's silver," she exclaimed, letting his comment go. "I recognize the chest. But maybe we should check inside to be sure."

Sky raised the lid and the broker's guarantee lay on top of the first tray. It verified that the contents were sterling, the maker Reed and Barton and the pattern La Perle. "You nailed it," Sky said, handing the guarantee to Annie. "Pawn shop owners have to know a lot about all kinds of merchandise, or they'd lose their shirts lending money to people they hope will come back to reclaim their goods, but rarely do."

"I hadn't thought about that. Isn't it against the law to deal in stolen property?"

"If they have reason to suspect it's stolen. Certain pawnbrokers have a backroom fencing operation, so to speak. This guy volunteered information about the silver, which I didn't have on my list, so I figure he's on the up-and-up."

"Oh, then I'm sorry he got taken." Annie lifted the chest out of the deep trunk of the aging Ford Crown Vic.

"Here, let me get that for you," Sky said. "I'll carry it to the house."

"That's okay. It isn't that heavy and you have two TVs to deliver. George Gilroy has a bad back, and Mike Spurlock's at work. I'm not sure if Missy is pregnant. Something she said the other evening made me think she might be. She broke down after the vandalism debacle and cried about the thought of raising children in this neighborhood."

"Huh," Sky snorted. "I'm an authority when it comes to that concern. My ex-wife's attorney drives it home every time they haul me into court hoping to derail my bid for joint custody."

"You have children?" Annie asked as he hefted the larger of the two TVs and slammed the trunk lid shut with more force than necessary.

"One," Sky answered. "Zachary's five."

Annie saw his jaw tense. She recognized his not-quite-checked anger. She'd seen similar reactions on numerous occasions during her work with broken families. She didn't know this cop well enough to sympathize, however. Besides, she was trained to remain neutral. "Just before you showed up, I was thinking of taking a break to have a glass of cold lemonade," she said lightly. "If you can spare a few minutes to join me on the porch after you deliver those

TVs, there's something I'd like to run by you—in your official capacity."

For a split second Skylar felt uneasy. But then, after glancing at his watch, he gave a brief nod.

Annie left to climb her porch steps. At the door she turned and called out, "Hey, thanks for getting back as much stuff as you did. I doubted you'd make the effort. My apologies for misjudging you, Cordova."

Sky nodded again, this time looking away. He hoped her apology was sincere. But if he went by past experience, it was entirely possible that she was trying to butter him up for some other reason. Not exactly an unfamiliar experience for him, since manipulation was a habit of his ex-wife's, he thought irritably as he rapped on the Gilroys' front door.

It took Sky twenty minutes or more to return the TVs and break away from the Gilroys' and Missy Spurlock's vociferous thanks. Almost wishing he'd turned down Annie Emerson's invitation for a cold drink, he checked in with Koot, hoping for a minor crisis that would give him an excuse to leave. As bad luck would have it, the lieutenant said all was quiet in the precinct.

Returning his cell phone to its holder on a leather work belt weighed down with a nightstick, a stun gun, handcuffs and a Glock, Sky trudged up Annie's steps. He saw several changes on the porch since his last visit. An old glider swing sported new cushions, as did four wicker chairs clustered around a glass-topped table. A pitcher filled with frosty lemonade sat there, along with two glasses. A shiny silver laptop rested on a sheet of paper Sky recognized as a plat map of Briar Run.

"How did the hoodlums miss stealing your laptop?" he asked, gesturing at it as Annie passed him a glass of lemonade.

"I had it in my rental car. I shouldn't admit this to an officer of the law, but I caught up on work email at stoplights between here and the funeral home." She gave him a wry smile.

Sky couldn't help laughing as he took a seat. She was a contradiction—a warm, everyday homebody mixed with a sometimes tough, cool professional. It unsettled him that he might not be so anxious to see her leave town. "I guess you're trying to calculate the worth of this house," he said after a long swallow. He wiped his mouth with the back of his hand and pointed to the map. "Since you probably want to get back to L.A. quickly, my recommendation, as I said earlier, is to sell all the contents in one giant estate sale, and put the empty house in the hands of a reputable Realtor."

"I, uh, phoned my supervisor in L.A. and tendered my resignation. I sublet my condo to a coworker who's going to ship my clothing and personal items like photo albums, CDs, books… and a special quilt Gran made… Oh, you don't care about that."

Sky straightened. "Pardon me for calling you a bit foolish, but the job market here is one of the most depressed in the nation. Plus, I would've thought a break-in might have convinced you about the sorry state of this town's general safety."

Annie tapped the map with a forefinger. "Don't you think it can be safe again? Do you know Briar Run was built before urban planning became a viable field? But it's laid out beautifully in a series of spokes around the town center. It was probably designed as a bedroom community for Louisville to accommodate the growth that was expected because of the Kentucky Derby."

"A bad calculation, since it was based on a once-a-year horse race," Sky muttered. "Thoroughbred horse owners, the folks with money, live on high-value real estate situated well outside the city. Not only is horse racing a sport that relies on transient labor, anyplace with big-dollar betting attracts criminals."

"You *are* cynical," Annie said. "I wish you'd seen this neighborhood the way I remember it, the way it was when I was growing up here. People took pride in their homes and yards, and they derived joy from socializing with neighbors." She moved the pitcher of lemonade and traced an area on the map. "There used to be manufacturing along our section of the Ohio River. Gran Ida worked for most of her life at one of the major lingerie-makers in the South. The owners sold the plant to a glove factory, which retooled and produced cotton and leather work gloves for export."

"And now they're gone," Sky said quietly.

"I know, but the building isn't. And a good-sized city park is a buffer between it and a residential area. South of the park are elementary, middle and high schools. When I was a kid, we all walked to school with friends. Briar Run was a great family town."

"Manufacturing here is defunct." Sky shrugged. "The park you remember so fondly has become a haven for drug pushers prowling for kids whose parents can't afford to drive them to school. I recommend you take another look at it—but in daylight. My force is too small to patrol everywhere

24/7. I figured your neighbors might've told you that lots of good people who used to live here have moved away. Take my lieutenant. You met Koot Talmage earlier. Koot and his wife, Sadie, moved to a safer town when their third kid was still in elementary. Sadie used to teach at the local high school. Now there's a forty percent dropout rate between middle grade and high school. Half the kids who do go on never graduate."

"Well, shame on them. And shame on all of you. People in positions of authority who shirk responsibility for whatever reason feed problems like the ones that exist here. If no one fights back, soon it won't be safe to live anywhere."

"Oh, right," he said, springing up. "I guess you've swept in from California and diagnosed all our problems."

"I don't know what you have against California or Californians, but it doesn't take a rocket scientist to see that one major problem here is apathy. On the part of residents, business owners and public servants like you and your lieutenant. You're like rats jumping off a sinking ship—you've written off this town. So has your city manager, who gave me the same song and dance the other day when I stopped in to ask if it was okay to hold a public meeting."

Sky set his now-empty glass down on the section of map that outlined the park. "Those of us who work in the trenches aren't apathetic, we're realistic. *That's* what we are."

"You're insinuating I'm not?"

"Look, all I know is that I'm doing my best to keep ahead of crime with a force that's been slashed twice this past year."

Annie got up, too, moved his glass and folded the map. "Fair enough. I understand that much of the bad stuff happening here is directed by criminals living outside Briar Run."

"At least we agree on that."

"Sort of." She opened a small leather notebook. "I informally surveyed a few residents. I believe their spirits can be improved by something as simple as home facelifts, like the one I've begun. Fresh paint. Maybe new drapes. Some rosebushes and weeded yards. Those things take sweat equity."

"And money. Paint isn't free. That kind of cosmetic change won't break the stranglehold gangs have on local teens. If you want to do something meaningful, get me the names of the gang leaders."

Annie refilled their glasses as they faced off across the table. "Maybe the gang leaders will give up and move on if we create the kind of community where families want to live. Pleasant surroundings restore hope. Hope creates far-reaching results."

"Perhaps that's true in prosperous neighborhoods." Sky drained his second glass. "Did any of the residents you talked to tell you how many hours a day they spend riding buses to Louisville and back to work minimum-wage jobs that barely put food on their tables? And those are the privileged few who actually found new jobs."

"I haven't totally gained their trust yet," Annie admitted. "But I plan to. I'll book a room at the library, and after setting a time and date, I'll distribute flyers inviting everyone to a meeting. Then I'll lay out my ideas in greater detail."

"Good luck." Sky handed her his glass. "Thanks for the drink. I need to get back to the job I'm being paid to do."

"I'd hoped I could enlist your support."

He clattered down the steps and strode along the walkway without so much as a backward glance.

Annie was fairly sure he'd heard her. She sighed as she collected the pitcher, glasses and her notebook, and carried them into the house. *What if Skylar Cordova was right? What if she and Gran Ida were wrong about her ability to help revitalize this neighborhood?*

SKY WENT BACK to the office. He called the pawnbroker to let him know he'd found the owner of the silverware. Afterward, he made up the work schedule for the following week. Aaron Loomis, the city manager, wouldn't let him authorize any overtime for his staff, which meant Sky had to take up the slack if any of his men needed a day off. When he posted the shifts to his calendar, he saw he had a dinner at Koot and Sadie's tonight. That was good. His pantry was bare, plus Sadie was a great cook. With nice weather, maybe they'd have a barbecue. And if the Talmage sons were there, the four guys could shoot hoops for a while. Sky could use a workout.

He'd just shut down his computer when the dispatcher notified him that a call had come in from a drugstore—a possible domestic dispute in their parking lot. Those had the potential of being especially difficult—and dangerous. Heading out, Sky called Teddy Saunders, his youngest officer, as backup. At six-three, two hundred and eighty pounds, Saunders often just had to show up and perpetrators got scared enough to beg for mercy.

Sky arrived at the altercation first and encountered a couple he'd been called out on before. Roger McBride reportedly had a problem with alcohol, and his wife, Loretta, had a problem with the amount of money Roger wasted on liquor. In the past there hadn't been any violence, so Sky canceled his call for backup.

Parking his cruiser a safe distance away from the arguing pair, Sky walked toward them and deduced that their spat was the same old thing. Loretta was outside Roger's car shouting at her husband, who sat behind the wheel.

"Loretta," Sky said evenly. "Roger." Sky nodded at the man. "Is Roger too drunk to drive?" That question he aimed at the woman.

"Not yet, but I just went to the bank with my pay and checked to see that his unemployment funds had come into our account. Who did I pass as I left the bank but this lazy bum on his way to spend money we don't have on Irish whiskey."

Roger glanced away, but not before Sky saw his unshaven jaw tense. "I only bought a pint," the man said. "Chief, don't I have the right to *some* of the money from my unemployment? This week I filled out four new job applications. I quit going to the tavern. Since Loretta got on me, for not doing anything around the house,

I've taken over all the chores. No matter what I do, she wants more. It's humiliating enough for a guy like me to let my wife be the family breadwinner."

Sky pinched the bridge of his nose. Man, where was the curb-appeal fairy who thought she could set local folks' world right with curtains and paint? He'd love to hear Annie Emerson's solution for this.

"Loretta, *is* Roger doing better?"

"I suppose." She plucked at the collar of her blouse with a work-roughened hand. Sky knew the couple was in their late fifties. Loretta worked at a fast-food restaurant. Roger used to be a production manager at the glove factory. Sky had heard the same kind of hard-luck story from a host of others in town.

"You're the one I'd have to charge with disorderly conduct today," he told Loretta.

"Don't do that," Roger broke in. "All she's guilty of is trying to pound some sense into my stubborn head. I'll return the pint." He grabbed the sack and got out of the car.

Sky and Loretta watched him jog back into the store. "I'm sorry," she said. "I shouldn't have made a scene, but my boss said today they may have to cut everybody's hours. I saw Rog headed for the store to get booze, and something snapped."

"It's okay. No harm done. I'm sorry life's so rough. If I hear of any work I think Roger can do, I'll call."

"Come by the house," she said meekly. "We had to let them shut our phone off."

"I'm sorry." Sky caught himself saying that a lot lately. The more trouble that was heaped on the heads of people in his jurisdiction, the more painkillers he took. He climbed into this car to scribble out an incident report and dug out a bottle he kept in the glove compartment, then shook out two pills and swallowed them dry. He hadn't quite finished his report when a call came in from the principal at the middle school. A fifth grader had been found with marijuana in his book bag.

Sky left the convenience store and drove four blocks to the school. He remembered getting in trouble once for taking a garden snake to school. It wasn't just that he'd taken the snake to class, but he'd put it in Julie Clark's backpack. Sky couldn't fathom what kind of mischief kids would be up to by the time his five-year-old son reached middle school. He hoped he'd have some say in guiding Zack through those awkward years. He wouldn't if it was up to Corrine.

During the school year so far, Sky had sat down with this principal more often than either of them would've liked. "I don't know what to tell you, Chief Cordova," Mrs. Beckerman said. "Billy Joe Wright swears he was set up."

Sky watched the scared kid who sat in the principal's waiting room. He was fair-haired and well-dressed. He didn't have on the oversize, low-slung jeans that seemed to be the gang-banger dress code. "What are his grades like? Have they slipped lately?" Sky asked.

The principal accessed the boy's record on her computer. "He's a surprisingly good student. I hate to admit it, but that's why I know so little about him. It's terrible that my days are spent getting to know all the children at the opposite end of the academic spectrum." She handed Sky the plastic Baggie filled with leaves. "But there is the fact that this fell out of his book bag in algebra class."

Sky opened a corner of the bag, sniffed, then made a wry face before sealing it again. "Potent weed," he said, coughing. "It's worth some bucks. Could be someone's bullying him, or else somebody's been coerced by a dealer up the chain to try and get him involved."

The principal closed the boy's record. "I'll talk to his mother. He said his dad's out of town on business. That could mean anything. It may mean he's in jail. If our counselor can handle one more case, I'll refer him and I'll sign a release for you to confiscate the bag. For now I'm inclined to give Billy a pass, but I'll try to keep him under surveillance."

All too familiar with the drill from past confiscations, Sky had come prepared with a notebook of release forms. Extracting one, he set it on her desk, and she signed it with a flourish.

Borrowing her stapler, Sky stapled the bag to the form. Mrs. Beckerman photocopied it, bag and all. "I hope I don't have to call you in again before school lets out for the summer. Not that I envy you having so many potential delinquents turned loose on the community for three months. I should warn you, the district cut all summer programs."

"Gr…eat." He sighed heavily. "Don't they realize it leaves the schools at risk for vandalism?"

She shrugged. "They claim they've wrung every possible penny out of the budget just to hire teachers for enough hours so our seniors can graduate."

"Thanks for the heads-up, Mrs. Beckerman. I'll see if I can arrange our schedules to include driving by the three schools several times a day."

"Do that. I'll pray for an angel to swoop down and keep our facilities protected."

Sky took his leave, fearing it was going to be a long summer. The news about no summer school felt like one more nail driven into the coffin of this dying town.

LATER, AFTER HE wound up his day, he went home, showered and changed out of his uniform before traveling eight miles to the town where Koot lived. Sky stopped at a flower shop and bought a potted plant as a hostess gift for Sadie Talmage. He knew she liked flowers. Continuing into the residential district, Sky couldn't help comparing these clean streets, well-tended lawns and inviting homes with those in his rundown community. He'd been to the Talmage home several times, but it struck him now that if he hadn't had a touchy encounter with Annie Emerson today, he wouldn't be making comparisons.

The safety of residents in his town was his first concern, not how the houses looked to passersby. Yet, Koot, a thirty-year veteran cop, had moved his family because he deemed this town far safer than Briar Run.

When Sky was hired as police chief, the city had a rule stating that its employees, especially police and fire, had to reside within city limits. Sky wasn't sure if they'd relaxed the rules for Koot, who was a fixture on the force and due to retire soon, or if the city manager wasn't aware he'd moved.

The main question still ricocheted inside Sky's head—was there truth to Annie's assertion that spiffing up the neighborhood would translate into safety? Sky hated to think that his reluctance to take her seriously could lie with the fact that she'd laid him out in her front yard, thereby threatening his masculinity. Preferring to put that incident and the woman out of his mind, Sky was glad to arrive at his destination.

SADIE ANSWERED HIS knock. She enveloped him in a hug, which was her way of greeting everyone. "Why thank you, sugar," she drawled when he gave her the plant. "Koot, are you too old to learn some manners from your younger boss?" she said with a laugh when her husband walked up behind her. She kissed his cheek to take away the sting of her rebuke as she showed off her gift. Koot flung an arm around her shoulders. His brown eyes twinkled as he feigned being stabbed in the heart by Sky, who grinned and followed his hosts through the kitchen and out to the back patio, where an outdoor table was already set. He felt the cares of the day recede. His friends had the kind of marriage he wished his had been.

"Grab a chair," Koot said, picking up a platter and a spatula.

Sadie handed Sky a chilled bottle of light beer and set one each in front of her husband's plates and hers.

"Prepare to eat the best pulled-pork sandwiches you've ever tasted," Koot called over his shoulder. He opened the lid on the barbecue and the scent of spices made Sky's mouth water.

"No kids tonight?" Sky asked when Sadie moved a tray of condiments to make room on the table for a green salad.

"Marcus is coaching a junior baseball team at the boys' club," Koot said, returning to the table with a platter of buns, piled high with meat oozing a tangy-smelling sauce.

Sadie used tongs to set a sandwich on Sky's plate. "Sam is helping his sister study for her bar exams. Poor Sam, he wishes he'd stayed in college instead of dropping out to get married. His job as a hospital orderly just pays the bills."

"He could go back and finish his degree," Koot said, whipping open his napkin.

Sadie defended their middle son. "It's almost impossible with two kids, and tuition fees climbing."

"I was lucky to finish college with some help from ROTC. Then I went straight into the police academy before getting called to active army duty," Sky said. "A lot of guys I met overseas hoped they could attend college after their tours," he added. "If they already had a family, it'd mean sacrifice. Maybe Sam will go back, though, if Koot keeps after him."

"I could have helped him out financially if I'd continued teaching." Sadie dished out salad and passed around dressings.

"You didn't need the hassle." Koot turned to Sky. "It got to where she was trying to teach kids who didn't care. You know how many times we get called to that high school. I wanted her and Diandra out of there."

"I picked up a packet of pretty high-grade weed at the middle school today."

"Middle school? Dang." Koot shook his graying head. "Can our job get any tougher?"

"Which reminds me. Apparently the school board voted to defund summer school. We'll have to be extra vigilant about keeping watch on the buildings."

Koot rolled his eyes. "Like that's gonna be

easy. If it didn't affect my pension, I'd retire tomorrow."

Sadie patted his hand. "Do it if you want."

"Don't you dare," Sky put in. "Guaranteed our city manager won't replace you."

"It's a shame everything's gotten so bad in Briar Run," Sadie said. "It's never made sense to me how things began to slide, and then one downward trend led to another. You may not believe this, Sky, but Briar Run used to be as nice as this town. What you need to do is find a miracle worker—preferably a volunteer."

"An army of them," Koot flung out. Sky mulled over Sadie's comment, which led back to his earlier thoughts about Annie Emerson. "Do you think one person could start a movement capable of turning a whole town around?"

Koot was quick to say no. Sadie seemed more willing to explore the possibility. "Briar Run didn't fall into decline overnight. We stuck it out for a long time. What happened was like a row of dominos. The first one that toppled was economic. The factory closed, and that affected the livelihoods of more than half the workers in town. One by one more dominoes fell. No job, no money. No money, fewer taxes paid. Fewer taxes, fewer city services, and so on and so on. You get the picture." She rose and collected their plates. "I'm going to the kitchen to get our dessert."

"Briar Run is in a hopeless spiral," Koot said after Sadie left. "I'm sorry you bought a house there, Sky. I know you took the job because it's near your ex. Unfortunately, conditions in Briar Run are so degraded, her lawyers can legitimately harangue you. The best hope you have is to keep sending out résumés for any comparable job in a forty-mile radius of your ex and her new hubby's horse farm. Ah, chocolate pie," he exclaimed as Sadie returned. "My favorite. Let's find a happier topic, so as not to give ourselves heartburn."

Sadie cut each man a generous slice of pie.

Sky continued to worry the subject the others had dropped. "If I understand you right, Sadie, are you saying that if people do stuff like painting the exterior of our houses, new landscaping, making the outside more appealing, it *won't* significantly improve their outlook? The city still lacks the economic development necessary to make folks less poor but wouldn't this make a difference?"

She gave a shrug. "Yes and no. I've long been interested in the effect housing design has on alleviating poverty. After I left teaching, I took design classes at the community college. One thing we learned is that housing developments with homeowner associations that have strict rules for keeping up homes and yards have happier, healthier residents. But...they still need funding."

Using the tines of his fork, Sky made a crater in the whipped-cream topping of his pie. "So... say, somebody got us all to gussie up our houses and maybe redo the park. Would that be enough to put a dent in crime? Will it encourage residents to get out and about?"

"Sounds like you wish a fairy godmother would wave her magic wand and turn Briar Run into utopia." Koot tipped back his head and roared with laughter. "Dream on, my man. Dream on."

Sky flinched. "Yeah, I see how the whole notion seems silly."

As the trio polished off their pie in silence, Sky thought how ironic it was that he'd mentally tagged Annie Emerson the "curb-appeal fairy." She *would* have to work magic, he realized, to accomplish even a tenth of the grandiose ideas she'd outlined.

CHAPTER THREE

ANNIE'S HOUSE PROJECT had multiplied. Her enthusiasm sparked some of the results she'd hoped for. Mike Spurlock liked the looks of Gran's Victorian after Annie's painting was under way. Mike had a few days off from his business travel and, at Missy's urging, borrowed Annie's sander. Within a few days, the Spurlock home was ready to paint. Peggy Gilroy got the bug next. Their siding was shingle; a good washing left it in shape to be painted before Annie finished her trim.

All the homes had been a dingy gray. Annie chose Wedgwood blue with navy trim to give the street a pop of color. Since her house sat between the other two, it looked even prettier after Peggy painted hers cream with chocolate shutters and matching gingerbread scrollwork. Missy loved both of their color schemes, but she couldn't make up her mind. She had Mike test sample paint on the back of their house until she settled on honey gold with dark green edging.

"I'm so excited about how good our homes look," Missy said the afternoon Annie climbed down from putting the final touches on three cupolas jutting from her third story. The Spurlock home was only two-story and less ornate. Mike had whipped right through painting it.

"They do, Missy, and they'll be even prettier after we've tackled the yards. That's assuming my body holds out," Annie added wryly as she rotated her shoulders. "Every night, what I wish for is some muscle man who'll cart my ladder around for a few weeks." The minute the statement crossed her lips, Annie pictured Sky Cordova, which jarred her until Missy spoke again.

"I could never climb an extension ladder the way you do, Annie. I get dizzy watching you. It was really nice of you to paint the upper section of George and Peggy's place. His back really bothers him. Peggy's gutsy for her age. She would've tackled it, you know."

"I do know. In a lot of ways she's like Gran Ida was." Annie paused, battling back the sadness that descended whenever her grandmother's name came up. "That indomitable spirit is why I was in denial when Peggy phoned to tell me Gran's health was failing. To me she never seemed to age. I still can't believe she's gone."

Missy threw both arms around her in an

impulsive hug. "I'm sorry for reminding you, Annie. She brought us a casserole the night we moved in. Mike, his brother and I moved everything we'd stored in his folks' garage into the house, all in one day. We were exhausted. And over she came with food. I called her an angel." Missy grinned. "She said we should call her Gran Ida because everyone did. She was proud as a peacock of you. I wasn't sure I'd like you, the way she made you sound like a saint."

Annie laughed self-consciously. "Stop already."

"I don't mean to embarrass you. I think it was sweet. What you're doing now, restoring the house, is exactly what she said you'd come here and do one day. Only she had grander plans. I'm sure you've seen the photo album that's filled with pictures of how every street in town used to look."

"I found it a few weeks ago," Annie murmured.

"Well, I'm sure you remember the park. It was beautiful, with rose gardens, benches and walkways. Looking at it now, you'd never know it's the same place. Peggy and I got together with Gran Ida most afternoons for tea and cookies and she'd bring out her album. She'd tell us that when you came home to stay, you'd get people to make the town look like it used to." Missy giggled delightedly. "See why I expected you to be a saint? Maybe Gran Ida wasn't quite herself toward the end, as Peggy pointed out, but I loved listening to her dreams. I had similar ones when we bought this house. Mike and I settled on a fixer-upper, which was all we could afford. I wish we'd known about the crime. I suppose it goes with the territory of low-income housing," she said, ending on a sigh.

Annie listened while she washed out paintbrushes. "Now you sound like our illustrious police chief. Missy, low income doesn't have to be synonymous with high crime. A family shouldn't have to sell and move away to feel safe."

"You can say that after all our homes were burgled in the same afternoon?"

Setting her clean brushes out to dry, Annie prepared to haul the ladder back to her garage. "Do you think that if people see what we've done, they'll want to do the same thing? That's my hope, anyway—that one set of highly visible improvements will encourage others in our community to follow our lead."

"Peggy said you plan to call a meeting. But if Mike's out of town I won't be there. We've decided it's not safe for us both to be gone at the same time. And I can't say whether what we've done will induce anyone else. Mike said yesterday that if you hadn't arranged for us to get such a deep discount at the paint store, we wouldn't have been able to afford this makeover. Same goes for Peggy and George."

Annie shrugged. She'd let them all think they were getting paint at a discount when, in fact, she'd made up the difference. She hoped they wouldn't discover what she'd done. They had no idea how much money Gran had left her. With those funds, she was in a position to underwrite other projects and fulfill at least part of her grandmother's dream. She'd told Gran's lawyer that she didn't want word of her inheritance to leak out. And she was more than willing to help families who pitched in by doing part of the work themselves. Mr. Manchester had said keeping the funding under wraps might be tricky. Annie guessed she'd deal with it if that became necessary.

Missy returned to her house and Annie stored her tools.

She walked to the end of her driveway to study the trio of newly painted homes, and thought they looked fantastic. It gave her personal satisfaction to see them so fresh and attractive—more satisfaction than she'd felt in a while. She'd thought she loved her job in L.A. But maybe the work had begun to weigh on her more than she'd realized. Her challenges here were more physical than mental. Here she used her creativity. Until now she hadn't noticed how long it had been since she'd done any cooking, sewing or gardening. Her main regret, though, was that she hadn't budgeted her time well enough to visit Gran Ida sooner.

Because her recent loss was still too raw, she distracted herself by installing the window boxes she'd bought. Soon she'd fill them with trailing roses. She wanted to tear out the old wisteria that covered a rock retaining wall. With Louisville gearing up for the Kentucky Derby, nurseries were selling gorgeous rosebushes. Annie pictured roses in a riot of color all across the front of this house, down the road and through the park again.

The next day, the weather turned from sunny and warm to muggy rain. Bad weather drove Annie inside. She alternately worked on kitchen curtains and a flyer to inform residents about her restoration planning meeting. The place, date and time were set. Darn it, though, she'd hoped to do some landscaping before she took pictures to put on her flyer. But the rain hung around for two more days, putting the kibosh on all her outdoor plans. She dug through Gran's boxes of fabric and found just what she needed for drapes.

KOOT TALMAGE BLEW into police headquarters on a gust of rain and wind. Shutting the door with some difficulty, he stamped water from his wet boots, then shook off his official yellow slicker and hung it on a peg near the door.

Sky saw him and stepped into the hallway, his coffee cup in hand. "Are we going to have a real gully washer today?"

"Already is," the other man grumbled as he met Sky at the coffeemaker and helped himself to a clean mug hanging on a wall rack.

"Is it causing flooding around Grandiflora or Hybrid Tea?" Sky named two streets that paralleled the river.

"Nothing like it used to before our city manager ordered storm drains installed. I remember how the people on those streets griped about the inconvenience when they tore up the intersection. Aaron Loomis won't be hearing any complaints now."

"That's good. Listen, I want all of us out on patrol about the time the high school lets out. Hopefully seeing our cruisers will slow the kids down. First big rain after a dry spell, young drivers tend to forget cars can hydroplane if they drive too fast. We don't need any of our kids ending up rearranging anyone's front landscaping."

"Speaking of landscapes, have you driven down Rose Arbor recently?"

Sky choked on a swig of his coffee. "Not really. Why?" he mumbled after Koot had pounded his back. Sky had made checking the street that suffered the three robberies part of his nightly routine. Because his checks weren't entirely of an official nature, but partly a personal interest he'd taken in Annie Emerson, Sky wasn't about to admit that he already knew about the improvements on Rose Arbor. He didn't *want* to feel any interest in Annie, but he did—and he wasn't about to admit that, either.

"Well, there've been big changes at the three homes where we investigated those break-ins."

"Changes?" Sky played along, even though he'd witnessed stages of the restoration via his car lights and one streetlamp. He knew Annie, the California cyclone, would get the credit or blame, depending on whether or not her plans to spearhead urban renewal caused upheaval among the rank and file.

"As soon as the rain lets up, you need to go take a gander. Those same three homes have been painted from top to bottom. The one in the middle is obviously being prepared for new landscaping. All those renos are pricy, Sky. I wonder if we've got ourselves a case of insurance fraud."

This time Sky did spew his coffee. "Sorry." He grabbed a paper towel, wiped the counter and bent to scrub part of the linoleum. "Tell me what brought on that conclusion."

"At least two of those couples claimed losses in the robberies. Ida Vance's granddaughter never provided us with a list of her stolen goods. After I saw what's going on over there, I started thinking the gal from California might be some kind of scam artist. The TV news is full of those tales. A lot of 'em are in Florida, but some are in and around L.A. She could've set it up so they all collected big on phony insurance claims."

Sky returned to his office. "Annie Emerson is no scam artist, Koot. And don't be saying anything like that around town. I told you I got back some of their stolen property that had been hocked. I even found silverware Ms. Emerson didn't know had gone missing. They're honest folks."

Koot followed his boss into his cramped office. "You sound pretty certain of that for somebody who claims not to have seen the work that's gone on there."

"Well, the day I returned the stolen goods I was able to track down, Ms. Emerson was sanding old paint off her house." He winced, remembering how she'd bruised his shin—and his pride—that day. Frowning, Sky sat in his swivel chair and beat a tattoo on his desk pad with a thumb. "Her biggest drawback isn't that she's a criminal, Koot. It's that she's too stubborn for words. Remember the night I had dinner at your house, and asked you and Sadie whether you thought one person could start a movement and turn this town around?"

"Yep. I recall thinking you'd gotten too big a whiff of that marijuana you'd confiscated from the middle school that day."

"What you said was that it would take a fairy godmother to wave a magic wand. Well, picture Annie Emerson with wings and a sparkly crown."

"There you go again, talking in riddles."

"I didn't come right out and say that our newest resident presented me with a nutty idea. She plans to conduct a town hall meeting and convince all our residents to paint their homes. She thinks that'll cure any ills Briar Run suffers."

Koot dropped heavily into the chair across

from Sky. "Why did you beat about the bush instead of telling Sadie and me the truth about what you knew?"

Sky stared at his coffee mug. "I don't know. Yes, I do know.... I didn't want you guys calling her a nut job. She's nice, but has misplaced ideas."

"Have you gone sweet on Annie Emerson?"

"No." Sky reared back, shooting Koot a scowl. "The thing is, she asked for my backing and I ran for the car like a scalded jackrabbit. Apparently she hasn't let that stop her."

The older man propped his elbows on his knees. "I've gotta say the houses look good. But, Sky, if she makes too much noise about believing that her urban renewal plan will drive out crime, won't that make the Stingers view her as a threat?"

Sky's nervous thumb tapped faster.

"I don't want to pile more worry on you, boss."

"You haven't said anything I haven't already considered."

"Maybe she'll decide that the amount of work or the cost isn't practical for most folks. Hey, if this rain slacks off, she'll probably get back out in her yard. I don't mind moseying over there again. I can compliment what she's done and see if she mentions any further plans."

"Compliments might encourage her," Sky said. "Better to let it go. Also, she gets her back up easily."

"Okay, it's your call, Chief. I'm due back out on patrol. If this rain *doesn't* quit, I can't say I'm sorry tomorrow's my day off."

"In my old job I got regular days off." Sky pursed his lips. "Not in this one."

"Not in the military, either," Koot pointed out.

"Nope. I'm talking about my last police job. Although come to think of it, working vice in Baltimore involved more personal risk than this one. We had some major crime to deal with."

"I'll bet that job came with a higher salary," Koot joked as he shrugged on his rain slicker.

"There was that aspect. But Corrine's marriage to a thoroughbred horse breeder didn't leave me with many other options. I should be thankful I landed this job. For now I can see Zack. Or at least I can see him between the times his mother dreams up reasons to haul me back into court."

"Any word on whether the court will advance the date of your big custody hearing?"

Sky shook his head. "My lawyer tells me the county docket is full. Chances of getting that court date advanced are slim to none. Sure seems like Corrine's attorney has more clout than mine does."

"Bummer. Sadie and I are ready to vouch for you. I hope it's a slow day here so both of us can go to court to say you're a good Joe."

"I appreciate it. That whole proceeding is nonsense. Kentucky Child Welfare has already demanded and received affidavits pertaining to every stinking second of my life."

"Yeah, well, stay cool. You know that her side is dragging this out, hoping for something that'll give them reason to file another injunction. That's why, even if you're sweet on Annie Emerson, forget it. Your ex's shyster lawyer will find some way to exploit it to their advantage."

Sky tugged his lower lip. "That burns me, Koot. Corrine divorced me while I was off fighting for our country. She claimed irreconcilable differences she didn't have to substantiate. I don't understand a system that lets her take my son from the state where we lived. She married an older dude with teenagers and nobody objected when she completely rearranged my kid's life. Yet, her side has the right to reject my home, my job and maybe whatever woman I may show a remote interest in wanting to date? Give me a break."

"I guess family law has to consider everything. Say, Sky, did you just admit you're interested in dating Ms. Emerson?"

"Koot, you old buzzard, don't try and put words in my mouth. I'll admit I find her intriguing. I'm reasonably sure that's not mutual."

"Hmm. I may have to ask Sadie to go strike up an acquaintance with the lady and invite you both over for an evening of food and poker. That way we can all get to know one another a bit better."

"Don't you dare! But before I forget, I'm scheduling myself a day off real soon to spend with Zachary."

Koot left, and Sky went back to his paperwork. Rain or not, he wanted to make time to drive down Rose Arbor Street in daylight for once.

It turned out that a series of fender benders caused by the rain played havoc with his good intentions.

The next day there were also several incidents that demanded his attention. By the end of a week fraught with headaches, Sky ran into the local café thinking he'd grab a take-out sandwich to eat in the car while he dashed by to inspect the paint jobs on Rose Arbor. They'd even caused chatter among his dispatchers and the two junior officers.

At the register where he handed over money to pay for his food, he happened to glance at a stack of flyers. They included a photo of the three homes he'd intended to visit. Sky snatched one up and perused it.

"Are you going to attend that meeting on Tuesday night, Chief Cordova?" the café manager asked as she gave him a brown bag with his sandwich and passed him a cup of steaming coffee.

"Huh?" He looked up from reading the flyer, which outlined all the points Annie had brought up earlier.

"The meeting at the library. I work a lot of hours, so I doubt I'll get to go. Nobody I've talked to seems to know much about the woman who's holding the meeting. Jim Morris said she's Ida Vance's granddaughter. You might've heard that Ida passed recently. She was a longtime do-gooder. She'd turn over in her grave at the thought of any relative of hers stirring up trouble in the town."

When he'd finished reading, Sky folded the flyer and tucked it in his shirt pocket. "What makes you feel this meeting might stir up trouble, Joanne?"

The woman shrugged plump shoulders. "As a rule, folks around these parts don't cotton to outsiders barging into our community, trying to tell us what to do."

"In her introduction, Ms. Emerson points out that she was brought up in this town and that she's inherited her grandmother's home. Doesn't that make her part of our community?"

"Not if she thinks she can throw around her fancy California ideas, it don't."

Sky saw he was on the losing end of this argument. And recalling that Annie had accused him of having it in for Californians, Joanne wasn't voicing much he hadn't said himself. "I should get back to work." He hurried out to his cruiser. The first thing he did was drive down Rose Arbor. Even before he reached the first of two speed bumps that required drivers to slow down, Sky noticed cars ahead of him traveling well below the speed limit as their drivers gawked at the three "painted ladies." In daylight, they were quite appealing. Sky tried imagining other streets with homes painted as tastefully. He hated to retract another set of objections. The other night he'd concluded to Koot and Sadie that mere paint would never boost the spirits in the neighborhood. Now he wasn't so sure.

THE FOLLOWING TUESDAY, Sky's initial plan was to run by his house at the end of his shift, change out of his uniform and sneak into Annie's meeting. He'd act like a casual observer at the back of the crowd. As with too many of his well-laid plans, things didn't go quite as he'd hoped. He had a man out sick, and the day presented an endless array of problems. It started with a group of half a dozen kids in the park. They'd skipped their first class, and had all contributed medicine from their households—both prescription and over-the-counter stuff—which they mixed together in a bowl and chugged with beer heisted from one dad's fridge. Thank heaven someone saw them and reported their activity before they could swallow everything in the bowl.

Koot had helped transport them to the E.R., where medics checked the kids' vital signs. A nurse hauled out the *PDR* and began matching pills to pictures in the book so they could identify the medications no longer in their original bottles. They all winced when an emergency room doctor ordered emetics.

Sky began the long process of calling parents, some of whom worked jobs they couldn't leave, others who couldn't be bothered to collect their little darlings. In between calls, he had to clean their vomit off his shoes. Five o'clock rolled around just as they handed over the last kid to a none-too-pleased stepmother.

Koot went home. Sky prepared to do the same, figuring he had time to shower and shave, and still make it to Annie's six-thirty meeting at the library.

He hadn't even reached the door when a call came in regarding a carjacking. "I'll take it," he told his dispatcher. "Koot's off duty and on his way home. Notify Morales, will you? See if he can come in a little early and meet me there."

Forty minutes later, Sky glanced at his watch as he signed the last report and turned the night shift over to Joe. It was seven-ten. He was closer to the library than his house. Even at that, it'd take him another ten minutes to get there—and he'd be arriving really late.

Sky drove straight to the library. He was sure he stank of sweat, and maybe still had vomit on the toe of one boot. Too bad. He wouldn't sit in the back row. He'd stand in a shadowy corner, out of everyone's way. According to Annie's flyer, the meeting would end at eight-thirty. With luck he'd be there for the last forty-five minutes—the part with audience questions and Annie's answers.

He'd attended a meeting in the community

room on a few other occasions. Thank goodness he didn't need to waste time hunting down the librarian to get directions.

The door to the room stood open. Sky softened his steps when he drew nearer so as to not disrupt the meeting. It was strangely silent inside the room, although he'd expected a controversial, maybe explosive give-and-take—his main reason for coming tonight. He wanted to make sure things didn't get too heated and out of hand.

He peered into the room. A side table held a large plate heaped with what appeared to be homemade cookies. The room smelled pleasantly of fresh brewed coffee. Sky spotted a big urn on the same table. Beside it sat paper cups, cream, sugar and napkins. She was ready for a crowd. At the front of the room Annie rested her forearms on the podium. All around her in half circles stood rows of empty chairs. Not a single soul had come to her event.

He must have made a noise at the door, enough for her to lift her head. Their eyes met and Sky's stomach tightened. He found himself deeply affected by the disappointment etched on her face.

"You must feel vindicated," she said, indicating the vacant chairs. "You told me this was a foolish idea. What I can't believe is that *everyone* stayed away."

Sky stepped into the room. "I didn't come to gloat. I came to keep the peace. After I saw your flyer, I thought you'd have a full house. Maybe it's the time. Six-thirty is early for people who work downtown and travel by bus. They have to get home, prepare and serve a meal and catch a bus back out to a meeting. That's why teachers at our schools start open house and parent meetings at eight."

"I didn't know that. So, you didn't hear a rumor that people were warned off by anonymous phone messages from gang members?"

Sky tensed. "No. When? Where?"

"A coworker of Mike Spurlock's claimed he received one of these calls late last night. Woke him up, he said, and he told Mike it was enough to make him stay away."

"Where are the Gilroys and Spurlocks? Why aren't they here to support you?"

"They're already part of the renovation project. But to be totally truthful, they've been edgy since the break-ins."

Sky felt edgy, too. He didn't like hearing that the Stingers had issued threats. The leaders—and few gang members knew who they were—had a vested interest in keeping neighborhood kids who did their bidding under their thumbs. They definitely wouldn't like the fact that one of the objectives on Annie's flyer indicated that beautifying the neighborhood was part of a larger strategy aimed at renewing family values and banishing gang activity. "It doesn't look as if anyone's going to show up, Annie. Why don't I help you clean up the room?"

"That's kind of you, but I see you're still in uniform. I'm sure you have other duties."

"No, I'm off. I intended to go home and get out of the uniform before dropping by here. But a late call tied me up."

"Then I accept your offer. I'll dump the coffee and go see if the librarians would like the cookies. They're open until nine."

Sky snagged a cookie and a napkin. He set it aside with a grin. "Those look tasty. I'll work up an appetite folding chairs."

"Here, take another." Annie added a second cookie to his napkin. "Do you want a cup of coffee, too, before I get rid of it?" She unplugged the pot.

"Hold on, that's hot and it's heavy. I'll pour us each a cup, then carry the pot to the sink in the men's room. You go ahead and deliver cookies to the library staff."

"You're being nice for a man who sounded

quite cranky about my ideas a few days ago. Why the change of heart?"

"Serve and protect is a motto I take seriously. My feelings toward this town are complicated. The other day I wasn't convinced your plan had merit. Part of my reason for coming tonight was to possibly be enlightened. Now I'll help you pack up, and then I'll follow you home. I don't like what you said about possible gang meddling."

"I don't need you to follow me home. And it's high time someone stood up to those bullies. That's all they are. Bullies who use scare tactics to frighten people and get what they want."

"Uh-huh. That's about the size of it. They're also very good at operating from the shadows. All the same, we'll do this my way."

"Okay, knock yourself out. Since you seem to be keeping track, my next move is to go door-to-door to speak to everyone in the neighborhood. Can they count on your force for quick assistance if I convince them to call 9-1-1 if they see a drug deal going down? Or if they spot gang members shaking down younger kids for school lunch money? I hear that residents often don't call the cops because your response time is slow or nil—and because of fear of gang retaliation."

"We do our best." Sky filled two paper cups

with coffee and set them near his cookies. "I can't make the promises you want on behalf of my department, Annie. Number one, my small force is already stretched thin. Second, I don't believe that in most cases it helps to arrest local kids for petty crimes they've been coerced into pulling off. It just adds to parents' misery. Especially poor parents."

"How else can you get the names of gang leaders if you aren't putting pressure on the kids you know are members?"

"You're assuming these local kids actually *know* who the leaders are. I promise you I hauled in a lot of kids when I first took this job. They were too frightened to rat out anyone. Fear is debilitating."

"But without cooperation from police, I doubt residents will commit to even the first small step in taking back our neighborhood."

Her dogged determination to go out on a limb to save a neighborhood she hadn't been part of for quite a few years baffled Sky. If he could sell his house he'd move from Briar Run in a second. "I'll go pour this out," he muttered, hefting the urn. "We can talk some more while we drink our coffee."

"Sure, but you're not going to talk me out of continuing. I hope you know that." Annie ripped open two packets of creamer and emptied both into her cup.

Sky didn't say what was really on his mind—that she was the most mule-headed woman he'd met in a long time. When he got to the men's room, he dumped the coffee and rinsed the pot. He had most of the chairs folded and stored on their carts before she returned from her trip to the main part of the library.

"Sorry I was gone so long. There weren't many patrons, and the librarians were chatty." She boxed the coffee can, sugar and creamer packets and the rest of the napkins. "The librarians think that what I want to do, motivating families to tidy up their homes and streets, is a great idea. But…" She sipped her coffee as Sky wheeled the last cart of chairs to the wall and walked up to claim his cup.

"But…" he prompted, gazing steadily at her over the rim.

"They're like the others, too scared to join in. It's only one gang, for pity's sake. In L.A. there'd be a dozen or more out roaming the streets."

"In L.A., like in other big cities, gangs fight one another for turf. They display their colors proudly, and cops know the members. They just have to catch them in the act of committing a crime."

"The gang here is sneakier, and that's precisely why I think there's still hope to wrest local kids from their clutches. In my work in low-income areas, I found parents willing to do whatever it took to give their children more opportunities for a better life. They'd risk a lot to keep them out of gangs."

Annie's fervor, coupled with her knowledge of people stuck in poverty, niggled Sky. "Something I may be able to do is arrange for a direct hotline during daylight hours, one that circumvents our dispatcher and goes instantly to the cell phones of whichever cops are on duty. It might shorten response time. Usually, when the dispatcher manages to get hold of one of us, the perpetrators have done the crime and gone to ground before we even reach the scene."

"That would be a start." Annie smiled at him, and jotted in her notebook. "It's something I can offer folks. Instead of another collective meeting, I'll go from house to house and discuss cleanup. If I get people to agree, I'll provide some incentives—like house paint. We can do one street at a time, ending up at the park. With their homes in shape, I bet everyone will be excited about helping replant the park."

Sky drained his cup, crushed it and tossed it in a wastebasket. "This is a darned good cookie. Did you bake them?" he asked.

"Yes, it was one of Gran Ida's favorite recipes. Everything I'm trying to accomplish here, I'm doing in her memory. So, I won't be distracted by compliments about my cookies." She tossed her empty cup in the basket from farther away.

Sky chuckled at that and picked up her box of leftovers. "I get the message, Annie. You're stubborn. Turn out the light, will you? I'll walk you out and stow this in your car. For the record, once I lay out a course, I follow through. Just sayin' so you can expect to see my cruiser glued to your bumper until you pull into your garage."

She didn't argue this time. She merely turned off the lights and directed him to the big pickup she'd bought and now drove in place of the compact rental she'd had. Admittedly, her mind sometimes strayed away from the business at hand and she thought about Police Chief Cordova in ways that were personal…and very unwise.

"Whoa, this is some serious set of wheels." Sky set the box in the cab after she'd unlocked the door. He walked around, admiring her shiny black Dodge Ram.

Annie shrugged. "I considered buying a car,

but decided I needed something capable of hauling ladders, tarps, paint cans and rosebushes."

He whistled through his teeth. "This baby oughta do that and more. Just don't assume you can ditch me at a stoplight with all your horsepower, though. My cruiser may look old, but it has a souped-up engine."

Annie laughed at that.

He assisted her into the driver's seat even though it wasn't necessary. Annie took a moment to reflect on his courtly manners as she saw his lights bob in her rearview mirror. She could no longer say she wasn't warming up to him. He had turned out to be nicer than she'd given him credit for. Cute, too, especially when his blue eyes grew serious. But he could use a haircut. On the other hand, she couldn't really dredge up any real objection to sun-tipped brown hair that curled appealingly over his collar. And a dimple. The chief had a deep one in his left cheek, which she'd bet he would deny was a dimple. No matter, she liked the way it softened his harshly masculine face.

Still considering his other attributes, such as trim hips and broad shoulders on a solid frame, she swung wide to make the turn into her driveway. She punched her remote garage door opener. As the door rose, her headlights and those of the cruiser behind her illuminated horrible black graffiti splashed across the disappearing door. Awful fat letters, along with skulls and wild arrows and curves, also left an ugly trail along the lovely blue siding she'd spent over a week sanding and painting.

Sky barreled out of his car, flashlight in one hand, his Glock in the other.

Numbed by shock, Annie was slower to descend from her vehicle.

Sky waved her back when she started to enter the garage. He uttered a low, angry growl as he flashed his light over the rest of the house. "Get in your pickup and lock the doors. Wait while I inspect the premises to make sure the guys who did this are gone, and that graffiti is the worst we're dealing with."

"What else could there be?"

"Oh, booby traps. Something set to explode the minute you open your house door. I hope to heaven you'll reconsider sticking your neck out to pretty up the town. Even if this warning turns out just to be graffiti, next time could be worse."

CHAPTER FOUR

HIS FLASHLIGHT CAST a muted yellow halo as Sky plunged straight into the varying degrees of darkness. His orders to Annie had been snapped out with a precision indicating he expected them to be obeyed. Like he'd said back at the library, he took his oath to protect and serve seriously. However, Annie had been in control of her life for a long time. This was *her* home and *her* ruined hard work, after all.

So, in spite of the fact that her legs didn't feel steady after Sky had casually tossed out the mention of a possible booby trap, she retrieved her house keys, threw her purse back in the pickup, then locked it, and struck out to follow his bobbing light.

She caught up to Sky in a narrow strip of yard separating her house from the Gilroys'.

Sky wheeled on her. "What are you doing? I told you to stay in your truck!"

"My house, my problem," she shot back in an exaggerated whisper. "If it blows up with you in it, I want to know where to point the fire marshal…and your replacement."

"Thanks," Sky drawled. "I actually doubt the place has been wired. This looks like the work of kids." He panned his light over a section of graffiti. "The little hoodlums sprayed as high as they could reach, and they can't spell worth a hoot."

Annie followed the light to words under a skull that said, "Leve town or next time dye." She put a hand over her mouth, but couldn't hold back a laugh.

"I'm glad you find it humorous," he chided. "Crudely written or not, the message is plain. Next time gang leaders might send someone capable of murder."

"Must be nervous laughter. And you're right, the message is clear—clear enough to make me spitting mad. I'm going over to the Gilroys' to make sure they're all okay. They haven't come out, even though we've made no effort to keep quiet."

"I'll go," he said. "You have a bad habit of forgetting which one of us wears the badge."

"You said you were off duty. And Peggy Gilroy used to babysit me. I need to make sure no harm comes to good people through my attempt to fix things around here."

"We'll go together," Sky said firmly as he shifted the Glock, gave her the flashlight and grasped her hand. "This time, do as I say. Stay behind me. I doubt your friends are dead, but in case I'm wrong about the group that did this, I'd prefer not to have to deal with you fainting."

"Brother!" Annie shook her head. "On my job, I saw death far too many times, and never once did I faint." She waved the light around, shining it directly in his eyes, which made him throw up his gun arm.

"Sorry." She managed to sound meek as she swiftly dropped the beam.

He snarled something Annie couldn't distinguish, which was undoubtedly just as well, since her companion used his fist to bang loudly on the Gilroys' front door.

They heard the shuffle of feet inside, followed by the hushed voices. Profound relief poured through Annie at the confirmation that her friends were okay. "Peggy," she called, putting her mouth near the door. "It's Annie. Police Chief Cordova is with me. It's safe to open your door."

The door opened a crack, as far as the chain lock would allow. George pressed one milky blue eye to the opening. "Peggy, it *is* Annie. Give me room to open the door." George accomplished the task, even though his wife, who must've been plastered against his back, eased out from around him to sweep Annie into a hug.

"We've been so frightened for you, dear. I called the library. Marta Jones said you were there and in your meeting."

"Well, I was there. Not a single person showed up at my meeting," Annie said. "Uh, except the chief." She motioned to Sky.

He broke into their conversation. "Mr. and Mrs. Gilroy, did you see who tagged Annie's house?"

"Tagged?" The couple exchanged puzzled glances.

"Spray painted," Annie explained. "Tagging is a stylized type of graffiti."

"Oh." This time Annie's neighbors reached for each other. Peggy's lips trembled as tears filled her eyes, and George tightened his embrace. "It was dusk when they came," George said. "We didn't see their faces, did we, Peggy?"

Sky's gaze flicked from one to the other. "I know it's frightening to witness vandalism, but my staff and I can't find and charge whoever did this unless someone gives us a tip to go on."

"Maybe Mike and Missy got a better look," George muttered, averting his eyes.

"We'll go see them," Sky said. "You folks

have a good evening." He took a deep breath as he hustled Annie out onto the porch. "They know something they're not telling," Sky said under his breath as he glanced back at the Gilroys, who were closing the door.

"Probably. I hope we get more out of Mike and Missy."

But they were stonewalled there, as well, even though Sky did his best to persuade Annie's younger neighbors to talk.

Mike thrust his wife behind him and said, "I didn't get a clear look, mind you. I think it may have been a couple of teenagers out for end-of-school hijinks."

Sky's vexation was more evident when the Spurlocks went in, and he and Annie were forced to pick their way down the neighbors' darkened walk. "I'll bet dollars to doughnuts these tags are the handiwork of the Stingers, despite what Mike thinks—or claims to think. If those kids were just out for end-of-year hijinks, yours wouldn't have been the only house they hit."

"You must have some idea which local kids are in the gang," Annie said.

"If I did they'd already be in juvie and I wouldn't have a couple of unsolved drive-by shootings at two homes where nice, studious kids happen to live—plus an unsolved rape. Koot and I are sure the victim knew her assailant, even though she insisted it was a stranger. Her family walked away from a house they'd paid into for five years. I'm telling you this so you'll understand that these no-name backers like the grip they have on Briar Run youth and won't give it up without a fight."

She pressed her lips together tightly. "I won't be driven from my home."

Sky geared up to say more, hoping to instill a healthy fear in Annie, but his cell phone rang, shattering the silence that had fallen around them. "Great," he muttered after checking the phone's readout. "Hello, Corrine. If you're phoning to give me some half-baked excuse as to why I can't see Zachary on Wednesday, prepare for my lawyer to file an objection with the family court. It's my scheduled visitation."

The night was still, without even the sound of cicadas. Annie clearly overheard an angry woman shouting at Sky. "I have no idea what dangerous case you're working on now, Skylar Cordova. We live miles away from you in the countryside. Fifteen minutes ago, a car sped down our private lane. Some crazy person heaved two big rocks through our living room window. There was a message tied to one. It says if *you* don't stop helping someone named Annie Emerson, our son will pay.'"

Annie jerked at the sound of her name, and so did Sky, who immediately snapped out questions. "Did you get a license number? Can you describe the person who threw the rock? I assume no one in your home was hurt, or you would've said so."

"Honestly," the caller shrieked, causing Sky to angle the phone farther away from his ear. "Archibald said to tell you to cease and desist whatever you're doing, or our attorney will petition the court to cut off all the visitation you now have with Zack. In fact, I think I'm going to request an interim hearing on the basis of this incident."

Archibald. Sky's anger flared. *Her new husband didn't have any say in anything involving Zack.* "You can't do that, Corrine. I'm a cop. A police chief, in case it's slipped your mind. A job I took so I could pay you the hefty child support the court set for Zachary. My payments are never late, and it's because of this job."

"I doubt that'll matter when a judge sees our shattered window and this note, Skylar. If you want to continue seeing Zachary, you need to move to a less dangerous town, and get a less dangerous job."

It was evident to Annie that the furious woman, Sky's ex-wife, had ended the call. All she heard now was his angry breathing. "I wasn't eavesdropping on purpose," she said. "But I heard every word. And I have to tell you, if I was a mother and that rock-throwing incident happened to me, I'd feel exactly the way she does."

"Of course you would," he said scathingly "But you don't even know her. You have no idea what kind of hoops she makes me jump through." His mouth tightened as he said this.

Annie gazed steadily at him in the glow of the flashlight. "No, but what I'm saying now is that you can opt out of helping me. If you're still planning to arrange for a direct hotline, don't include your phone. Residents can contact your staff. Oh, thank you for escorting me home and checking out my house. I'm going in now, so you can leave. I'll deal with the graffiti tomorrow."

Over Sky's objections, Annie climbed into her pickup, drove into her garage and promptly hit the automatic door closer.

Sky held his breath until a light came on in her living room, followed by another one in her kitchen. He hadn't looked indoors, darn it. But, after standing watch where he was for a few more minutes, he assumed that if anything was amiss in there, he would've heard a commotion. Annie would have used her martial arts skills to stomp on an intruder like she had him. All the same… He walked toward her house again. *Ah, there she was. He could see her moving around the kitchen.* Still, he was oddly reluctant to return to his cruiser. Once he did and turned the key, he was struck by a mind-boggling thought. Annie had willingly put his problems before her own. Sky couldn't remember when he'd run across any woman that unselfish. She'd stood in front of her vandalized home, but after hearing Corrine rail at him, Annie's uppermost concern had been for him—and his fight to spend time with his son. That rattled him.

Driving home, Sky recognized that despite their confrontations, Annie Emerson stirred a long-dormant yearning in him, a desire to have a home like the one he'd been raised in. A home with a loving family. He'd fought for people in war-torn lands who'd had nothing to cling to except family. Yet here, it seemed, too many of his peers were cavalier about splitting up a marriage, breaking up a family. So, yeah, he'd grown jaded.

There was something else that was different about Annie, he decided, pulling into his own garage. In voicing her unselfish opinion, she'd made him want to be the kind of cop he used to be. He'd let his life get derailed. Now he didn't much like what he saw as he took a hard look inward.

He locked up, went into his bedroom and took off his uniform.

He knew that when he'd come home from his last tour, it had been easy to fall into blaming Corrine for making him feel like a failure as a husband—as a man. It'd been easier to blame her, because she'd remarried and taken Zack at a time Sky's whole life was turned upside down. He'd been dug into the side of a godforsaken mountain, with the very real prospect of dying, when she'd had her lawyer send papers requesting a divorce. He'd been too weary, too numb, to fight her. Since then, nothing had kicked him in the butt and made him step up to seize his old life—*until tonight. Tonight, and Annie.*

As he stood under a hot shower, letting the day's grime wash down the drain, reality elbowed its way in again. Not one single thing in the world meant as much to him as his son. However, if he let the Stingers or anyone else run roughshod over him, he wasn't the man he wanted to be in Zack's eyes. He needed to set an example.

Decision made, Sky wrapped a towel around his waist. He sat on the bed and phoned Koot. "I know you're not on duty tonight," Sky said after hearing his friend's sleepy hello, "but I wanted to catch you up on some gang activity that went down a few hours ago." Sky laid out the details in crisp cop fashion, and the older man listened. Sky finished, saying, "I'm more concerned for Zack's welfare than I let on to Corrine or to Annie, who's hot under the collar thinking punks did this and got away with it. I'm sure she'll redouble her efforts to continue this mission of hers to save the neighborhood. She claims it was her grandmother's last request. I've heard that Ida Vance did a lot for others and wasn't one to ask favors. This particular favor is a huge one, if you ask me. But Annie has guts."

"I knew Ida Vance, Sky. Her life wasn't any bed of roses. Uh, Sadie's standing here reminding me that Ida was a good neighbor to anyone and everyone in Briar Run. She was color blind, always ready to lend a helping hand. Sadie wants to know if there's anything she can do to help Miss Ida's granddaughter."

"Well, Annie has a lot of ugly graffiti to scrub off her house or paint over. I'm going there tomorrow. I've also got Wednesday off, remember? I'm supposed to have Zack all day. Unless Corrine's successful at getting her attorney to block my visit…"

"That's just wrong, Sky. A judge shouldn't hold your job against you."

"Yeah, well, I agree. I'll let Corrine calm down for a day, and take Zack to the zoo in Louisville. We can spend most of the day there. She objects if I bring him to my house. She calls it a dump and has other choice words to describe the town. I'm tired of fighting her, so I listed my house with a Realtor on a by-appointment-only basis. I haven't had any lookers yet."

"You haven't talked much about your ex, but from what you *have* said, I've always thought she sounds like a piece of work. Not that it's any of my business, Sky, but how did a nice guy like you fall for her in the first place?"

"She wasn't always like this, Koot. I met her in Baltimore, where she was vacationing with her horsey crowd. I'd volunteered for some extra duty in the form of a weekend security detail at the Pimlico Race Course. Corrine was in town for two weeks taking in the festivities connected to the Preakness. She flirted with me. We hit it off. It was fast-track dating that ended in marriage."

"Ah, those dates must have been hotter than jalapeno pepper seeds."

"We'd both been in the dating game a while. We were two people looking to settle down at the same time, I guess. Then I went to war and she had buyer's remorse."

"It happens. Hey, Sadie's jabbing me. She wants me to tell you to give her a call tomorrow when you head over to Ms. Emerson's. Sadie will bring buckets and brushes and join you. I'm on duty, so you know where to find me if I'm needed."

"Okay. Thank Sadie. The more hands, the better. That reminds me of something else. I'm going to ask our phone rep to arrange a tip line that bypasses dispatch and rings one of us directly."

"I wonder why no one thought of that before. It should cut our response time, Sky. I say, go for it. We're all frustrated about not getting our hands on the real troublemakers."

"I agree. I'll set it up first thing tomorrow." They signed off, and Sky went through his case notebook to locate Annie's phone number on the robbery report. He'd decided to give her a heads-up.

She answered the phone tentatively; he supposed she didn't get too many calls at night.

"It's Sky…Cordova," he added. "I know you said I should steer clear of your place for my own sake, but I have some free time tomorrow. I'm coming by around ten to help you get rid of that graffiti. Koot's wife is coming, too." He waited a heartbeat and all he heard was Annie's sharply indrawn breath. "You can thank us later," he said pointedly, and hung up. He still wore a grin as he climbed into bed and turned off the light. He didn't know her well, but he'd quickly figured out that Annie liked being in charge. He didn't mind throwing her off balance a little—partial payback for the way she'd thrown *him* head over heels.

Sky stifled a yawn and rolled over, vowing to make time to brush up on his own martial arts techniques. At the police academy he'd been adept at hand-to-hand combat. He'd even taught new recruits. It still rankled that he'd let Annie, who probably weighed a hundred and fifteen pounds, get the drop on him.

Eventually he fell asleep.

IN THE MORNING, Sky spoke to the department phone representative, who said that he could have a hotline working by noon.

Next he touched base with the night dispatcher. He might be officially off duty the next day, but he was still responsible for the department. Joe Morales, the quietest of the three cops on his force, liked the night shift. It was no big surprise that none of the others fought to make him rotate. Not even for the twenty percent night differential Sky had persuaded the city manager to add to Joe's weekly pay.

Sky poured orange juice as he listened to a summary of Joe's report. "Looks like Joe had a three-pot-of-coffee yawner," the dispatcher, ready to go off duty, told Sky. "He had one incident at midnight. Two kids trying to steal cigarettes from a convenience store. Joe drove in and the boys took off, dropping the cartons. That's it. If this trend continues, you'll be able to run the squad from a rocking chair, Chief."

"That'll be the day, Margie. Leave a note for day dispatch that Koot's the main man tomorrow. Today I'll be a phone call away if there's any trouble. Tomorrow I hope to take my son to the zoo."

"Will do. Enid just walked in. Enjoy your days off, Chief. Hope you've got something fun planned for today."

Sky hesitated to mention his plan for helping Annie. In Baltimore the precinct dispatchers had too much to do to involve themselves in the day-to-day lives of the cops. He'd expected the same in Briar Run. But after a week on the job, he'd realized that their two long-time dispatchers rivaled a twenty-four-hour newscast. The word *discreet* simply wasn't part of their vocabulary. "I've got a busy day on tap," he said after a moment. "You ladies take care." With that he hung up.

He found a sander amid a pile of tools in his garage. He also found a paint sprayer. Untangling the cord, he debated whether or not to toss that in, too. He had no idea if the three of them—Annie, Sadie and him—would even get around to painting today.

As he backed out of his garage, Sky felt almost guilty for going to help Annie when his own house needed work. Not that it looked any more run-down than anyone else's on Dusty Rose. Most of the homes he drove by were well past their prime. Maybe it was because this was the first time he'd really studied them, but he could suddenly imagine the benefits of Annie's ambitious project....

He parked down street from her driveway. Sky had thought ten a reasonable hour to fire up the sanders, but Annie must have been at it a while. She'd finished the garage door, and was working on the L that connected the garage to the front of her house. He punched in Sadie

Talmage's number. "Hey, it's Sky. If you're still planning to throw your lot in with the graffiti patrol, do you mind picking up coffee and doughnuts?"

She laughed. "Now you've gone and spoiled my surprise. I know you cops need coffee and doughnuts to run on. The bakery was already on my list."

"Thanks. Annie must have started at dawn's early light. This project won't take as long as I expected. See you soon." He hung up and retrieved his sander, taking care to circle around so Annie could see him, rather than risk startling her again.

She shut off her sander and lifted her goggles. "You did come." She rotated her neck. "On the one hand, I don't want anyone to retaliate against your family. On the other, I'd be a fool to turn down a second pair of hands."

"Third," he said. "I just spoke to Sadie Talmage. She's on her way. Let me spell you. Give your back a rest."

"I'll rest once all the graffiti's gone."

Sky saw the determined set of her jaw. He knew when it was pointless to argue. He sauntered off and plugged his sander into an outlet near the porch, one he'd spotted last night. Donning gloves and goggles, he started his machine.

Both sanders whirred steadily until Sadie stood on the walkway and shouted Sky's name.

Dusting off his hands, he got Annie's attention. "Coffee break," he called. "Come and meet another volunteer."

Annie set down her sander and jogged over to the porch, where Sky already had the doughnut box open. He made the introductions before taking a bite out of a delicious-looking cruller.

"He's such a man," Sadie said, giving a throaty laugh. "Annie, I'm delighted to meet you. I don't know if Sky told you about my interest in interior design. Seeing the huge improvement you and your neighbors have made painting these three homes, I'm ready to sign on as a permanent volunteer. We used to live on the next block, and by the way, I knew your grandmother. I used to run into her at the grocery store and hear her concern about how the town was declining."

"I wish she'd said something to me before her illness brought me home."

"She probably didn't want to worry you. Are you thinking of trying to get a grant? I know they have some for environmental development."

"That's a possibility." Annie wasn't going to mention her inheritance.

Sky handed out cups of coffee, and passed the doughnuts. "Sadie, I think her plan is to fire up residents with her unbridled enthusiasm, so they can't wait to jump on her bandwagon like you just did."

Both women looked sheepish.

"Hey, there's nothing wrong with that," Sky said, popping the lid off his coffee. "In fact, when I left home today, I was ready to nominate my street as your next candidate."

"I'll consider it," Annie said, "if you catch whoever had this paint party last night."

"Like I wouldn't do that if I could?"

Sadie sent a quick glance between them. She cleared her throat. "Annie has a point, Sky. She can't keep on cleaning up the same mess. I lived here long enough to know the Stingers rule by intimidation."

"Darned straight." Sky glared at Annie.

She licked the sugar from a doughnut off her fingers and set her cup aside. Picking up her sander, she left the porch, returned to the artistic skull she'd been obliterating and switched on the sander. Paint flew, and the high-pitched squeal had Sky and Sadie moving to the other side of the porch.

"She's too obstinate to be afraid," Sky said. "I told Koot the gang leaders spread various threats that kept everyone from attending her meeting. It wasn't by accident that her house is the only one of the three newly painted ones that got tagged. It's like she has a target on her back, Sadie."

"And you care enough to spend your limited free time over here. I can see she's blind to that and you wish she wasn't."

"Huh? No way! She's stirred up some bad elements in my jurisdiction, that's all."

Sadie rolled her eyes. "I wasn't born yesterday. Plus, I know cops. The tougher they are, the longer it takes, but the harder they fall." She put her cup down and went to get a bucket and sponges out of her car.

Sky watched her fill the bucket from the water spigot, then begin wiping down the sanded garage door. He took his sander and moved to the other side of the porch. The next time he looked up, a few women who didn't normally venture out much had joined Sadie's bucket brigade.

He took a call from Koot before he stopped to figure out what that meant. "Hey," Koot said, "I'm on my way to pick up a submarine sandwich for lunch. Can I bring you hard workers some eats? I assume my wife's still there since she didn't answer at home."

"She's here, along with Annie, me and, let's

see…four women from the neighborhood. Do you have enough cash to buy seven subs?"

"Maybe I'll get a four-foot one with a variety of things on it and have it sliced up."

"Sounds good."

Koot showed up in short order with food and soft drinks to go around. The other women were shy, but Sadie and Annie included them in the chatter.

"How did you happen to know about the work going on here, Mrs. Gonzales?" Koot asked one of them.

"Bad news travels. Neighbors phone neighbors," she murmured. "We all hate what's happened in our schools, and to our town." Her pals nodded just as Koot's cell phone chimed.

"Hot dog, Sky. This is our first tip on the hotline! An anonymous call about a possible drug sale two blocks away," he said, jumping up.

Sky got up, too. "I'm not in uniform, but I have my badge, so I'm going along." The men sprinted for Koot's cruiser, leaving the women to comment among themselves. A hard expression crossed the face of one neighbor.

"Margie Dumas, the night dispatcher, lives next door to me. She told me this morning that the chief started a new tip line. It's about time! My daughter's away at college, thank goodness.

I'd be worried sick if I had a kid at our high school. I hear the boys are all pressured to join the gang. Pressured and threatened."

Annie listened to the women. She took it all in, and after they settled down to work again, she worried about the fact that Sky and Koot hadn't returned.

Midafternoon the four helpers who'd pitched in walked up to Annie and said they had to leave. Rita Gonzales extended a hand. "Good luck. We wish you the best, but we can't risk coming again tomorrow. Word of this will get out, and our houses will be tagged or worse. It's happened before whenever anyone tried to buck the Stingers."

Annie hugged them all and thanked each one for her bravery in coming. "We'll meet again soon to discuss painting *your* homes."

Once the women were out of earshot, and she and Sadie had taken over the painting, Annie said, "I've worked in some rough neighborhoods, but never where so many people were afraid for their jobs—and their homes. It's not right."

"At the time Koot and I decided to sell and move, gang activity had just started infiltrating the schools. I taught there, but the adults weren't hounded." She shook her head. "Those women's stories are unnerving."

"Yes."

The pair fell silent then. Conversation became more difficult when Annie went to the other side of the porch to paint the area Sky had sanded.

The men didn't return until nearly five-thirty. Annie and Sadie had finished painting and were washing up brushes and rollers when they drove in.

Sadie straightened and set her hands on her hips. "You two goof-offs sure know to stay away until the work's all done." She flung a hand out to indicate the drying paint that had restored Annie's home to the blue it'd been before the vandalism.

Koot bounded up the walkway and swept his wife into his arms. Sky paused to study their finished paint job.

"Careful who you call goof-offs," Koot scolded his wife. "We nabbed ourselves a teen dealer and two drug buyers. The users were underage, and since they didn't have priors we had to release them to their parents with stiff warnings. But we confiscated some street equivalent of *oxycodone*. Aka *hillbilly heroin*."

Sky reached Annie as she dried her hands on

a towel. "I've heard the term," she said. "The dealer's a teen? Is he out on the street again, too?"

"He's seventeen," Sky answered. "Old enough so we can hold him overnight, or until his family gets a lawyer and posts bond. He's a scared, desperate, local dropout. His folks are unemployed and his story is that what he brings in selling these pills feeds the family."

"That's a shame," Annie said.

"If it's true," Koot responded. "He claims to be afraid of the gang, but seems more afraid of his dad. He said he'll provide the names of a couple of guys higher up the chain that he splits his take with if we'll intervene with dear old dad. The dude apparently hits the sauce hard, and sonny pays. Sky thinks he's being truthful. I guess we'll see."

"Oh, there's no happy ending is there?" Annie frowned. Sky glanced at her. "There rarely is when kids go off track. But you'd know that."

"Yes, I'm sad to say. Listen, that *is* good news about maybe getting some names. I have a suggestion. Since it's late and we're all tired, why don't I order pizza for a celebratory dinner of sorts. I know Franco's delivers."

"Works for me." Koot was the first to accept. "Sky and I probably managed two bites of our subs at lunch." He turned to his wife. "Okay with you?"

"Sure thing!"

Sky looked as if he might decline, but after checking his cell phone, he nodded. "While we were waiting for the parents to collect their kids, I texted Corrine about my plan to take Zack to the zoo tomorrow. I asked her to text back if I needed to adjust my plans. No news from her is good news. So, I agree with Koot. My stomach is empty and pizza sounds great."

They trudged into the house behind Annie. Sadie immediately spotted the drapes Annie had hung. "Did you make these?" she asked.

"Yes. Gran has stacks of fabric. I love the colors, and I like how they turned out, but they don't really match Gran Ida's old furniture."

"What about recovering the couch and love seat? It wouldn't be difficult. And furniture built today doesn't have the life span these old pieces do."

Annie got out the phone book. "Let me order our food, then we'll talk sewing. I love the idea of upholstering these pieces, but I'm not sure I have the time or expertise." Pausing, she asked what toppings everyone wanted, then placed the order. Storing the phone book, she got out money for the delivery person, even though the men wanted to pay.

"Tell me more about fixing up Gran's furniture while I set the dining table, will you, Sadie?"

"Annie has an ancient TV," Sky informed Koot in the other room. "I guess we might as well pass on the game." He smiled at Annie through the archway as he said it.

Koot folded his long body into a big overstuffed chair. "Hey, Annie, you need to keep this chair for sure. It's really comfy."

"So's this couch," Sky admitted after he sat down.

"Hard to tell if the women even heard us," Koot murmured. "They're too busy trading decorating ideas."

"I noticed. That's nice." Sky eyed the women working together, talking a mile a minute about upholstering, quilting and other crafts.

"This is a treat for my wife," Koot said. "After Sadie quit teaching, she missed her teacher pals. If Annie's serious about spiffing up homes around here, she and Sadie might make a good team. Sadie's a whiz at decorating."

"You know, Koot, I can't recall a single time during our marriage that Corrine made an effort to socialize with the wives of my buddies."

"There's partly why your marriage didn't pan out. If a woman doesn't have a circle of girlfriends, avoid her like the plague. There's something wrong with her."

"Corrine had friends. But they didn't live in Baltimore, they lived here—the highbrow horse crowd. We met in that environment and I let her drag me to their parties for a couple of weeks. She assumed I moved in those circles, and was shocked to learn I didn't. It was hard on her when my army reserve unit got called up for active duty."

A knock sounded at the door. Sky stood to answer it, but Annie beat him there. She paid the delivery boy, then let Sky, who was right behind her, take the boxes to the table where Sadie was pouring iced tea.

Koot passed around the first slices of pizza, which now filled the room with a spicy aroma. Sighs of appreciation followed as they began eating. A sharp crack followed by a second pop rent the air. The large window behind Annie's chair splintered and glass flew everywhere.

"Someone's throwing rocks," she yelped, looking shocked as she ducked.

"Not rocks, bullets," Sky and Koot cried in unison, each dragging a woman to the floor. Sky covered Annie's body with his. She went still under his weight, and for a protracted moment the only audible sound was the combined breathing of the two couples. Then through the shattered window came the screech of tires.

Sky sat up and tugged Annie upright. Their eyes met as he reached out to dust sparkling glass particles from her long dark hair. "Your cheek is cut," he said, starting to touch it, but she pulled away and wiped away the trickle of blood herself.

"Sadie's been hit. Her arm, I think." Koot scrambled to his feet, pulled her close and grabbed a napkin from the table. He shook glass out of the napkin with one hand, and with the other tossed his Sig Sauer to Sky. "Here, boss. I noticed you weren't carrying, and you'll have to give chase. I need to get Sadie to the E.R."

CHAPTER FIVE

SKY SPRANG UP and, with a last glance at Annie, raced for the door. "Call the paramedics, Annie, and have them check your scalp. You have glass shards in your hair."

Annie bent over. After shaking her hair vigorously, she straightened, grimaced and dug out her cell phone. Her hands shook so hard she misdialed the first try and had to start over. When the call connected, she explained the situation, then repeated her address. Hanging up, she said, "I'll get you a clean towel from the kitchen. You need to apply more pressure to that wound, Koot."

It was plain that the man who was a thirty-year veteran of police work was badly shaken because it was his beloved who'd been hit. "Don't faint on me, honey," he pleaded with Sadie.

"I'm okay except it stings like fury. Don't *you* faint on *me*," she said, attempting to joke back.

"Paramedics should be on their way." Annie

returned from the kitchen and handed Koot a white towel. She'd brought in a broom and dustpan but, instead of sweeping, watched Koot carefully bind Sadie's arm without removing the cloth napkin he'd first used to stanch the flow of blood.

All three were startled when Sky unexpectedly burst back in through the front door. "I hear sirens a block or so away. Help is almost here. How are you all doing?"

"That was the shortest chase in history," Koot said, sinking back to his knees. His relief at seeing that their intruder was Sky—and not some gang member—was palpable. But he didn't sound too happy when he asked, "Why aren't you chasing our shooter?"

Sky paced to the wall and back. "A neighbor across the street flagged me down. He said he'd opened his gate, intending to walk his dog, when he noticed a dark blue Caddy driving past real slow. His name is Dawson. I had to drag that out of him. Annie says that according to the other neighbors, he's a bit of a recluse. Anyway, he said he ducked out of sight and kept his dog quiet because it looked like the same car from the other night. The car that let out two young guys, then peeled out fast. He saw them from an upstairs window that night and he thought they were teens based on their builds. They wore dark clothes and acted furtive. But later, they apparently made no effort to hide as they spray painted Annie's place. Like you said, Annie, he didn't report it because he was afraid of retaliation. The other night, he didn't see who picked the guys up."

"Did he get more information on the Caddy? Did he read any part of the license number?" Koot asked halfheartedly, his attention still on Sadie.

"No, and by the time I took his statement—and he insists on remaining anonymous again—it was too late for me to pick up a trail. He did mention that the car was lowered all around and had pricy chrome spinner hubcaps. I sent the Louisville cops a bulletin saying we have an official interest in locating a car like this."

The siren drew closer, then stopped, and Annie, who was stationed by the door, opened it and welcomed in four firemen. In spite of the fact that they knew Sky and Koot, the newcomers took charge of the scene and of Sadie, who had suffered the worst injuries.

"How bad is she?" Koot hovered over a medic breaking open a Ringer's IV to restore Sadie's fluids.

"I've seen worse," the medic said. "We have

to transport her, Talmage. You can meet her at the hospital. Hey, calm down. She's not in serious danger. It's a flesh wound and the bullet passed clear through the underside of her arm. Your time will be better spent figuring out the slug's trajectory and digging it out from wherever it landed for evidence."

"We'll do that," Sky said, but he hovered as one man dabbed an antiseptic-saturated gauze square to a deep cut on Annie's cheek. "We'll take her, too," the fireman told him. "This cut may take more than a butterfly to close. Besides, she's got glass all through her hair. The E.R. nurses are better equipped to remove the particles without doing further harm. Right now your cuts look minor," he said, returning his full attention to Annie. "I'll cover your hair with a sterile plastic cap. You won't win any beauty contests—" he gave her a wink "—but it'll keep glass bits out of your eyes and from falling on your shirt."

"I should stay here," Annie fretted. "I need to cover the window. And there's glass to sweep up in every corner of this room." She clutched the broom, but Sky pried it out of her hand.

A third man, who'd begun to pack up the medical kits, indicated the open, almost-full pizza boxes on the table. "Somebody did a number on your supper. Whoever cleans this up, be sure to secure the leftovers well before you toss them in an outside garbage bin. We frequently see homeless folks and hungry kids riffling through cans around the neighborhood."

"That's terrible," Annie said. "I had no idea hunger was such a problem here. Oh, Sadie," she cried, transferring her concern to Koot's wife. "I couldn't be sorrier that this happened to you in my home." She held Sadie's uninjured arm and helped a little as a fireman and Koot settled her onto a gurney.

Sadie's beautiful complexion had gone pale from pain and anxiety. Her color began seeping back after the medic gave her a shot of mild painkiller. Now she did her best to smile as she patted Annie's hand. "Don't worry, I'm going to heal and be good as new. I promised the women who helped us today that they could count on my help with their homes. I intend to keep that promise. It burns my you-know-what the way those cowards bully innocent people." She continued her rant as two of the men wheeled her out.

Koot took a couple of steps to follow his wife, then stopped and shot Annie a helpless expression.

"It's okay." She waved him on. "I won't hold her to anything she said tonight."

Sky shifted the broom to his left hand and urged Annie toward the door. "I meant what I said about you going along to the E.R. for treatment. And the paramedic expects you to go, as well. I'll stay and sweep up the glass, and see what I can find in your garage to cover that window until morning. Then you can call a glass company to repair it properly."

"Again." Annie sighed. "Repair the window again. I had it fixed the afternoon of the break-in. I should've kept the glass company's invoice," she lamented. "Wait—George Gilroy called them. Maybe he's still got their phone number."

"That's another thing," Sky said. "I'll check with the Gilroys and Spurlocks. Maybe they saw more than Dawson. I know your next-door neighbors are skittish, Annie, but I'm surprised they haven't come over to see if you're okay."

A fireman who'd lingered to escort Annie to the aid car arched an eyebrow. "Cordova, it sounds as if you're battling something bigger than standard, low-level gang mischief. If it's a vendetta against this woman, then maybe you should arrange a safe house for her after the docs fix her up tonight."

Annie sputtered objections from the doorway as her escort hustled her out. "My poor neighbors are probably huddled in their bedrooms in the dark, afraid for their lives," she called back to Sky. "Please don't frighten them more."

Sky stepped to the door, assuring her he'd be calm and composed when what he wanted to do was put his fist through a wall. He hated feeling powerless against this gang. He hated the fact that they'd retaliated against Annie for no reason other than her unwillingness to hide. Instead, she cleaned the graffiti off her house and refused to back down from her plan to organize folks and take back the neighborhood. He didn't like that they were stepping up their crimes. And to have this drive-by happen right under his nose galled him no end.

After the entourage left, Sky spent a few minutes guessing at the angle of the first bullet. He took photos with his cell phone and experienced some satisfaction when he found a slug in the wall. Leaving it, he went out to his car for an evidence kit. He carefully removed the slug and saw that it bore trace evidence of blood, obviously Sadie's. He recalled the second shot, which exploded the window, going wide of the table. After a few minutes' examination, he discovered that slug embedded high in the wooden molding that framed the dining room ceiling. Climbing onto a chair to retrieve it, he then tucked the evidence bag in his shirt pocket and turned to the task of sweeping up glass. He also heeded the words of the fireman who'd warned them about properly disposing of the leftover pizza. Ultimately he decided to put the trash bag in his car to throw in the Dumpster behind the police station. Sky doubted even hungry drunks were stupid enough to rummage through the department's garbage.

As bad luck would have it, Annie didn't own a board big enough to cover her window. Sky visited the homes on either side of hers to see if the neighbors had anything he could use. Neither couple answered his knock. Annie had probably been right that they were hiding in fear. Since he couldn't force them out, he made do with some two-by-sixes that were in Annie's garage. He nailed two of them in a big X over the jagged opening and put two others on the inside. Once he'd completed that, he recalled the last comment made by the fireman who'd been helping Annie, a suggestion about finding her a safe house for the night. His department budget didn't stretch to putting any victim up in a hotel. But he was afraid gang leaders might send someone back here tonight. He debated the options that were open to him as he gave the house a final once-over. Having done the best he could with cleanup, he left a light burning over Annie's kitchen sink, locked up and headed for the hospital.

Fifteen minutes later, Sky turned into the parking lot of the nearest trauma center, which served lower Louisville and Briar Run. He met Koot driving out. They stopped their cruisers beside each other and both rolled down their windows.

"How's Sadie?" Sky peered into the car, where she sat beside Koot with her eyes closed. "And where's Annie?" He didn't see her in the backseat.

"Busy night in the E.R.," Koot said. "A doc was just going in to evaluate her. She insisted I take Sadie home, so I told her I was sure you'd be along shortly. Thank heavens Sadie's not as bad as I feared," the older cop admitted, relief evident in his voice. "The bullet grazed the underside of her arm. The doc said she was lucky. It's soft tissue, which is why there was so much blood. I should've known that," he said with some irritation. "But it's hard to think like a cop when the person bleeding all over you is someone you love."

"It's okay, Koot. You don't have to apologize for being distracted, I understand. You get Sadie home. I'll go see what's up with Annie. If they finish with her and I'm not around, I wouldn't put it past her to call a cab."

"I noticed she's pretty unflappable. In fact, we ought to be plenty proud of both our ladies, Sky."

Sky pulled his lower lip between his teeth for a moment. "Yeah. But Annie's not my lady. She's a taxpayer in our district—that's all. And considering the way she's setting off the Stingers, she's our department's personal pain in the butt."

"Really?" Koot's comment was mild compared to his expression, which implied that he thought Sky was full of baloney.

Flustered by his coworker's insinuation, Sky rolled up his window and drove on. His nerves jumped as he exited the car in the lot. To keep his hands steady, he buried them in the back pockets of his jeans. Sky didn't know how he felt about Annie, and wasn't sure he *wanted* to know. She piqued his interest on several levels. But he wasn't happy his feelings were transparent enough for Koot to see that interest. After all, look at the disaster he'd made of his marriage. What did that say about his ability to pick a woman? *The right woman.* Chin lowered, Sky stiff-armed his way through the emergency room glass doors.

Yowza! Koot hadn't exaggerated when he'd said it was busy. People in obvious pain wriggled uncomfortably in their seats. A drunk jabbered out loud to no one. Kids and babies squalled. A fresh-faced boy looking too young to be a father walked his moaning, very pregnant wife past overflowing chairs. They avoided a pasty-faced woman vomiting into a bucket.

A harried nurse stepped out of a door marked Private and called out a name. She glanced at Sky and, on recognizing him, said, "Chief Cordova, Lieutenant Talmage said you'd be in to collect the patient in examining room D. If you'd like, you could come on back and join her."

Sky weighed the possibility that they might have put Annie in a dressing gown. The thin gowns could reveal more than the wearer wanted. *Oh, what the heck.* "Thanks, Lou. I'll go let her know I'm here at least."

He made his way down the corridor to room D, and poked his head around the curtain. Annie lay on an examining table with her head tipped back. An aide stood behind her, running a large comb with big teeth through Annie's long black hair. Even from the doorway he could hear the tinkle of glass as it fell into some kind of container. "Hi," he said, moving fully into the room. "Lou sent me back here," he informed the aide he wasn't familiar with. Sky couldn't say whether he was happy to see Annie in her own clothes, or whether he was just a touch disappointed not to find her wearing one of those short, revealing gowns.

Aaak, he should feel guilty even *thinking* that…but he wasn't.

"I'm almost done," Annie said, lifting her head. "Koot said Sadie's arm was a flesh wound. That's a relief, isn't it? I don't need a stitch in my cheek, either. The other cuts to my scalp are minor."

"And thanks to this lice comb," the aide interjected, continuing to gently comb Annie's hair, "she'll soon be free of glass."

"That's good. Annie, I found both bullets," Sky said, propping one shoulder against the door frame. "If it's okay with you, I'd like to stop at the office to send the slugs and the photos I took off to the lab. The sooner we can find out if there's any match to known gang activity, the faster we'll run down our shooter."

"If you need to go now, I'll call a cab to take me home."

Sky laughed and the women both eyed him speculatively. "I'm laughing," he said, "because I told Koot in the parking lot that if I didn't get in here to take you home, you'd call a cab. I bet you had no idea you were so predictable."

Annie shrugged as the aide said, "That's it, Ms. Emerson, you're free to go." She set aside the comb and plastic basin, and separated a form from a clipboard. She passed a copy to Annie. Bending closer, the aide asked in an exaggerated whisper, "Why on earth would you call a cab, honey? I wouldn't if *I* had a big, handsome chauffeur come for me."

Sky flushed as Annie slanted him a long, assessing look. "Don't take the handsome part too seriously," he said, placing a hand at the small of her back to guide her out of the room.

"I should have a comeback, but my brain stopped functioning about the time you threw me on the floor, pounced on me and said we'd been shot at."

"So you *are* human?" He said it teasingly.

They stopped at checkout, and Annie paid what was owed on her bill. Outside, Sky directed her to where he'd parked. He unlocked and opened her door, then shut it again as soon as she was settled. He was in the process of backing out of the parking space when his cell phone rang.

"Cordova," he said, punching the speaker button on his dash.

"It's Corrine. What are you doing at the hospital with that Annie person? I tried reaching you a few minutes ago. When you didn't answer I called dispatch. Margie Dumas said you and some other people were shot at while you were eating dinner at that woman's home, Skylar. And you don't see why I'd object to letting my son go off with you tomorrow?"

Sky's jaw tensed and he wrapped his hands so tightly around the steering wheel his knuckles turned white. "Zack is my son, too. I called my lawyer last night. He assured me that tomorrow's my scheduled visitation day. You can't stop me from taking Zachary to the zoo, Corrine."

"Our lawyer told us the same thing," she said unhappily, "but Archibald says if you had any decency, you'd skip tomorrow and any other visitations until whatever mess you and that woman are involved in gets cleaned up."

"Have Zack ready at nine-thirty in the morning. If he still has the backpack I gave him for Christmas, load it with a snack and some juice or water. I'll have him home at five, although technically I'm allowed to keep him through the dinner hour." He punched the off button so hard, the plastic knob popped off and landed in Annie's lap.

Without saying a word, her expression benign, she snapped it back in place.

Sky altered his tone. "I'm sorry she kept calling you 'that woman.'"

"I've been called worse by a few clients I had back in L.A. And you're the one who has to deal with her on a regular basis, Sky. I'll never meet her."

He pulled into precinct parking. "Here I was about to ask if you'd like to go to the zoo with us tomorrow."

"Now why would I do that?" Annie asked, giving him a hard look.

"Well, partly because we haven't caught the people responsible for the attacks on your house. All evening I've been thinking about a remark made by one of the firemen. He said I should get you into a safe house tonight. I don't have money in the department budget to put you in a hotel. I do have a spare bedroom at my place. It's not the Hilton, but it's got a bed, a dresser and its own bathroom. The next problem I see is that I won't be around tomorrow to look out for you."

Annie sucked in a breath, then blew it out. "I appreciate your concern, but I can't go home with you and leave my house empty and vulnerable to whatever attack those idiot gangbangers dream up next."

"I was afraid you'd say that. Stay in the car for a minute while I toss the trash from your dining room. Then we'll go inside and I'll ship off the evidence kit to the lab. It'll take me another two minutes to inform our dispatcher that if she gives my private information or whereabouts to my ex—or anyone—ever again, she'll be fired."

"I'll wait in the car. That's not my problem. I have enough of my own."

"That you do. Problems, may I point out, that you've brought on yourself. What you should do is put out through the grapevine that you've decided to stop trying to save the neighborhood."

"But I haven't. Other women came to help me today. They're willing to let me help them paint their homes. And they want the gangs run out of town, too."

"You can't be a one-woman army, Annie."

"No, but it only takes one ant to start moving a mountain."

"You know what? I've exhausted my arguments for now." Sky picked up the evidence bag, slid out and hit the door locks. He went to the back of the car, opened the trunk and hauled a trash bag to a big bin behind the police station. Then he went into the building through a back door.

Annie leaned against the head rest and shut her eyes. Her nerves were frayed. What if Gran Ida's dream of revitalizing Briar Run was totally unrealistic? Peggy Gilroy and Gran's doctor said she'd tended to ramble and lose herself in the past. Annie hadn't witnessed much of that. But what if Gran's faith in her ability to make a difference was part of a dear old lady's desire to turn back the hands of time? Annie's early attempts to fulfill Gran Ida's wishes were causing havoc for good people. The Gilroys and Spurlocks were afraid to leave their newly painted homes. Sadie Talmage had embraced Annie's plan and it got her shot. And Sky— Sometimes you just knew when a man was good. The more time Annie spent around Sky Cordova, the more she felt that way about him…and wished she didn't.

Sky returned to the car in the middle of Annie's reflections.

"Hey, are you just dozing off, or are you suffering belated effects from our trauma?"

Rolling her head, she gazed at him from heavy-lidded eyes. "It's been a long day. I should've taken a cab home. Dropping me off takes you out of your way. But there isn't much we can do about that now."

"Ah, you've lost some of your fire." He remembered what Koot said. "According to Koot, you held up like a champ. Better than him, he told me."

"They're a great couple. Sadie's a woman with unbelievable guts."

Sky started to comment when his two-way radio came to life. "A unit in south Louisville just stopped a vehicle matching the description you sent in, Cordova. You reported two men in the car. All we have is a driver. He's wanted on priors so we're taking him to the station if you'd like to drop by and ask him some questions."

"You bet. Did you find any weapons in the car?"

"Negative."

"Hmm, okay. I can be there in about twenty minutes. Do you mind checking his hands for residue?"

"Will do. See you in twenty, Cordova." The light on the radio went off.

"Is that the car involved in our incident?" Annie faced him, drawing up her left knee and bracing it on the console that separated their seats.

"Could be. But they picked up one guy and no weapons. Your neighbor saw two men."

"That doesn't mean he won't give up his companion if the police make his life uncomfortable enough," Annie said.

"Are you telling me how to do my job?"

"No. Er, of course not. Well," she said brightly, "here we are at my house. Thanks for the lift." Annie had her door open the minute Sky stopped in her driveway, her door key in hand.

"Wait! I'm going in with you to do a walk-through. I locked the place when I left for the hospital, but—"

"I'm sure everything's fine. The street's completely quiet."

"Yeah." Sky did a cursory glance all directions. "I couldn't find a solid piece of plywood to cover your window. But I didn't leave a hole big enough for anyone to crawl through."

"It's fine. You go see if the guy they picked up is connected with what happened here."

"Right, I know you're Ms. Black Belt." Sky put the Crown Vic in park. "If it's all the same to you, I'll wait until you open up and turn on some lights."

"Not black belt. Red stripe in a white belt, but I'll wave if everything is okay." She hopped out and hurried up the walkway. Annie hadn't noticed before how dark her sidewalk, yard and porch were at night. Because of all the incidents that had occurred, plus the boards nailed over her broken window, she couldn't help feeling jumpy. She unlocked the front door, went in and flipped on the living room and porch lights. Turning, she lifted a hand to signal Sky. After that, she locked up quickly, then stood at the window and watched him back out. His departure left a great black hole outside, and she couldn't suppress a shiver as his taillights disappeared around the corner.

She kept a light burning in her living room as she went into her bedroom and got ready for bed. She'd lived alone in a neighborhood worse than this one for a long time. *Yes, but you were never shot at before.* Hoping to silence the little voice in her head, Annie climbed into bed and opened the notebook filled with her preliminary plans for beautifying the area. Tomorrow the sun would come up, and she'd begin anew. She tapped her pen against her lips. It might not be a bad idea to spread the word that her primary goal centered on helping residents paint their homes. She could downplay the more distant objective of ousting the Stingers. That could come later, once people started to feel confident again. Confident and hopeful…

ANNIE WOKE WITH a start to someone pounding on her front door. She'd fallen asleep while working on her notebook, and she hadn't even shut off her lights.

With her heart thumping like the biggest drum in a parade, she threw on her robe and tiptoed to the door. All the while she told herself that people out to do her harm wouldn't announce their presence by knocking. So perhaps George Gilroy or Mike Spurlock had noticed her lights still blazing at—she checked Gran's living room clock—1:00 a.m. Yikes, that was late for anyone to stop by. "Wh-who is it?" she stammered, her mouth pressed to the keyhole. She hated how thin and reedy her voice sounded.

"It's Sky. Are you okay?"

Annie was so relieved to hear a friendly voice, she undid the chain lock and the bolt lock and yanked open the door. "I'm fine. Sort of fine," she corrected, scraping back hair that had fallen out of the half twist she'd put it in before heading to bed. "What's wrong? Why are you here in the middle of the night?"

Barging straight into the house, he dropped a duffel bag at his feet. He'd had it slung over one shoulder.

"Where's your car? I don't see it in the driveway." She craned her neck to peer around him, up the street and down, before he locked the door.

"I walked over from my house."

"You live near enough to walk?" Annie blinked.

"I live two blocks east. Annie, listen up. I believe the car and driver my colleagues in Louisville picked up earlier does belong to a Stinger member. A guy ordered by higher-ups in the gang to scare you into leaving Briar Run, all because that brochure you put out targeted their hold on the town. The driver of the Cadillac has a mile-long rap sheet. The team in Louisville got a warrant and searched his apartment. It takes time to get a warrant, which is why I'm so late." He waved his arms. "Anyway, the upshot is they found an arsenal in one of his closets. None of the weapons were registered and he has no permits to own or carry. None of those weapons were fired recently. I know from what Mr. Dawson said that there were two men in the car when it left this neighborhood. The perp refuses to cooperate or give up a companion, assuming he was part of the duo who pulled your drive-by." Sky smoothed a hand down hollow cheeks. "Smug as the jerk acted throughout his questioning, I came away with a bad feeling.

So, I'm bunking on your couch for the rest of the night."

"The night is half-gone and everything was quiet until you banged on my door. Babysitting me goes beyond the call of duty, Sky."

"Forget about duty. I don't want your dead body on my conscience." He found himself shouting because he didn't want to give her the impression he'd come because he *cared* about her. "Just go back to bed," he said wearily. "I'm sorry I woke you. When I drove by on my way home, I saw all your lights on. I assumed you were up."

Annie studied him a moment, then climbed down off her high horse. "I'll get you a sheet and blanket. I admit I felt anxious, so I purposely left a bunch of lights on." She spun around, hurried down the hall and rummaged in a closet. Then she returned with her arms full of bedding.

Sky hadn't intended to touch her, and he shouldn't, but the look on her too-pale face, along with her admission, had him reaching out to smooth back her hair. She'd just deposited a set of sheets, a blanket and pillow on the couch.

"Get some rest. My being here is just a precaution—so *I'll* sleep better," he said, his voice low.

"Thanks," she murmured, touching his hand

before she turned again and padded barefoot back to her room.

He expected to hear her lock her bedroom door, but he heard nothing. When the light shining out from under the crack in her door went black, he felt a knot lodged under his breast bone dissolve and spread like liquid warmth.

The truth was, he felt tired, too.

Sky shook out the sheets and covered the couch cushions. He sat and took off his boots. Earlier he'd returned Koot's Sig-Sauer, and now he removed his Glock from the holster at the small of his back; he set it within easy reach as he removed his shirt and loosened his belt.

Tomorrow he'd lock the weapon in his glove compartment, or otherwise Corrine would pitch a fit—like she did not long ago. He'd been running late and had worn it when he showed up at their farm to take Zack out for ice cream. He didn't blame her for complaining about that. Kids and guns didn't mix. The problem was that she took every opportunity to rag on him about being a cop. But it wasn't as if she hadn't known that when they met.

Unable to stop a yawn, Sky flipped off the living room light switch and burrowed into the comfy old couch. Despite his exhaustion, his mind refused to shut down. Normally, thinking about spending a day with Zachary made him happy and let him relax. Even though he looked forward to taking his son to the zoo, Sky's thoughts kept going back to Annie, wishing she'd accepted his invitation. That also perturbed him—the fact that he'd invited her. Never before had he met a woman he'd wanted to share Zack with. Sky couldn't understand why he'd chosen someone as prickly and as obstinate as Annie Emerson.

But she had a softer side, too. Her hair was soft, and so was what he'd touched of her skin. He flopped over onto his side, and smiled about that. He was getting close to sleep when the strong, pungent odor of smoke curled past his nose. Thinking he must have been dreaming, he checked the time on his cell phone. According to the backlit display, it was after 3:00 a.m. He no longer thought he was dreaming the strong acrid scent of smoke in the room.

Shooting up off the couch, Sky yelled out to Annie. She materialized at his side so fast he knew the smoke had awakened her, too. She snapped on the floor lamp that stood at the foot of the overstuffed couch. It gave off enough light that Sky was able to see smoke rolling into the room from under the front door.

He snatched up his gun and unfastened the

locks. "Stand back," he ordered Annie, who pressed the length of her slender frame against his back. She moved slightly. Not wanting to wait, Sky turned on the porch light. Smoke continued to billow through the sides of the door, but the middle wasn't hot to his touch. "Go to the kitchen and get me a pitcher of water."

She complied at once, and though some water slopped out onto his stocking feet, she'd gotten back with most of it. He yanked open the door and immediately spotted a pile of newspapers smoldering right in front of the door. Sky doused the burning papers.

Wrinkling her nose against the acrid odor, Annie took back the pitcher, ran to the kitchen again and returned with it full to the brim.

Sky had jumped over the bundle. "I think whoever did this is long gone," he said, emptying the pitcher, and making sure the whole bundle was out. "It's another warning," he muttered, glaring at her.

For the first time he noticed what Annie, who hovered in the doorway, had on. She wore an oversize Dodgers T-shirt that doubled as a nightgown, and big slippers on her feet that looked like alligators. In her left hand she clutched, of all things, a rolling pin. Seeing her so exposed touched a soft spot in Sky that up to now he'd reserved for Zack. It seemed natural to gather Annie into his arms. He smoothed his hands up her taut back, then tucked her head under his chin, and realized he needed a shave when her hair rasped on his whiskers. "This is too much, Annie. I want you to get dressed, and I don't care what you say, we're spending what's left of the night at my place. The smell of smoke will linger here for hours."

"No, Sky." She felt him tense, and she wrapped her arms around his waist. "Listen, I'm not being contrary, I swear," she said against his solid shoulder. "This home of Gran's is all I have of my past. And it meant everything to my grandmother. I don't know if I told you she raised me. I'm scared to death the firebug will come back. But what kind of caretaker, what kind of *person,* would I be if I left for the sake of my safety, but risked the home that represents my whole history? Not only that, I'd be risking the lives of innocent neighbors who own tinderbox houses next door."

Sky touched his forehead to hers. "I can't argue with that kind of logic, Annie." Tucking his Glock into the back waistband of his jeans, he brushed both thumbs over her cheeks. "It's possible that someone planned to burn this house down and I scared them off when I got up and shouted for you. Or maybe they hoped to smoke you out. I didn't hear scampering feet, but I may have been just groggy enough to miss any sound. I was scared to death you'd be overcome by the smoke."

Annie took her arms from around his waist and wedged a space between them. She sensed a shift in him, in his attitude toward her, which she wasn't prepared to deal with. She didn't know what to do about a warm, protective man who loosened her tightly bound and controlled desires. She'd been dumped by one guy she'd loved. And looking at the track record of the women in her family…most of the relationships hadn't panned out. Gran Ida's only love had died, leaving her alone to raise their child—a child who grew up and ran off with an unreliable man. That had broken Gran Ida's heart.

Annie had decided that giving your heart to any man was risky. She'd systematically avoided the possible perils of falling for anyone again—successfully, too, until Police Chief Sky Cordova appeared and disrupted her well-ordered world. And why *him?* Heaven knew she'd tried to discourage him. He continued to show up and show his concern for her. And darn it all, he left big, muddy tracks across her wounded heart.

"I guess sleep is out of the question," he

said. "I'll go make a pot of coffee. Do you play poker?" he asked hopefully.

"I play cribbage."

"Good, you can teach me."

"I'm wide awake. You don't need to stay."

"Ah, yes, if the firebugs come back for a second try, you'll hit them with your rolling pin and bite them with your alligator slippers."

She looked down at her feet. "I like my slippers. A pair of abused twins I got into a great foster home bought these for me last Christmas. They said the alligators reminded them of how hard I fought to help them."

"Hmm. That says a lot about your work ethic—and your compassion. Out of curiosity, did you leave behind a brokenhearted Dodgers fan when you moved here from L.A.?"

"What? No! Why would you ask such a thing?"

"That's definitely a man's T-shirt you're wearing. A big man."

For all of two seconds Annie thought about lying. She thought about inventing a pining lover. However, she didn't lie well. "I'm a huge Dodgers fan," she tossed over her shoulder as she stomped toward her room on her floppy alligator feet. "By the way, you might do well to heed one of Gran's favorite sayings, namely that curiosity killed the cat."

"Uh-huh, but satisfaction brought him back to life."

Sky laughed as she threw up a hand and said, "Pfft!" She slammed her bedroom door. Unable to stop chuckling, he stepped into his boots and collected his shirt from the couch. She was one of a kind. Despite his concern that the Stingers had it in for her, Sky almost had pity to spare for the unsuspecting gang leaders.

CHAPTER SIX

ANNIE SNIFFED THE air as she walked into the kitchen after changing into jeans, a clean T-shirt and sneakers. "The smell of coffee almost wipes out the smoke. Maybe it won't take as long to air out the house as you thought."

Sky held up one of two mugs sitting on the counter. He waggled the glass coffee carafe at Annie. "I can't recall if you put anything in your coffee. Should I leave room at the top or fill it up?"

"I prefer cream, but I've been known to drink it straight up in a pinch."

"Your house, your coffee, your call." He left room in her mug and watched her rummage in the fridge for a jug of milk. Even though he chided himself, he ogled her nicely rounded derriere. In his appreciation for how snugly her jeans fit, he overfilled his cup and burned his fingers while trying to wipe up the spill.

Annie straightened, saw his dilemma and tore off two paper towels that she handed him. "Do you need ice for your fingers? What happened? Did you misjudge the size of the mug?"

"Something like that," he muttered, and mopped harder.

Annie added milk to her coffee, then set the jug back in the fridge. She carried her mug to the table and sat at the end, where she'd been eating her meals since Gran Ida's death. "I started thinking about your zoo trip," she said. "Will you manage okay on next to no sleep?"

Sky sat beside her. "On this job and others I've had, it's common to work around the clock. You adjust."

"Those don't sound like fun jobs. What others have you had? I assume you were a cop before coming to Briar Run."

"Yes. When I got out of college, which I'd gone to on an ROTC scholarship, I went to the police academy, then stepped into a job with the Baltimore P.D. Big city, big force, lots of crime. Kept us busy. I also served in the Maryland Army Reserve. It took some juggling to keep up with my reserve duties, but my supervisors were good about the schedules. At first I only had me to worry about, so I was footloose. I advanced through the ranks and was promoted to sergeant, then lieutenant. I was in line for captain when I met Corrine. I look back now and see that we married too quickly. Six months after our wedding I was called into active military duty." Sky let a few minutes tick by as he ran a finger around the rim of his mug.

"About four months into our marriage, we learned Corrine was pregnant," he finally said. "I left an unhappy, pregnant wife behind, and Uncle Sam tapped me for three back-to-back tours. Rotations stateside were brief at best. Corrine was ready to go out and socialize, but all I wanted to do was sleep." Taking a drink, Sky set his mug down and gazed into space.

Annie waited for him to go on. She'd deduced, of course, that his marriage hadn't ended well. But hearing how he'd been forced to leave a pregnant wife to fend for herself reinforced her own skepticism about marriage. Sky's ex had remarried. Not all widows or women left to their own devices did—at least not in her family.

Sky planted his elbows on the table. "You've heard enough about me. Let's talk about you."

"Boring!" Annie idly shuffled the deck of cards she'd set out, along with a cribbage board. Suddenly she asked another question. "So, is being police chief of Briar Run is a nice step up from being an almost-captain back in Baltimore?"

"Not necessarily. Oh, I know how attached

you are to this town, but I head up a skeleton crew charged with protecting folks who feel terrified and don't really care what we do. The factory closed and that paralyzed everyone. They choose to live in apathy. Compared to families struggling to survive in other parts of the world, life here is still pretty cushy."

"What other choices are there for the residents?"

"They could move to where there's jobs or pool their resources and keep the small businesses operating. What the average Joe doesn't understand is that this city's going broke. It's a matter of time before all services are cut, and the town dies."

Annie eyed him a moment. "Pardon me for saying it, but that sounds defeatist on your part, too. I don't believe anyone likes living in poverty. Picking up and moving, like you did, may have been easy for a single guy. Not so easy for a family with three or four kids and a family dog—oh, and with a run-down house to sell. When life beats good people down, Sky, they find it nearly impossible to get back up. Not being able to support your family causes loss of self-esteem. You feel isolated, as well as defeated. That's why I believe that if I can help paint homes, it may reboot people's community spirit. I see you're looking skeptical again. I'm not so naive as to think that's the whole answer. But improving the look of their surroundings may boost people's initiative, their willingness to dig in and find ways to solve other problems."

"I think you *are* naive, Annie. Fewer than one in five home owners in Briar Run can afford to paint. Renters don't care, and wouldn't buy paint even if they had the money. If landlords cared, they'd have spiffed up their properties long before now."

She sat silently, and had to glance away from the cynicism in his eyes. As she wrapped her hands around her coffee mug, she looked up again. "Gran Ida left me the means to do a lot of the work that needs to be done, Sky."

"You can't… You're paying?" Sky rubbed the back of his neck. "Annie, now I'm doubly worried about your safety. If that news ever leaked out…" Breaking off, he continued to stare blankly at her.

"I shared the information with you because you just said you understand the issues, yet you continue to try to dissuade me. I let the neighbors think I negotiated a ridiculously low price per gallon of paint. Last night I started thinking that maybe I could tell the next set of home owners I found a store going out of business and they practically gave me the paint."

"Annie, Annie, Annie…even little white lies told for a good cause have a way of coming back to bite you."

"And that worries me. I've never been good at lying. Gran Ida always knew if I was trying to put something over on her."

"You said she raised you. What happened to your parents?"

"My mother was a teen runaway," she said, her voice laced with sadness. "Her history is pretty much lost. I only recently learned that my grandmother hired a private investigator who found Mary Louise living on the street in L.A., but she refused to come home. I knew she ran away and maybe lived on the street somewhere in southern California. I didn't know Gran had located her. All she ever told me was that one rainy night my mother showed up at her door, deathly ill and nine months pregnant."

"I take it she was married, since your last name is different from your grandmother's."

"So she claimed. Her supposed husband is another empty limb on my family tree," Annie said with a shrug. "My birth certificate is blank where his name belongs. But my mom is listed as Mary Louise Emerson. Don't get me wrong,

Sky, Gran was wonderful, and I'd never want to hurt her. I never told her I spent years phoning Emersons in and around L.A." Annie sighed. "Even lacking a first name, I made a gazillion calls asking if the person answering the phone at a particular Emerson household knew Mary Louise Vance. No one ever did. I'm sure Gran suspected that was why I applied for scholarships in southern California and stayed there to work. I hit so many dead ends, ultimately I gave up. Gran Ida never stopped hoping I'd come home. It was too late for her, but I eventually figured out that this is where I belong."

Uncharacteristically, Sky reached out and caught hold of her restless fingers. "As a Johnny-come-lately outsider, it strikes me that you turned out okay. Better than okay." He skimmed a finger over her nose. Then, as if embarrassed, he pulled back and stumbled a little on his next statement. "I, uh…it's just as well you didn't run the guy to ground. No one who's fit father material—or a decent human being— would abandon a woman he got pregnant."

Annie nodded. "You're probably right. As a social worker, I found food and beds for a lot of homeless men. Most were like fog that dissipated when the morning sun came out. I can't understand the appeal for living in the moment like that. The constant drifting, often bunking in culverts or under bridges. Their lives are anathema to the way society expects grown-ups to act. A few of them were rehabilitated. Most didn't want to be. Even if my biological dad fell into that category, it doesn't mean I wouldn't prefer to know if he was an alcoholic, prone to addictions, mentally challenged or just a jerk, since I carry some of his genes."

Sky started to say something, but stopped and half rose out of his chair. He put a finger to his lips, and pulled out his Glock with his other hand. "Shh. I think we have uninvited visitors in your backyard."

Annie strained to hear, and sure enough there was a slight rustle, as if someone was shuffling through her flower bed. She glanced at the clock and saw that she and Sky had been talking for nearly two hours. Oddly, instead of concern that a new form of trouble was about to descend, what popped into Annie's head was that she hadn't taught Sky how to play cribbage. And another thing—how he seemed to accept her background.

Sky dropped into a crouch and duck-walked past the sink, staying out of sight under the window.

Slipping out of her chair, Annie followed his lead.

The minute he noticed, he motioned for her to stay back. But when he moved, so did she.

"This is serious, Annie," he whispered. "I heard a rattle—could be a gas can. I'm going out. Stay back. Please." He stood up, threw open the back door and made a flying leap off the back porch. He landed in the flower bed where he'd gauged the culprit to be, and took a would-be arsonist by surprise.

Annie emerged with a flashlight she'd stopped to retrieve from a kitchen drawer. She snapped it on and the beam bounced off a red gasoline can still rolling on the ground. She swung the light in Sky's direction. He'd trained his weapon on the guilty party, a scared kid with a box of matches at his feet.

"Police!" Sky yelled. "Turn around. I'm cuffing you. You have the right to remain silent, and the right to engage an attorney. Outside of that, buddy, you're in a heap of trouble."

"Sky, stop. He's shaking in his shoes. Can't you see he's just a boy?"

"Yeah," Sky said, turning to scowl at her. "He's a boy, all right. A juvenile delinquent planning to burn your house down."

"I didn't want to," the kid babbled. "Please. Some older guys said they'd hurt my sister if I didn't pour gas around this house and set it on fire. They left the gas and matches here. Oh, my mama's gonna kill me."

"Bring him inside, Sky. All of this commotion will wake my neighbors."

"Annie, for Pete's sake, he's a felon. I'm calling Joe Morales, who's on midnight to eight, to transport and book him. You go back in. I'll handle this and ride to the station with Joe."

"He'd only be a felon if he'd actually sprinkled gas and lit the match. He's a child, and he's going to die of fright before you take him anywhere. What's your name? How old are you?" she asked the boy, shifting the light away from his eyes.

The kid's teeth chattered so much, it was all he could do to get the words out. "I'm De…Deshawn Cul…ver. I'm ta…twelve, ma'am."

"See, Sky? He has manners. I don't want to be the cause of the boy's mama killing him over this, do you?" She gestured toward her open back door with the flashlight.

Sky said something she couldn't really hear. But he hooked the cuffs back on his belt, grabbed the collar at the back of the kid's too-big plaid shirt and marched him up the porch steps. "One wrong move, kid, and you're toast. You got that?" He gave the kid a sound shake as they entered the kitchen.

All the boy seemed able to do was bob his head, which was tucked turtlelike between thin shoulders that shook. His whole body shook, Annie noticed. She shut the back door. "Now then," she said, bending to get a better look at him. "Deshawn, where do you live?"

"Oh, for Pete's sake," Sky said, repeating himself. "Annie, you can't interrogate my suspect."

"What suspect? He's twelve!" She shot Sky a dark frown.

"Sheesh! Come on. Next you'll be handing our young hoodlum a plate and inviting him to join us for breakfast."

The skinny kid seemed so hopeful, Annie darted a glance from him to her stove and then to Sky, who still held on to the boy's shirt. "Well, Chief, that's an excellent suggestion. You two sit at the table. I'll whip something up. How do pancakes, bacon and spicy apples sound?"

"An...nie!" Sky stretched out her name, revealing his frustration, and threw up his gun arm in disgust.

"What? You don't like the menu? I can do French toast or waffles."

"I love pancakes," Deshawn ventured, gazing worshipfully at Annie. "We ain't had no breakfast at home most all week. It's the end of the month, and Mama's paycheck done got shorted 'cause the bus she takes to work broke down.

She missed most of one day cleaning rooms at the hotel, so she didn't get tips, either."

Sky's eyes clashed with Annie's over the boy's bent head. This time he released Deshawn's collar and threw up both arms in defeat. He tucked his weapon back into his belt and nudged his young perpetrator toward the chair where Annie had been sitting earlier. "There's no reason I can't question Deshawn over breakfast," he said, pulling out another chair. "I'll ask the questions and, Annie, you butt out."

She smiled and said sweetly, "Ask away. I'm just going to cook." Opening a cupboard, she pulled out a skillet and pancake fixings.

"Where do you live, and who all lives there?"

"Me, Mama and my sister, Chantal, she's fifteen," Deshawn said. "We, uh, live at the far end of Dusty Rose Street, down from you," he told Sky.

That seemed to shock Sky, who traded surprised looks with Annie as she handed him plates, napkins and flatware. "Why don't you start at the beginning and tell me the whole story. How did you happen to be sneaking around this neighborhood before sunup, aiming to set fire to this lady's house? A lady I'll guess you don't even know."

"I don't know her," the boy admitted, his

words laced with guilt. "That's why I figured I could do what those two guys said. They beat me up after school. If I didn't, they told me they'd hurt my sister." Tears sprang to his dark eyes. "She's smart, and the choir director at our church says Chantal's got loads of singing talent. We don't got no dad. He's dead. Since the glove factory shut down, Mama works two jobs in Louisville. She used to have a good job, and she was always home before and after school. Back then we had food to eat all month long, mister. Uh, am I s'posed to call you Chief Cordova?"

"Chief is okay," Sky said, lifting his eyes from the paper napkin he'd been frantically scribbling on.

Annie had put strips of bacon in a hot frying pan, and the smell permeated the kitchen. The boy kept darting glances at her, and every so often licked his lips. "Do you want milk or juice?" Annie asked the two at the table as she delivered glasses.

"I love milk," Deshawn said. "But it's expensive so I'll drink water."

Annie sucked in a deep breath and made sure she conveyed to Sky her horrified reaction to the boy's comment. "You'll drink milk," she said firmly, and pulled a gallon jug from the fridge and set it on the table with a thump. "Have as much as you want." She brought the first four pancakes to the table and offered them to Sky, along with slices of crispy bacon.

He let her fill his plate, but as she did, he connected with Deshawn's eyes, which could only be described as *hungry*. Without a word, Sky exchanged his full plate for the boy's empty one.

Moved by that, Annie rested a hand on Sky's shoulder as she set down a bowl of spicy apple slices that she'd taken from the fridge and reheated in the microwave. "More pancakes coming right up," she announced with a warm smile.

He stared at her mouth until he shifted in his chair and lowered his eyelids.

Both adults took note of how fast their morning guest had tucked into his food, which was disappearing rapidly. But the fact that he said "thank you" wasn't lost on Sky or Annie, who beamed at the boy before poking Sky's upper arm as if to say, "See?" With the griddle hot, the next batch of pancakes didn't take long to cook. Annie filled a plate for Sky and one for herself. Realizing Deshawn had almost finished his stack, she discreetly plopped two pancakes from her plate onto his. Then she sat. "I know you wanted to ask all the questions, Sky, but you're busy eating, and I'm curious about how

Deshawn and Chantal have stayed clear of gang activity up to now. I mean, I gather this gang's been operating in Briar Run for a while."

"Two years," Sky said, pausing to pour Deshawn more milk. "You would've been ten," he noted.

Deshawn wiped his lips on his napkin. "Mama's real strict. She's got big hopes for Chantal and me. We do chores before and after school, plus homework. If Mama's not home by supper, Chantal fixes us food, and I do the dishes." He pulled the wry face one would expect from a boy who'd rather do just about anything rather than dishes.

"Do you walk to and from school together?" Sky asked.

The boy shook his head. "We carpool. There's four moms who used to work on the line making gloves. They all got laid off when the plant closed. All of 'em have kids. Miz Hall's heart has problems so she can't work anymore. Mama, Miz Poole and Miz Morino pay Miz Hall to drive us to and from school." He shuffled his feet under the table. "She gets some money from the state, but Mama says she's proud and we can't talk about that. I could eat a couple more pancakes if you've got 'em," he said, and turned to look hopefully at the stove.

"I have more batter." Annie hopped up. "Sky, shall I put a couple more on for you?"

"No, thanks, I've had plenty." He eyed the boy. "I've never seen anyone put away as many pancakes as you. Don't eat so many it'll make you sick."

The boy blinked a few times. "It'll be a while before I get to eat again. Chief Cordova, you've got to take me to jail."

"Why? So your mom doesn't kill you?" Sky asked with a grin as he folded the napkin with his scribbles and stowed it in his shirt pocket.

"I know what I said, but Mama loves me." He fiddled with his plate as Annie slid three more steaming pancakes into the center of it. "Mama will yell at me for sure, but I think the gang guys who gave me the gas and matches, they're gonna kill me. Or beat me so bad I'll wish I was dead. If I went to jail for a couple days, and word got out that a cop had the house staked out, that'll prove to the gang I tried."

Annie leaned against the kitchen cabinets. "So you mean if the gang thinks you were arrested, your stock would go up and they won't beat you up?"

"Stock? Huh?" Deshawn said, pausing with a forkful of pancake halfway to his mouth.

"Annie, you're doing it again," Sky warned.

"He's my perp. And you can't deny the fact that he came here intending to do harm."

"On behalf of people a whole lot older—who have a grip on this town. I'm getting the picture here. The poor kids who live in Briar Run are pawns in the gang's chess game. Deshawn," she said, ignoring Sky, "do all the good kids have to stay in their homes whenever they aren't in school? What about sports? What about playing kick ball or softball in the street?"

"Can't," the boy said. "It ain't, uh, isn't safe. There are drug pushers all over the place.…"

Annie began to pace.

"*Now* what's going on in your head?" Sky groaned. "You've got that same look you had when you were talking about your residents' meeting."

"Making homes in this area nicer won't go far in helping single moms like the ones Deshawn mentioned. I'm beginning to see that the core problem in Briar Run—and this pertains to two-parent families, as well—is that beauty's only skin-deep."

"Huh?" Sky stacked the dirty plates, but it was plain Annie had lost him.

"One universal truth I discovered while working in the poorest and roughest neighborhoods in L.A. is that kids are a parent's number-one priority. All moms and dads want the lives of their kids to be better than their own. Better than what circumstances thrust on them. I found it true regardless of background or ethnic origin."

"I get that. But fact is fact. The Stingers are targeting kids, and no matter how big our police force is, we can't possibly safeguard all kids day and night."

"Safeguarding doesn't have to just fall to the cops, Sky."

Deshawn's head whipped from one speaker to the other. His face remained impassive.

Getting up, Sky carried the dishes to the sink. "I'm sure you're dying to tell me how you're going to wiggle your nose and make all of that happen. However, it's almost 6:00 a.m. I need to grab my duffel bag and collect the gas can and matches for the evidence file. Then I'll hand Deshawn off to Joe Morales. It's my day off, remember. I'm going to the zoo."

"Six? Cripes," Deshawn exclaimed. "Mama gets up at six. She finds I'm not in my bed and man, oh, man, I'm gonna be in so much trouble now."

"Sky, you take the evidence and do whatever you need to do with it. I'll give Deshawn a lift home. I'd like to have a word with his mother if she can spare the time."

"Annie, you're interfering in a police case."

She raised an eyebrow. "Is it a police case if I choose not to press charges?"

"You don't have to. I caught him red-handed."

"And I need to go get myself booked." Deshawn sided with Sky.

Annie glared at Sky and he glared back. She broke eye contact first. "We'll all go to the station. You'll book Deshawn, or pretend to, so word of his arrest gets out to the gang. If you don't phone his mom, I've got no doubt that when she discovers he's not in his bed, she'll call 9-1-1. I'll be there to talk to Mrs. Culver when she comes for him."

Deshawn propped his skinny arms on the table and buried his head in his hands. "I am so gonna be cooked no matter what. I should've told Roy Dell and Heywood I wouldn't do what they said and let them beat the stuffing out of me."

Annie and Sky whirled on the boy, but it was Sky who went down on one knee next to Deshawn's chair. "Roy Dell who, and Heywood who?" he demanded in his steeliest cop voice. "Are you saying that all this time while you sat here wolfing down pancakes, you had the names of two gang members and kept them to yourself?"

The boy uncovered his face one half inch at a time. "They said if I snitched they'd cut off my ears. See, they didn't used to be bad." Giant tears formed in the corners of his eyes and trickled down his cheeks. "That was after Roy Dell said if I didn't set this house on fire they'd hurt Chantal. Heywood used to like her...." He grabbed his stomach. "I ate too much. I'm gonna puke."

"No, you're not," Sky said. "We'll work this out. You, me and Ms. Emerson," Sky said, rearing back to pin Annie with a serious gaze.

"Yes, we will," she reiterated. "And since you walked over here last night, Chief, I'll drive us all to the police station in my pickup so we can start the process of helping Deshawn." She grabbed her purse from the counter.

For a drawn-out minute Sky seemed unsure about her suggestion. Then, rising slowly, he let a sigh trickle through his tightly compressed lips. "So help me Hannah, if you say one word at the station that even sounds like it undermines my authority, I'll...I'll..."

"Yes?" Annie asked, her exaggerated smile dripping sugar.

Deshawn sniffled, but took an interest in

what had been said. "Who's Hannah? I thought her name was Annie."

"It is," Annie assured the boy. "Chief Cordova gets confused when he's been up all night on a stakeout." Tossing another smile at Sky, Annie nudged Deshawn through the archway into her living room and out another door into her garage.

With the boy trudging ahead of them, Sky had a chance to lean close and murmur in Annie's ear, "Are you a thorn in everybody's side? Or just mine?"

"Oh, I'm an equal opportunity thorn," she said, giving him a cheeky grin.

Sky's shoulders relaxed and his lips curved up in his first honest smile since he'd caught Deshawn.

CHAPTER SEVEN

THE THREE OF them entered the station in single file, Sky bringing up the rear. Koot Talmage rushed to meet them. "Hey, Sky, I didn't expect you today. I thought you'd be halfway to horse country by now."

"The zoo doesn't open until ten. We have new business." Sky turned to Annie and Deshawn. "You two sit down out here." He indicated a few chairs scattered about a narrow entry. "Deshawn, phone your mother. If she can't come to the station, tell her someone will bring you safely home." Sky pointed to an old-fashioned wall phone.

A much-subdued boy wearing a hangdog expression walked over to the phone, his shoulders slumped.

Sky beckoned Koot into his office and shut the door.

Through the glass beside the door, Annie watched both men talking and gesturing. Nei-ther sat, but since she couldn't hear them, she

studied the small but serviceable police station.
A short hall to her left led to three barred cells,
all vacant. In a second office about the size of
Sky's a woman wearing headphones sat behind
a large monitor. Annie assumed she was a dispatcher. A large open room held more desks
than Sky had officers. Three had computers
and were messy with strewn papers and coffee
mugs. Four were cleared of everything. Annie
figured the empty desks had to be another sign
of Briar Run's decline. Sky had said that money
problems had forced cutbacks, and Aaron Loomis, the city manager, said the same thing when
she'd asked him about holding her first town
meeting.

Deshawn came back and threw himself into
the chair next to Annie's. "Like I said, I am so
screwed."

"Is your mother coming to the station?"

He nodded. "Only, she said her boss at the
hotel told her if she was late one more time,
she's fired. She's more worried about me, I
guess. I feel really bad about making her cry."
He picked idly at a broken fingernail.

Annie patted his knee. "Did you tell her Chief
Cordova said he'd work everything out?"

"Yeah, but she don't think our kind can trust
cops."

"What do you mean 'your kind'?" Annie asked sharply.

"You know." He shrugged.

She didn't know what he meant for sure, but she could guess. She'd encountered distrust toward all government authority figures among the minority populations she'd worked with in L.A. In some cases they distrusted with good reason. *But not this one.* "Deshawn, you could be charged with attempted arson. That's serious. Chief Cordova wants to work out some kind of arrangement to let you off with a warning, but he doesn't have to. You strike me as a smart kid. I hope you appreciate what we're doing to help you out of a mess that's at least partly of your own making. So you need to cooperate where you can. The fact is, you made a bad decision to go along with what those gang members asked you to do."

"I know." The boy slid lower in his chair, his expression glum. He lifted his eyes to the man who'd walked up to them in midconversation. "I swear I wouldn't have lit no match," he said, looking straight at Sky. "I was too scared."

"I'll take your word for that, son. Annie, I need to go. I'm leaving Deshawn in the hands of Lieutenant Talmage. I'll check in later." He took two steps toward the door, then turned back.

For a minute his gaze seemed to center on Annie's mouth. "Try not to cause any more trouble while I'm gone," he muttered.

She raised her chin in a mulish way, but held her tongue.

Shaking his head, Sky left.

Koot beckoned to Annie and Deshawn. They hadn't quite reached the office when three women and a very pretty teenage girl burst through the main door. Two of the women started to wail, but the tallest, an attractive dark-skinned woman of maybe forty, rushed up to Deshawn and gathered him in her arms. "Deshawn, baby, what have you done?"

He burst into tears and sobbed out his story until Koot put his fingers to his lips, whistled shrilly and said, "Y'all stop this caterwauling."

Annie almost smiled because they did stop as if their weeping was turned off by a single switch. Koot ended up taking Deshawn and his mother into the office. Annie sat in the waiting area again and struck up a conversation with Burdette Poole and Chantal Culver, Deshawn's sister.

"Ah, so you'd be Gran Ida's relative from California," Nina Morino said after introductions were made. "You're the one who came to town and stirred up the Stingers."

Annie's mouth thinned. "That bunch should've been stirred up and sent packing long before they got their hooks into the people of this town."

Chantal, who'd said nothing to this point, piped up. "They got their hooks into the good kids by acting all friendly-like. They claimed to have backers who promised to build us a teen center. Instead, they skulked around, figured out who was weak and got them to sell drugs or steal stuff. And they do it by threatening our families."

Annie's ears perked up. She dug her notebook out of her purse and flipped to a clean page. "What do you think a drug- and alcohol-free teen center would have to offer if it's going to lure kids away from gang activity, Chantal?"

"Dances, for one thing," the girl said. "The high school and junior high principals canceled all after-school events 'cause of fights and stuff. Teachers said they don't get paid enough to police the grounds before or after school. So we don't have sports, either. It's not safe to hang out with friends when class lets out," she said.

"And the city doesn't have enough cops to handle all the problems," Burdette Poole, one of the adults, elaborated. "Parents can't be in two places at once. Many work more than one job."

"Tanya Hall, another of our friends, heard

you've got big ideas to do stuff Gran Ida used to talk about," Nina said, eyeing Annie. "Nobody paid attention to her, 'cause we thought Ida was a bit senile. You know…" The Hispanic woman lifted one shoulder in a shrug.

"Are you aware Ida was my grandmother? She wasn't as out of touch as you think. It's a cinch the houses in this town can do with paint and yard cleanup, which is one thing my grandmother wanted, right?"

"Nina didn't mean to speak ill of someone who passed on," Burdette chimed in. "Nor did Tanya. Gran Ida had great ideas. It's just…none of us have the money or the energy to fix up our homes."

She looked so disheartened, Annie reached over and squeezed the woman's plump arm, smiled and said, "Painting may not be that costly, Burdette. Drive down Gran's street. Two neighbors and I painted three of the Victorians. I got a fantastic deal on paint if you're interested. Other people on our block pitched in yesterday, so we're painting their homes next. I hope to keep going with this project."

"Why would you do that?" Nina asked suspiciously.

"To carry out my grandmother's dream,"

Annie said softly, and the women nodded as if they suddenly understood.

Davena Culver and Deshawn rejoined the others. Mrs. Culver leaned down and impulsively hugged Annie. "Lieutenant Talmage said I owe you a heap of thanks for listening to my boy. And you fed him, too," she said, her eyes filling with tears. "If I can do anything in return, you only have to ask."

"As a matter of fact, I wondered if you sewed that cute dress Chantal's wearing."

The woman looked startled. "Yes, I did. I love to sew. I don't have the time for it like I used to, or the money for material. Oh, I hope you don't want me to make you a dress." Her face fell.

"I don't need a dress, but I'm hoping to find a couple of women to sew drapes. The lieutenant's wife's going to help after her arm heals. What I have in mind isn't a one-time job, but something ongoing."

"I'm sorry, but I already have two jobs. Well, I did have. One's gone."

Annie glanced at Deshawn. "I understood that if you came to the station you'd lose your main job. Mrs. Culver, I think I can match what you made in hotel housekeeping. And sewing would let you work at home. So you could be there when your kids get back from school? I'm also considering setting up a teen center, a place free of riffraff."

Davena Culver clasped a hand over her heart, but still seemed unsure.

"Listen, I realize you don't know me. I grew up here. Gran Ida raised me, and I owe her more than I can ever repay. It may seem too little, too late, but I intend to live up to the faith she had in me. Part of which was her staunch belief that I have what it takes to return Briar Run to the town it used to be."

"Won't be easy," Burdette murmured. "Impossible," Koot predicted from behind them. "And Sky's not going to be happy about your teen center idea. You'd better wait on that until he gets back."

Annie looked defiant. "Ladies, and Deshawn, if we're all squared away here, I suggest we go someplace where we can nail down our plans." Annie herded them all toward the exit, ignoring Koot's admonitions.

ABOUT THREE THAT afternoon, Sky stopped his cruiser on the street in front of Rita and Homer Gonzales's home. The faint beginnings of a headache that had started in the noisy chimpanzee section of the zoo began to throb in the back of his head as he sat watching Annie paint siding. She stood high on a too-tall ladder. The house, which yesterday was a dingy white, now appeared fresh in a new coat of pale cream. Three women wielded rollers and brushes. None were as far up as Annie.

Sky didn't know how to get her attention. Once again, she kept the world at bay as she worked, listening to songs streaming into her earphones.

Rita Gonzales noticed Sky's approach and beamed at him. "Chief Cordova. Isn't this the greatest improvement?" She waved a dripping brush.

"Mmm," he grunted. "Is there any way to have a word with your foreman?" He stabbed a finger toward Annie.

"Daddy, Daddy," exclaimed a boy who ran up and tugged on Sky's pant leg, "That looks funner. I wanna paint. Can I? Can I, huh?"

Sky glanced down in surprise. "Zachary, how did you get out of your booster seat? Didn't I ask you to stay in the car?" Sky massaged the back of his head where the drumbeat had grown more insistent.

"Booster seats are for babies. I'm *five*." The boy held up his hand, fingers splayed. "I won't get paint on my shirt, I promise. In day care we hafta wear big men's shirts. Mama makes me wear Papa Archibald's shirt, but it smells yucky." The little boy wrinkled his nose.

Those words had Sky swallowing his next lecture. He knew he shouldn't be glad that his son thought his stepdad's shirt smelled yucky, but he was tempted. He got darned tired of hearing about Saint Archibald Fleming from Corrine.

While Sky was occupied with his son, Rita went over to Annie's ladder and gave it a couple of hard shakes.

Sky saw the ladder sway. "Rita, her ladder isn't on a solid footing," he called. "Stop, before you make Annie fall."

The rocking of her ladder did gain Annie's attention. Looking down, she peered at Rita, who jerked a thumb over one shoulder. Turning farther, Annie saw Sky. She pushed her goggles up into her hair, shut off her music and laid her brush across a paint can perched on an aluminum tray jutting out from the ladder. Then she descended step by careful step. The minute she noticed that Sky had grabbed hold of the lower sides of her ladder to steady it, Annie sent him a grateful smile.

She jumped the last three rungs and landed with a thud between Sky's arms. Laughing, she turned around—until they stood chest to chest.

Their thighs brushed, and Sky's blue eyes went dark and smoky.

"Daddy, are you gonna ask that lady if I can paint?"

Annie was the first to break free, dispelling the tension between them. "Oh, hello, you must be Zachary," she said, ducking beneath Sky's muscled arm. "I'm Annie." Bending, she smiled and stretched out her hand.

Taking it, the boy said, "I like your name. I like to paint. Can I help you?"

Annie straightened. "That's up to your dad. I have grungy paint clothes on, and you guys are dressed for the zoo."

The boy squinted up at her. "How did you know we went to the zoo?"

Annie debated saying she'd just guessed, because Sky was frowning. She knew how kids blabbed, how they tended to say whatever came into their heads. She wasn't sure if Sky's displeasure was at her for barging in and introducing herself to his son. "I think your dad mentioned it," she said as the boy clearly expected an answer.

"I like animals," he said. "We saw the giraffes, two big elephants and polar bears.... Daddy, what were their names?"

"Qannik and Siku," Sky said, coming over to set a hand on his son's tawny curls.

"Yeah, that's them. And we saw tigers and snakes and frogs and a big white alligator, huh, Daddy?"

Sky's earlier frown dissolved in an instant, and his blue eyes, so like his son's, crinkled at the corners with his smile.

Annie saw the family resemblance in their eyes and in the shape of their faces. Except that Sky had stronger cheekbones, and his hair was more brown than gold like Zack's. His son might grow up to be slighter of build. Something Annie really liked about Sky's looks was that for a tall man he was wide across the chest and not too narrow in the hips. He was built solidly—a man who could handle any emergency. Maybe Zack would fill out as he got older. Hard to tell at this age. "So can I help Miz Annie paint, Daddy?"

"Maybe another time. I stopped by to have an official word with Miz Annie. Son, I need you to go buckle yourself back in your seat."

"Aw!" Pouting, the boy kicked at a pile of trim that had been removed from around the house windows.

Annie felt for the child. She took a piece of light sandpaper from a pouch in the carpenter's belt she wore. "Zack, maybe your dad will let you sand that top piece of trim while he and I talk. They need a light going over before Mrs. Gonzales paints them."

Zachary's eyes lit up.

Sky darted another frown at Annie.

"He wants to help, Sky, and that's admirable. The boards have already been cleaned of old paint. At the most you'll have to dust off his shirt and pants."

"Okay, sure, Zachary. Let me show you how to sand," he said, plucking the sandpaper from Annie's hand.

She stood aside and surveyed the work already accomplished on the Gonzales home and thought it looked good. Engrossed, she gave a start when Sky latched his hand around her upper arm and moved her some distance away from where his son was now busily sanding.

"I talked to Koot half an hour ago. He said you stuck your nose into what's sure to be another hornet's nest."

"And that would be?"

"A teen center. I can't think of many things likely to cause my department bigger headaches than gathering a bunch of teenagers together at a single location in a town understaffed by police. A town you know darned well is rife with gang activity. Honestly, what are you thinking?"

She yanked on the bill of her Dodgers cap. "The truth is, as I talked to Chantal Culver, her mom and the others, it struck me that this town's been held hostage for too long. Kids shouldn't be afraid to meet their friends after school or do things outside their homes. I haven't worked out the details yet. Maybe I could hire a couple of handymen once I find a place. I'd hoped you could steer me toward a cheap, empty building not too far from the high school. Ideally it needs property out back big enough to fence and set up a basketball court."

He threw both hands up in the air. "Are you bull—uh, kidding me?"

"I'm dead serious. Oh, I hired Mrs. Culver to make drapes for the front windows of the homes we've painted. It was dumb luck that she and I stumbled across the most fantastic sale of perfect fabrics. I know it'll be a while before Sadie Talmage is healed enough to sew, and Davena needs work…. Anyway, I think Sadie's design expertise can be put to better use decorating the teen center."

"You're certifiable!"

"I don't agree. People are getting involved. By the way, I plan to paint homes on your street next, starting with Davena Culver's place at the end of your cul-de-sac." Turning aside, Annie opened a cooler sitting near the porch and removed two bottles of water. She handed Sky one, and smiled over the lip of hers as he rolled his cold bottle across his forehead. "Would it be okay to give Zack an orange pop as a treat for sanding?" she asked.

He checked his watch. "Sure, why not mess up my whole day? I'm going to get yelled at, anyway, for bringing him home late, all because Koot mistakenly thought I could drop by here and talk some sense into you. So, when Corrine takes a strip off me for ruining Zack's dinner with a soft drink, it's a mere ripple in my life."

He dug out the bottle of orange soda buried under ice in the cooler. "Zack," he called. "Give Miz Annie her sandpaper and come get a drink. We need to head out to the farm. We're already late. You can drink this on the way."

The boy trotted over and gave Annie the crumpled square of sandpaper. "Did you ask Mama if it's okay?" he said, querying his dad. "Papa Archibald doesn't let his kids or me drink soda, 'cause he says it rots your teeth."

Sky wrenched off the bottle cap. "I drink the occasional soda. My teeth are fine. Please try not to spill on your white shirt." Under his breath in an aside to Annie he muttered, "Who sends a boy to the zoo in a white dress shirt?"

"I'm in enough trouble with you, Sky. I won't be stepping into *that* trap."

"Mmm." He opened his water and took a long drink. "The main problem is…I'm worried about you, Annie. Worried about the lengths Stinger leaders will go to maintain a grip on their turf."

Annie's heart caved, just a bit. "I, ah, thought I'd annoyed you."

"There is that." His slow smile was lopsided.

"Daddy, you said we were gonna be late. Can we come back another time and help paint?" The boy turned his eager face up to Annie.

Sky answered for her. "Zack, let's see how our next visit coincides with Annie's schedule to paint my house."

"She's gonna paint *your* house? What color? I like red."

"It won't be red."

"Why?" Zack juggled his drink as he gazed at his dad. Already the boy had orange staining his lips and chin.

"Have you seen any red houses?" Sky asked.

Zack skipped backward a few steps. "Nope, but Grover says it's okay to be different from everybody else."

"Grover who?" Sky had started walking toward the street where his car sat, but he stopped to question his son.

"You know, Grover on TV."

Annie, trailing a few steps behind the pair, said, "I think he means Grover from *Sesame Street*."

Zack nodded vigorously and his soda did slop onto his white dress shirt.

Sky glanced at Annie as he straightened the bottle Zack held. "How do you know so much about a kids' TV show?"

"We had a TV going 24/7 in the waiting room of our counseling offices. Believe it or not, the characters on that program dispense a lot of sage advice."

"Maybe, but all the same, don't you be painting my house red."

Annie smothered a laugh. "I'd never do that. You get to choose your own colors. I gave Davena Culver the folder of exterior colors I picked up before I painted my house. She'll pass it along to the residents on your street. If you stop to check on Deshawn, his mom can tell you who has it. Once you've seen it, you can phone me with your color choices."

"How have you organized such a big operation in one day? You've hired a seamstress, circulated a color chart and you've added some painters, I see."

They'd progressed to where Sky's car was parked on the street. Zack's head continued to swivel between the two adults as he gulped his orange drink.

"It all began with me painting my own house. Isn't it great that all my grandmother's wishes are coming together? Oh, something I didn't tell you," Annie said. "At lunch, Mrs. Gonzales introduced me to an unemployed iron worker. I've retained him to make decorative coverings for the windows and doors on the homes we've completed. I saw some of his work. It's exactly what the neighborhood needs to ward off more break-ins of the type experienced by the Spurlocks, the Gilroys and me."

"Annie, for crying out loud! You can't go around hiring every out-of-work Tom, Dick and Betty in this neighborhood."

"Why not?"

"Because…because…" he sputtered.

She rolled her eyes. "*Because* doesn't strike me as a valid reason."

"Okay, how about this… When the Stingers hear about the amount of cash you're shelling out—and they will—you might as well *ask* the gang to grab you for whatever ransom pops into their heads." Sky's gaze and Annie's locked in another feud.

"Why are people going to grab Annie, huh, Daddy?" Zachary's childish giggles broke the intensity of Sky and Annie's argument.

She rearranged her defiant features into a warm smile for the boy. "It was a pleasure to meet you, Zachary. Thank you for sanding that molding for me. You were a big help."

The little guy puffed out his chest. "It was fun, but I'd rather paint. Or nail. I like nailing stuff, too."

"Well, a lot of those things will need doing before we finish this project. Maybe I'll see you again if your dad brings you around."

"Will you, Daddy?"

"Maybe, after Annie and her friends start painting my house. But we'll have to clear it with your mother." Sky took his son's hand, opened the back door of the car and boosted Zack into the child seat.

Even from where she stood a distance away from the vehicle, Annie heard the boy's complaint. "Mama will talk to Papa Archibald, and he'll say no. He does what Mama wants, and she doesn't like your house. Do you think she'll like it better if Annie paints it a pretty color?"

"Mmm." Again Sky answered with a non-committal noise.

Zack, once buckled in by his father, waved and waved and waved at Annie.

She envisioned more of the orange soda spewing onto his shirt thanks to those energetic waves. He was a cute little guy. And sharp. It saddened her to know how many hoops Sky had to jump through to have access to his son, whom he so obviously loved. Her squabble with him seemed minor compared to the wrangling he must go through with his ex-wife. Her mood softer, Annie raised her hand in recognition of Zack's goodbye. She made sure Sky saw her, too, as he ducked into the driver's seat.

"Bye," he called, maybe yielding a little, as well. "You be careful climbing around on tall ladders...and doing other things. We'll touch base later."

Annie resisted the urge to watch Sky drive out of sight. However, her mood swing from happy to pensive didn't get past Rita Gonzales.

"Chief Cordova is worried about you Annie. It's easy to see he's got a thing for you."

Annie paused as she put on a pair of work gloves. "The thing he has for me is that he's convinced I'm making his work life more difficult."

"No." The older woman shook her head. "He

may not admit it, and he may not *want* to care about you, but it's written all over his face. You two are shooting off enough sparks for anyone to see."

Annie choked off her laugh, because it was plain that Rita believed every word she'd said. "I don't mean to make fun of you, Rita, but Sky Cordova and I have shot sparks of a different kind from the day we met."

Rita grinned. "*All* the sparks that fly between a man and a woman are rooted in desire. Mark my words. He'll keep coming around and keep coming around with one excuse after another. Some may be pretty lame before the truth knocks one or both of you upside the head."

Anne gave a wry shrug. "You're a romantic, Rita, but I'm not. As for Sky, he was burned badly by his marriage. In my job as a social worker I've met other guys like him—men who become cynical after divorce. I saw so many bad and broken marriages I've developed a cynicism toward getting into a relationship myself. Two cynics do not a good match make," she joked.

"Well, Homer says I have a sixth sense when it comes to forecasting which couples will end up together. I'm just giving you fair warning, Annie. Even though we don't know each other well, I predict I'll dance at the chief's and your wedding."

Snickering at that, Annie climbed back up the ladder. She thought humorously about Rita's predictions for a while and considered them total nonsense. But painting was a mindless task and left too much time for her mind to wander. Even after being dumped by her high school sweetheart, she'd only dated coworkers once or twice. Mostly she'd been too busy. Looking back she could see the lack of real attraction, of *sparks,* between her and any of them. Heaven knew she'd helped untangle enough messes that occurred with clients and their exes; she wasn't interested in being the hated *other* woman. And all too often, ex-wives did consider any woman who dared to date a former husband the *other,* even if they'd instigated the split themselves.

The more she slopped on paint and let her mind roam back to her encounters with Sky, the more it occurred to her that he touched some sad, needy place in her soul. The fact that she still *had* sad, needy places surprised and irritated her. She liked to think she was strong and independent. However, she'd gone to California after high school because of her various unresolved issues—a romance turned sour, the history of a footloose mom she'd never met and a no-name father. In college psychology courses, it became clear that she'd felt abandoned by everyone except Gran Ida. Annie had told herself that she'd banished those feelings and left them behind.

She wrestled her wandering thoughts under control as she got off the ladder and moved it to begin painting the next section of siding. That physical act broke the cycle of wayward memories and let her concentrate on her plans for the town.

HOMER GONZALES ARRIVED home from his day job around seven-thirty. He carried a lunch box and a bag of groceries. Rita, Annie and the others had finished painting the house and were starting on the gingerbread moldings they'd sanded.

"I can't believe the difference a coat of paint made to our house," Homer exclaimed. "I'm late because I stopped for groceries, Rita. Mrs. Tompkins raved to me about how nice our house looks. She told everyone within earshot to come and see our street. She went on and on, calling you an angel, Annie. Oh, by the way, I ran into our chief of police in the checkout line and he asked me to give you this note." Homer pulled a folded paper out of his pocket and passed it to Annie, who shifted her paintbrush and took off one glove.

She opened the note and saw what appeared to be an address. "Did he say what this is?"

"No. I assumed it was self-explanatory."

"Excuse me a minute while I call him. Homer, if you feel up to nailing some of this trim to the fascia boards, your house will be done, and tomorrow we can start on Evelyn Dodd's place next door."

"Let me put the milk and bread in the house and I'll get right on it."

Turning away, Annie found Sky's cell number on her phone, and punched Send.

"Cordova," Sky answered briskly.

"Hi, it's Annie. Homer Gonzales gave me a note with an address, but I'm afraid I'm in the dark."

"You said you wanted a place to open a teen center," he said gruffly. "On the way home from the farm, I remembered hearing about a warehouse that's reverted back to the city in a foreclosure. I drove by. It's two blocks from the high school. It has a sizable back lot, already fenced. I have no idea what's inside. Maybe one big room." Silence hung between them for a moment after he stopped speaking. "Annie, are you still with me?"

"I am. I…guess I'm getting over the shock of this. The *pleasant* shock. Before, you sounded as if you were a hundred percent against my idea of opening a teen center."

"Yeah, well, I was…am. I assumed you'd do it, anyway."

She heard him move his phone and pictured him flustered at being caught doing something nice for her. Annie lightened her tone. "Would you have brought the address to me yourself, or would you have carried it around until you ran into someone like Homer, who could deliver it for you?"

"I intended to sleep on it tonight and make a decision in the morning. I met Homer at an opportune time for you, because I decided to pass it off instead of letting it give me another headache."

Mesmerized by his low voice, Annie almost didn't say thank you before Sky clicked off. Still, she was left smiling, and was once more reminded of Rita Gonzales's speculation that Sky cared for her.

That thought stuck with her all evening. As a result, she was eager to check out the warehouse and hunt him down the next day for further discussion.

CHAPTER EIGHT

IN THE MORNING Annie answered an early knock at her door. Facing two men, strangers, she grappled for her phone, ready to speed-dial police dispatch.

The pudgier, red-haired man with a crew cut spoke quickly. "My name is Roger McBride. This is my friend, Charlie Fitzpatrick. Last night the police chief came to see me. He said you might be hiring general laborers. Me and Charlie can do anything."

Once again Annie was stunned that Sky would refer people to help with a project he wasn't shy about saying he'd rather she dropped.

"At this point, the work I have going is more of a neighbor-helping-neighbor thing, mostly painting houses. I don't own a business, so I'm not offering real jobs. Not the kind where you fill out applications and get paid regular wages. Right now, I provide lunch and supper if we paint that long. Yesterday I gave all the volunteer workers credit coupons to a local grocery store by way of added thanks. And I supply paint for the homes of workers who pitch in."

"Food coupons are worth a lot to those of us who've lost our jobs and can't find work," Roger McBride said. "And Loretta, that's my wife, says just about every week that she'd like to paint our house dark gray with wine-red trim."

"I like what you've done on Rose Arbor," Charlie chimed in.

Annie eyed them and judged them both to be in their fifties. Of an age when even in a good economy they might have difficulty getting hired. "What did you used to do?"

"We were managers at the glove factory. Prior to that, when the Honeycutts produced lingerie, we kept the machines running and did other general maintenance. We both worked there from the time we graduated high school."

"My grandmother sewed lingerie for many years. Ida Vance, did you know her?"

"Yes, ma'am," they said together.

"Miz Ida made a heap of undies in her day." Roger smiled. "Wore out two machines during my tenure. My wife and I were sorry to read about her passing. We would've gone to the funeral, but Loretta couldn't get off work. She's in fast food."

Charlie echoed his friend's sentiment.

"Thank you." Annie cleared her throat. Talking about her grandmother's death was still hard. "I may need your skills a bit farther down the road if another plan of mine takes shape. Evelyn Dodd's home is scheduled for painting today. Her husband power-washed it yesterday. If everyone who worked on the Gonzales house returns, and if you two pitch in, we could finish early enough to move on to the Mickelson bungalow. The other home owners on Rose Arbor Street are waiting to see how it goes."

Charlie, the shorter of the men, tilted his head to one side. "Rumor has it that you aim to gussie up the whole town, Ms. Emerson."

"Call me Annie. My hope, Mr. Fitzpatrick, is to start the ball rolling and encourage all our residents to get involved."

"I don't know about that," Roger said, rubbing a hand over his short hair. "Folks in Briar Run, we're all down on our luck. A lot of us, like Charlie and me, are about to run out of unemployment benefits. We'll tackle anything to earn a little extra."

"Why did the glove factory close? Seems to me gloves are an item people always need. Maybe they're not quite as essential as toilet paper," Annie said with a smile, "but between sanding and painting, I've gone through a few pairs."

Roger nodded. "We all thought that. The Honeycutt brothers retooled to make gloves after they lost the lingerie trade to China. Gloves did real well at first. Then Bill Honeycutt died. His brother got cancer, so he sold to a conglomerate. Lucy Portallis, our accountant, said the new owners bought the factory as a tax write-off. After a year we all noticed orders tapering, then a comptroller from outside cut our shifts. One day, two suits met us at the front door and said the plant was closed. We should've seen it coming, but no one did."

"Hmm." Annie nibbled on her lip. "Since the factory was the economic lifeblood of this community, it's a shame they didn't sell the business again instead of shutting it down."

"The conglomerate's board didn't care. They outsourced the contracts. They didn't know the folks who worked there. Three generations of Honeycutts lived in Louisville. They had skin in the game, so to speak. The shame was that Bill never married. Harold did but he never had kids to pass the company to like their daddy did."

Annie stared into space a moment. "I see. Did they come in later and sell off all the equipment?"

"Not that I know of," Roger said. "Do you, Charlie?"

"Nope. But I don't think so. Kids broke some windows in the back of the building. The police chief before Cordova, Jimmy Heilman, he ordered the place patrolled. Eventually the kids lost interest."

Annie glanced at her watch. "I'm late to go pick up paint. If you two want to work, meet me at the Dodd house in half an hour. It's the second one from the end of this street. I'll bring over some paint and supplies, and then I have a few errands to run. I'll swing past the paint store again later to get paint for the Mickelson place."

"Sounds good," Charlie said, pulling a pair of cotton gloves from his pocket.

Roger let his friend walk away, but he hung back. "Uh, Chief Cordova said I had to tell you that since I lost my job, I had a drinking problem for a while. I swear it's under control and you won't have to worry about it if you need handymen later."

"I appreciate your honesty, Roger. I'll contact you and Charlie if another project I want to do actually happens. For that, I may be able swing paying a bit above minimum wage."

"That would be good. Real good," he said,

lowering his chin before he trotted after his buddy.

Annie's cell phone rang as she closed her door. "Hello." Her greeting was tentative since not many people had her number.

"It's Sky. I wanted to let you know that I told a guy to contact you about work. He may bring a friend by to see you today."

"They've been here. I have to say I wondered why you'd be drumming up workers who need to be paid when you were worried it'd get out that I inherited money from Gran Ida."

"Sorry, I didn't think about that. Like I said, I know you're going to carry on one way or another. But I did have another reason for sending them over. I've noticed a lot of gawkers driving down your street. We can't be sure they're all friendly locals. Some could be gang members. I'd feel better if you had some hefty guys around in case anybody tried to cause you more grief." He paused. "Speaking of grief, I called the high school principal and got last names to go with the first names Deshawn accidentally spilled. Roy Dell Carter is a dropout. Heywood Brown is a junior, still attending school, but it's hit and miss. Both kids' recent histories suggest they're prime candidates to be your graffiti-painters. In the principal's view, even if those two strong-armed Deshawn into torching your house, someone pressured them first. It's unlikely either one is our shooter. Apparently they talk big, but gossip among the students says that Heywood would opt out of the gang if he could. Roy Dell's been heard to say he wishes he'd stayed in school. Louisville police still have our main suspect. They hope he'll rat out a partner. What I'm doing is scrabbling for a reason to question Roy Dell and Heywood that won't implicate Deshawn."

"While you're figuring that out, is there any chance you could meet me at the warehouse? Maybe in an hour? I looked it up online and the size and what it'll sell for is perfect."

"Can you wait until this afternoon? I received a summons a few minutes ago to be in family court at nine. Corrine's lawyer got someone to take her complaint about the dangers of my job—and the town—seriously." He sounded bitter.

"Then this isn't the custody hearing Sadie told me about, where she and Koot will give character references on your behalf?"

"No. This is what I call a nuisance hearing. My ex doesn't even have to attend. She made a complaint and her lawyer filed it." Sky's irritation vibrated through his statement. "I have to go with my attorney to register opposition, or the judge automatically rules in Corrine's favor. I found that out the hard way in Maryland when I skipped a hearing I thought was nonsense. I'm convinced she and her lawyer sit around thinking up all this aggravating crap so they can drag me into court. Stuff they know takes me away from my job and costs me money because I have to pay my attorney. And if the judge rules in her favor, I get stuck paying court costs, too."

"I know how that works, Sky. I used to help some of my single-mom clients get those types of complaints before a judge. We didn't consider them frivolous. My preference in most cases was for the couple to meet without their lawyers and work out their differences rationally. I mean, if it's a case like yours where there's no history of child abuse, and both of you love Zachary and ultimately want what's best for him, involving lawyers and courts just muddies the waters."

"Now *you* sound like a lawyer, Annie. With Corrine and me, it's gone beyond being able to talk. You heard her screaming at me on the phone. Do you call that rational?"

"I don't know her, Sky, so I should have kept my opinion to myself. I seem to have difficulty doing that. My only excuse is that these are the kinds of situations I worked with a lot in L.A."

"Yeah, well your name came up this time. You remember that our dispatcher told Corrine about the drive-by at your house and said I was there having dinner? Yesterday, Corrine was ticked to hear that I took Zack to one of your work sites. She says I'm irresponsible for allowing him to sand boards that might have had rusty nails in them. Oh, and giving him an orange soda was a cardinal sin as far as she and Archibald are concerned."

"Why is she so angry at you, Sky?"

"Both the lawyer I had in Maryland, who was referred by the military, and my lawyer here asked that. I don't know, so you'd have to ask her. I thought we had an okay marriage. Apparently she claimed I'd deserted her. Like I could tell the military I wasn't going on tour. At one hearing her lawyer said she felt our marriage was a mistake and wanted out."

"For Zack's sake, you two should communicate. Otherwise, you can't hope to build an amicable relationship."

"We're way past amicable. Listen, Annie, I need to run. I have to go by the station and make sure patrols are covered for the time I'm in court. You haven't said if you can wait until later to check out that warehouse?"

"Okay. I'm picking up paint for the Dodd house in half an hour. Speaking of paint, did you get the folder from Mrs. Culver? You know," she said thoughtfully, "a judge might like the fact that we're upgrading Briar Run, and that you have plans to repaint your home. Once the work's done, you can request another evaluation by a child welfare investigator."

"What business is it of theirs where I live? I'm gainfully employed and I pay an inflated amount of child support every month. A family court judge combed through my military records and I submitted to a battery of psychological tests they claimed were necessary to prove I hadn't come back with PTSD. What did Corrine's new husband have to undergo? Nada!"

An uncomfortable silence ensued for several seconds.

"Uh, perhaps you should rethink that attitude, Sky."

"There's nothing wrong with my attitude."

"It's hostile," Annie said evenly.

"For good reason," he returned. "Listen, I really need to go. So, what about the warehouse this afternoon?"

"I think two o'clock should be fine. Call if

you can meet me there. If I don't hear from you by one-thirty, I'll see if Sadie feels up to going. I intend to ask her to design the layout inside if I'm able to buy it."

There was a lingering testiness in his reply. "I'll be in touch."

Annie held the phone longer than necessary after Sky had ended the call. She shouldn't have said anything, shouldn't have commented on his family problems. All the years she'd worked with couples in similar cases should have taught her that when it came to divorce and child custody, very few people could be clearheaded about their own circumstances. Second marriages and stepfamilies added a whole other complicated dimension. Sky wasn't one of her cases, and she should have better sense than to befriend someone mixed up in a custody battle.

Were they friends, she and Sky? That thought knocked around inside her head as she backed out of her garage and drove to the hardware store. For a few minutes she reflected on the evolution of her relationship with Skylar Cordova. *Tense* and *heated* were words that described their early encounters. Friendlier, yet mercurial seemed to define their more recent exchanges. So why did they continue contacting each other? *That was the sixty-four-thousand-dollar question, wasn't it?*

Luckily she arrived at the hardware store and was able to put those musings on a back burner.

Something stood out the minute she walked into the store where she'd been buying paint for over three weeks. Michael, the clerk who always rushed over to greet her, took off in the opposite direction. Brian Townsend, the store owner she'd negotiated prices with on her first visit, hurried toward her. And it wasn't just her imagination that Brian was acting...nervous.

"Ms. Emerson, we don't have the paint you requested."

Ah, so that was the problem and no one wanted to admit it. "That's odd. I phoned in my order to Michael yesterday," Annie said. "He verified that the moss green and ginger colors for the Dodd home were in stock and available, as was the coffee brown I said I'd get for their neighbor at the same time."

Townsend started moving her along toward the front entrance. "I'm no longer handling that company's paint. It's a franchise matter," he mumbled, distinctly anxious for her to leave.

She noticed that his gaze flicked everywhere but at her as he made his excuses. Annie braced a hand on the door casing, determined not to be hustled out. "It's fortunate, then, isn't it, that you stock other brands. I'm sure another company will have comparable colors, and we can negotiate a multiple gallon price. Mrs. Dodd's choice isn't out of the ordinary. But I will need a new brochure. I gave the others to home owners on the street where we'll be working next."

Townsend literally wrung his hands. "It pains me a great deal to tell you this, Ms. Emerson, since you've been my best customer in months. Heaven knows business is slow. But…I can't sell you paint at all. Someone wants to halt your operation."

"Who?" It had slowly dawned on Annie that this problem wasn't merely a matter of the store changing paint brands.

"I don't know. But my mother raised me as a Southern gentleman, and I'm thoroughly ashamed to admit I've let a threatening letter drive a reliable customer away. I've been at this location serving Briar Run for almost thirty years. Maybe the letter is a hoax, but…" His voice trailed off, and this time he did look at her, his eyes filled with worry.

Annie readjusted the sunglasses she'd shoved up into her hair. "I'm sorry if I've brought trouble to your establishment," she said earnestly. "It's probably not a hoax. I wanted to buy locally to help local merchants. And now that I think of it, didn't you have problems *before* I started buying here? On my first visit, you said you'd installed a burglar alarm because your store was broken into twice."

"Yes, but insurance covered those losses. This letter threatened physical harm to my family and the families of my clerks if I continue doing business with you."

"Did you report the letter to the police?"

The store owner shook his graying head. "The instructions in the letter were very specific. If I quit selling you merchandise, nothing else will happen. They attached a copy of a flyer where you said you were hoping to organize families to boot out the gang."

"If store owners like you cave, Briar Run will suffer more and more criminal activity. Longtime residents are moving out due to the decline of a once-safe town. And that's without even considering the drugs that are being openly sold near our schools and in the park."

The man stared at Annie as if she had two heads. Sighing, she lowered her glasses to hide the frustration she felt. "Can you at least direct me to the nearest big paint store?"

He rattled off an address. "That's in Louisville proper. I do appreciate that you bought here, Ms. Emerson, but the truth is the bigger store can offer you a better price break than I can."

"The convenience of buying here meant more to me. It's sad that we can't band together and force out the scum that's sucking the life out of Briar Run."

"You need to be careful. The tone of that letter was hateful."

"You're telling me? They shot out my living room window," Annie said, this time shoving open the hardware store's front door.

As she unlocked her pickup, she cast a furtive glance around to see if anyone was lurking, watching her leave without the paint she'd come for. She felt like shaking a fist in the air and shouting to any intimidators out there that they weren't going to drive her away. After all, her mother and grandparents were buried in Briar Run, and she had a deep vested interest in this town.

But the street in front of the hardware store was vacant, just as it had been on most of her previous visits. It was as if residents had stopped shopping at businesses on this street. It was the first time Annie had noticed that the pet shop next door was chained shut. So was an equipment rental store down the block. A liquor store had heavy iron bars on both windows and the front door, but looked open. If she had to bet, she'd put her money on the operator of that establishment having a sawed-off shotgun under his cash register. Or maybe he was beholden to gang leaders. In L.A. she knew that was sometimes the case. Certain store owners paid protection money. People didn't think stuff like that happened in the States, but they were wrong.

She phoned Mrs. Dodd. "This is Annie. Your house paint isn't ready yet. Will you please tell any workers who beat me to your house that I'll be along shortly? And, Evelyn, two new guys may show up." Annie listened a moment. "That'll be great if you want to serve them coffee and muffins. I'll be there as soon as I can."

The clock on her dash said nine. She spared a thought for Sky's trip to family court. She hoped his morning was off to a better start than hers.

SKY SAT WITH his lawyer outside the private office of a family court judge. It was the first time one of his hearings wasn't assigned a number on the court docket.

"This is an informal hearing," his lawyer said in answer to Sky's question about the difference. Glancing up, the lawyer added, "There's our opposing counsel. We're all here, so this shouldn't take long. Answer the judge's questions, Sky, but don't say any more than necessary."

Sky nodded. He dug an antacid out of his pocket and stuck it in his mouth. It didn't seem to matter how often he'd appeared before a judge on his own behalf, it always tied his stomach in knots.

His lawyer nodded to Corrine's attorney. Sparks was his name. Sky thought of him as *the shyster*. But when he'd asked around in the police community, he was told the guy had a reputation for being a bulldog and winning.

A clerk Sky had seen before stuck her head out of the office. "It looks as if everyone involved in the Zachary Cordova case is present. Judge Martin has reviewed his history and the current complaint. She's prepared to see you all now." The woman opened the door wider and swept a hand toward the interior.

Sky let the two lawyers go in ahead of him. The judge, an older woman, wasn't wearing judicial robes, but had on a plain tan suit. He hated to look nervous, but recognized his own tension when he raked a hand through his hair. Thank goodness he'd gotten to the barber for a trim.

"Please be seated," the clerk said, indicating chairs in a semicircle facing the judge's desk. "The Honorable Sara Martin is presiding." The clerk slipped into a chair behind a digital steno machine.

The judge peered at the assembled trio over the top of her half glasses. "Zachary's case-worker can't be here, since she was called away on an emergency. I hope we can resolve this based on her report and our meeting."

"Your Honor, we can resolve it," Mr. Sparks said. "My client again requests total custody, this time due to a very upsetting incident that occurred at her home. I submitted a photo of the rock and a copy of the note tied to it that was thrown through Mr. and Mrs. Fleming's living room window."

"I reviewed the evidence," Judge Martin said. She turned her attention to Sky. "I believe that after the rock-throwing, you were shot at?"

He shifted on the hard chair. "I'm a law officer," he stated, linking his hands in his lap.

"He's chief of police in Briar Run," his lawyer clarified.

"Yes, I know. I did some checking. The city has lost population and has therefore reduced police and fire protection. Is that right?"

"Yes." Sky felt a slow burn start in his stomach. He wanted to defend his job, his city and his rights, as Zack's biological father, to have unrestricted access to his son. Except… His most recent conversation with Annie rang in his ears, particularly the part where she accused him of having a hostile attitude, and her insinuation that he'd get farther if he curbed his temper. "Cities of all sizes across the country have been adversely affected by a sluggish economy, Judge Martin. Small towns suffer most. I came to the department at a time of substantial budget cuts. Despite being a limited force, we give the town twenty-four-hour coverage."

"I read that you served in the armed forces. That's laudable, don't you agree, Mr. Sparks?" She pinned the Fleming lawyer with a needle-sharp glance.

"The number of tours he served left his ex-wife alone to have her baby. She was separated from family and friends. And Mr. Cordova didn't see his son until Zachary was almost two years of age."

Sky's lawyer objected. "While Skylar served his country, his wife chose to file for divorce and flee with his son to Kentucky, where she promptly married Mr. Fleming. All of that has been hashed and rehashed, Your Honor. Our contention has always been that Mr. Cordova has done everything required of him by the court to allow for unfettered joint custody. And still Mrs. Fleming wants those rights restricted."

"Not merely restricted, Judge Martin," Mr. Sparks put in smoothly. "Terminated. We are asking for termination because of continued unsafe conditions in the town where Mr. Cordova works and lives."

Sky felt the judge's scrutiny return to him, and he bit his tongue to keep from lashing out. Twisting his hands together, he stopped short of cracking his knuckles.

"Is there gang activity in town?" the judge asked, again leafing through the file.

Feeling his heart dive, Sky lifted his head and met her eyes. "Yes. I believe they orchestrated the rock-throwing incident and the drive-by shooting. The encroachment of the Stingers didn't have much opposition before...well, before," he finished, reluctant to name Annie and effectively throw her under the bus.

Sky's lawyer had no such compunction. "Before a former resident, a woman from California, came back home. Her efforts to rally residents and revive the town has upset gang leaders. She unwisely announced her intentions on a flyer."

Both lawyers shifted their gazes to Sky, who said, "Ms. Emerson inherited her grandmother's home. Her dying request was that her granddaughter would make Briar Run the thriving place it once was. The Stingers clearly don't like her intervention. She's…fearless and won't be dissuaded." Sky stopped talking when his lawyer poked him.

The judge gave a slight smile. "It so happens I have a good friend, whom I won't name, living there. I took the liberty of speaking with her. She's seventy, but in her day was also fearless. She's quite enthusiastic about the restoration, and plans to paint."

"What is this nonsense?" Sparks burst out. "The Emerson woman is who Cordova was dining with when they were shot at. His lieutenant's wife was hit by a stray bullet! Even after that, Cordova had the nerve to take little Zack to that woman's construction site. It is simply not acceptable to his mother or me."

"Mr. Sparks," the judge said, "it's my job to determine what is acceptable. As someone who has worked in family court for years, I can tell you that the majority of cases we see involve mothers who petition the court time and time again, hoping for a shred of cooperation from their children's dads. Here we have a willing father. My decision, for now, is to continue his visits. In fact, seeing his son once every two weeks when they live less than an hour's drive from each other seems miserly. I'm increasing his access to once a week, with visits to be worked around Chief Cordova's work schedule. By that I mean some weeks his day with Zachary will be a weekday, and other times it'll be on a weekend. Mr. Sparks, I'll leave it to you to inform Mrs. Fleming of this change. Out of curiosity, why isn't she present?"

"Why should she be subjected to being in the same room with a man she divorced?" Sparks asked bluntly.

The judge removed and folded her glasses, then set them on the fat court file. "Need I remind you there's a reason we call this *family court,* Mr. Sparks? Our single most important goal is to facilitate the conditions that are best for the offspring of couples who feel they can no longer live together."

Sparks reared back, a slight sneer on his lips. "I speak for Mrs. Fleming when I point out that she resides on two hundred and fifty acres at Fleming Horse Farm, in an elegantly appointed home, while Mr. Cordova lives in a seedy suburb of Louisville. There's no comparison to what Mrs. Fleming can offer Zack."

Sky would have liked to wipe that sneer off Sparks's face. He let the thought churn in his belly. However, the elation he felt about getting to see more of Zack won out over the anger he felt toward Corrine's lawyer.

"I beg to differ," the judge said, jotting a note before she closed the file. "Zachary's case-worker attests to the fact that the boy, in his own words, loves his dad. It's plain from the number of hoops Mr. Cordova has already jumped through that he loves his son in return. In my book, love beats living in a castle. This case is dismissed. I'm requesting an update back here in my office in October. My clerk will give you all a date before you leave. And, Mr. Sparks, I'll expect to see Mrs. Fleming, too, or she'll be in contempt." The judge rose and everyone else did, too. She handed the case file to her clerk, and disappeared through a back door.

Sparks slammed his papers into an open briefcase. "I'll be in touch for that next court date," he told the clerk. "I plan to file for a continuation with the previous judge," he informed Sky's attorney. Sparks left without so much as looking at Sky.

"Can he do that?" Sky asked in an undertone.

The clerk heard him, and smiled. "He can file. But Judge Martin is the longest-serving judge in this county's family court. And when she takes an interest in a case, I've never seen it revert." She passed Sky's attorney a card with information for their next appearance. After thanking her, the men walked out.

Sky felt like jumping in the air and clicking his heels together.

"I'm pleased to see that things finally broke your way, Sky," his lawyer said. "I wish I could take credit, but we were scheduled to go in front of Judge Keating, who's been sympathetic to Corrine. I got a call last evening saying he'd gone into the hospital for emergency gall bladder surgery. I expected I'd be calling you to say we were canceled. Instead, we were assigned to Judge Martin, who usually has the most packed schedule in this court. You must have acquired a good fairy somewhere."

Maybe it was the curb-appeal fairy. That thought ran through Sky's head. Annie deserved praise. Her jab had kept him from an outburst in court matching that of Corrine's lawyer—comments that went against Sparks, and made Sky wonder why the man seemed to lead the charge against him.

"We'll be in touch, Sky. I'll follow up on this ruling with your ex. Between you and me, I don't trust Sparks to relay the whole truth. He takes clients who can pay well for his services, and he doesn't like to lose."

"Hmm. Corrine won't be happy with today's

outcome. She and Sparks never cut me any slack even when they know I have résumés out to find a job in a safer town."

His lawyer nodded. "They're determined to gain sole custody. But today was positive."

The men shook hands and went their separate ways. Sky had promised Koot that he'd rush straight back to the station after his court date. At the last minute, as he entered the city, Sky detoured onto Rose Arbor Street. Annie was the first person he wanted to share his good news with.

He saw her painting the Dodds' garage door some shade of green that also dotted the threadbare jeans she wore. Today her hair was pulled back and covered by a triangle scarf. Giving no thought to the possibility that his surprise visit might end up with him flat on his back—again—Sky got out of his cruiser. He ran up behind Annie, scooped her up, paintbrush and all, and with her feet dangling, he laughed like a maniac and danced her around.

"Sky? Stop! What are you doing? I'm dripping paint all over your nice shirt."

"I took your advice and reined in my temper today. It paid off. A new judge granted me more visits with Zack every month. So I came to thank you," he said, lowering her to the ground.

Annie clung to his shoulders, her head still whirling. His hard body pressed against hers. His smile grabbed her. His smiles were usually a bit cynical, but the one today came from his heart and touched hers. She smiled in return, enjoying the delicious pressure from each of his fingertips splayed across her back. And when he loosened them and slid his hands up and down her spine, she felt tingles all the way to her toes.

"I'm thrilled for you, Sky. Truly thrilled. But, uh, if you don't let go of me, we'll be the subject of gossip all over town."

"I don't care." He was extremely slow to release her. "Don't give me that teacher look. I really *don't* care."

CHAPTER NINE

THROWN OFF GUARD by Sky's admission, Annie swiped at the paint that had dripped on his white shirt. "Sorry, I made that worse. If you're headed straight home, run that spot under cold water. It should wash out. But if you aren't in a rush, I'll give you a paint roller," she said, teasing to cover the fact that she still felt the warm imprint of his hands on her back.

"I have to get to work." He'd stuck one arm of his sunglasses in the open collar of his shirt and now shook them out and put them on. "Are you still planning to check out the warehouse at two?"

"Would three be okay instead? I got a late start here." Bending, she laid her brush across the open can of paint. "I'll walk you to your car and tell you what happened at the hardware store to make me late." Annie matched his stride while succinctly relaying her exchange with Brian Townsend.

Sky's jaw tightened. "Darn it, Annie. So far

most of what the gang's doing is meant to scare you away from getting the residents to band against them. The Louisville cops think the shots into your house were a warning and I agree. The ricocheting bullet that hit Sadie was almost certainly accidental, which is why the dude they picked up hadn't ditched the car. That's not saying Stinger leaders aren't capable of moving past scare tactics and into even more serious stuff."

"I'll grant you I should have been more circumspect in wording that flyer, but I'm not giving in, Sky." She waved a hand at the Dodd house. "Do you see how many helpers showed up this morning? Every day we've attracted twice the people we had the day before. Have you noticed that the porches on homes we've already painted now have outdoor furniture? Those home owners are starting to feel comfortable being outside again. It's no longer just me. It's a movement. The people here want to take back their town."

"Well, the gang leaders see you as the ringleader," he said grimly. "I don't like your plan to drive into Louisville for paint. Can't the store deliver?"

"I did ask about a delivery fee and on small orders it's astronomical. It exceeds what it would cost in gas. And that's why I bought a pickup, Sky—for chores like this."

He caught her hands as she waved them about. For a long moment he said nothing, but he rubbed his thumbs over her paint-splotched knuckles. Tugging her against him, he brought both her hands to his chest. "See if you can get someone to go to the paint store with you. Whatever you do, promise me you'll vary your times and routes. It'll confuse any tail they might put on you."

Annie smoothed out a few wrinkles in his shirt to hide the involuntary flexing of her fingers within his grasp. "I promise. I know you think I'm too impulsive."

"I don't." He gripped her hands harder.

"Foolhardy, then," she said, giving a twisted grin as she tried to tug free of his hold.

"Not that, either." He exerted enough pressure to carry her hands to within an inch of his lips. As if belatedly realizing what he was about to do, Sky dropped her hands and in one fluid motion reached around her and opened his car door. "You're a rare woman, Annie," he said, his voice low and solemn. He began to add something, then ducked into his cruiser and lifted a hand in farewell. "See you later." Slamming his door, he revved the old engine and peeled out in a cloud of dust.

Annie's head spun as she tried to ignore the warm feelings that seemed to pool in her stomach. She didn't want them, darn it. Shaking them off, she plunged back into her work until it was time to break for lunch. As she'd told her two new workers, she dashed out and returned with burgers and soft drinks all around. On her way back, she'd stopped at city hall to pick up the keys to the empty warehouse.

"Hey, Roger," she said, "I met your wife at the burger bar. She's very nice."

"Loretta is better than I deserve," he responded, pausing to dry his hands on his shirttail after he'd rinsed them off with the hose. His confession sparked a round of good-natured teasing among those who knew him. As the crew relaxed in the shade of a decades-old magnolia tree in the Dodds' side yard, Annie explained the mission she was heading off to undertake later—looking at property for a teen center.

Peggy Gilroy gestured with her still-wrapped burger. "I swear, Annie, if you don't slow down you'll keel over."

"There's so much that needs doing, and I'm impatient," Annie said. "Oh! No slowing down anytime soon." Pointing to the street, she got up and dropped her unwrapped burger back in the bag. "Here comes the first set of our decorative iron. Peggy, some of it's for your house, and the rest is for mine and the Spurlocks'. If everyone likes how our homes look once the iron's installed, I'll have the shop continue measuring more of the finished houses."

She led Peggy off and left the other workers buzzing about the changes coming on Rose Arbor Street.

"Missy phoned me while you were picking up paint, Annie. She was too sick to lift her head off the pillow, so that's another indication she's pregnant," Peggy confided with a chuckle.

"Why doesn't she go see a doctor? Or at least take a home pregnancy test?" Annie asked as she signaled the truck driver to back into her driveway.

"Mike's parents are old-school, I gather. His folks don't know she and Mike lived together before they got married. Missy's afraid that a doctor will confirm she got pregnant before their wedding, and that Mike's parents will be upset with them."

"That worry is probably making her symptoms worse. Why doesn't she tell them to go jump in the lake? They should be ecstatic at the prospect of a grandchild." Annie checked the bill of lading, signed for the delivery and talked to the ironworker about homes she might want done next. "Peggy, do you mind checking on Missy to see if she's okay with the noise of drilling and hammering?"

"She'll be fine. She's still so spooked about our break-ins, she's too scared to leave the house. It's a very generous thing you're doing, paying for this iron grating. George is concerned that you're out of a job and you're running through your savings like water just to honor your grandmother's wishes. But she's already gone and you shouldn't be putting your own livelihood at risk. He says—"

"Tell George not to worry," Annie broke in. "I launched this project out of love for Gran Ida, not out of guilt."

Mollified then, the older woman struck out for the Spurlock home. As Annie watched the men unload the iron, she chewed her lip anxiously. If friends like George and Peggy were speculating about the source of her funding, how long before people gossiped—and Stinger leaders did the math? Sky had said if and when they did, she'd be in even greater danger. She needed to circulate more rumors about deep discounts, or talk about how she'd applied for grants. That was true. In the evenings she *had* applied for grants that would help fund and staff a teen center.

Workmen had fit Annie's window grates by the time Peggy and a pale, bedraggled Missy emerged from the Spurlock house.

"Oh, that's going to look fabulous," Peggy exclaimed.

Missy simply threw her arms around Annie. "Mike was afraid the houses would end up looking like a row of jail cells. Take that, you burglars," she said, making her friends laugh out loud.

Peggy stayed for a while, then said, "I'm going back to paint. I can't wait to finish Evie Dodd's house so we can start on Jane Mickelson's, which is the last one we're doing on Rose Arbor since the Dawsons and those two others up the street opted out. Can you tell I've been bitten by your refurbishing bug?" She laughed again. "Oh, and I promised Davena I'd go with her to see some drapery fabric she found on sale."

"I may be back or I may not, Peggy. I'll stick around until they finish putting up the iron, but don't forget I'm inspecting a building for a possible teen center this afternoon. If the fabric's a good deal, just charge it and I'll pay you later, okay?"

Nodding, Peggy strode off down the street. Missy turned to Annie. "I'm younger than either you or Peggy, but I don't have a tenth of your energy." The words were barely out when she covered her mouth with one hand and clutched her stomach with the other. She hurried back into her house, obviously to throw up. Annie watched Missy's mad dash and felt sorry for her friend. She could only imagine what it would be like to be pregnant during the muggy heat of a Southern summer. For that matter, what it would feel like to have a tiny human growing inside you, regardless of the time of year.

Annie reflected on all the babies she'd held, rocked or bounced on her knee during her tenure in L.A. Some were so adorable she recalled telling coworkers she wished she could take one home. Their usual response was to tell her to get a puppy. And they'd all laugh. Still, sometimes her biological clock ticktocked like crazy. She shook her head to clear it, trying not to think about a baby of her own. In these all-too-familiar fantasies, her baby's father always stood off to one side, shrouded in mist. Life had taught Annie she could raise a child alone. Many mothers she'd met did fine. Gran Ida had.

But not her. Annie always swore she wouldn't. The absence of a father in her life had affected her more than she'd ever let on. It was why, in her old job, she'd worked the hardest to help single moms.

The ironworkers drilled holes and set screws at a good clip, yet when the last piece was in place and they'd loaded their tools and left, Annie's stomach growled, reminding her that she'd missed lunch. Still, she wanted to stand there for a few minutes, admiring the work that had just been done. Walking back to the sidewalk, she gauged the effect of this final touch on their three homes and smiled in satisfaction.

A car screeched to a stop at the curb inches away from Annie, and she whirled around in concern.

Sky threw open his door and bounded out to stand beside her. "Hey, you're turning the old neighborhood into a little N'Awlins French Quarter with all that wrought-iron curlicue stuff."

"My thought was more a Spanish village," she said, turning away from the houses and inspecting him from head to foot. He'd changed out of his paint-splotched white shirt into a crisp blue one, teamed with darker pants and a navy tie that denoted the official Briar Run police uniform. A badge pinned to his left shirt pocket gleamed like gold in the afternoon sun. A wide black belt bracketing his hips was weighed down with the tools of his trade All in all, he looked mighty fine to Annie. Solid. Manly. Appealing.

But perhaps she was still in the grip of her recent daydream about babies and motherhood. Unless her real problem was a light-headedness due to hunger. Feeling slightly off-kilter, she wet her dry lips with her tongue. There was no doubt that, next to Sky, she appeared grungy in her rumpled, paint-spattered jeans and blouse. "It's close to three," she said to break the spell his sudden unsettling arrival had cast over her. "Did you stop here to beg off meeting me at the warehouse?"

"I came to give you a lift."

"I can drive myself."

"I know you can. But if gang leaders *do* have someone keeping tabs on you, it's better if I drive. They'll figure I'm making a routine check of an empty building."

"Are you in the habit of taking regular citizens along on official checks of empty buildings?"

"Do you get a charge out of being obstinate?" She cracked a smile at that. "Apparently."

"I'll give you points for honesty." He swept a hand toward his vehicle. "If you're done here, we can go on over to the warehouse now."

"Let me get a notepad and tape measure."

"I have both in the car."

"I'm a mess. I'd planned to clean up first."

"An…nie!"

"All right. All right. Neither of us has time to waste. All the same, I need to get my notebook and my bag out of the truck." She retrieved them, locked her vehicle and rounded the back of his, then yanked open the passenger door. "Do you want me to sit in back so it looks like you're taking me to the scene of a crime or something?"

"Just get in," he said, his nightstick hitting the console with a crack as he heaved himself into the driver's seat.

His tone said he'd reached the end of his patience. She climbed in—not meekly—but nevertheless withholding further comment.

His car mobile phone crackled to life. "It's Saunders checking in, Chief. Koot said you're not available for an hour or so, but it's a lazy day in town, so I'm going to grab a break at the burger bar, okay?"

Sky depressed a button on the mike. "Roger

that." He clicked off and clipped the mike back in its holder.

Annie leaned against the headrest. "I didn't mean to sound stubborn back there. But the way you whipped up to the curb gave me a fright. I do appreciate you taking time from your busy day on my account, Sky."

"I didn't see you standing there at first. I was too focused on the work you've done. The paint looked good, but that iron...*bello!*" He kissed the tips of his fingers and made an approving gesture.

"So you like it?"

"Oh, yeah."

"I wasn't sure if you'd think I'd overdone things."

"If you can keep up the pace, you *will* turn this town around."

She angled toward him, raising her left knee. "So you actually believe that now?" She smiled. "But why would we slow the pace? I expect it to increase once people see what's possible."

"This town has a lot of homes, Annie. You've painted how many...five or six?"

"That's in a few weeks. I painted my place alone—well, the first time, anyway. I had help painting over the graffiti. Two of us painted Gilroys'. Mike pretty much did his own. With every home after that, we've doubled our work force. At that rate I figure all the houses here could be painted in one year. Most could have wrought iron, too."

"Not if you go off on other tangents."

"What does that mean?"

"Like this." Sky pulled up to a chain-link fence around an old single-story, redbrick building.

"Oh, this is the warehouse! How lovely. Sky, it still has some landscaping in front. It's absolutely *perfect* for a teen center."

"See? That's what I meant about going off on other tangents. This teen center idea is bound to tempt gang activity. Besides, the time and energy you'll spend here is time you're not spending painting homes."

"People don't need me to paint."

"Maybe…"

"Honestly, Sky, you can be so frustrating sometimes. Why 'maybe'?"

"Can't you see that you're the driving force? Your enthusiasm is infectious. You make people want to do better. Be better." He lowered his voice. "You've had that effect on me."

"Wow, when you put it like that, it feels like a heavy burden." Annie's brow knit.

Sky shut off the Crown Vic's engine. Lips

pursed, he skimmed a finger down Annie's nose. "Let's go take a gander inside."

She fumbled a ring of keys out of the flowered, quilted bag she'd grabbed from her truck. "I picked up the keys from the city clerk after I got our lunch order today. I can't believe she handed them over to a virtual stranger."

"More proof that your reputation precedes you," he said, and sprang from the car to rush around and open her door.

"Why don't I think you meant that as a compliment?" Brushing past him, she tried two keys before one opened the lock on the chain looped around the gate. Sky refastened the chain, while Annie repeated the key trials with the front door lock. She had it open by the time he caught up with her.

"I was afraid it'd be pitch-black inside," she said, and her voice echoed in the empty building. "There's tons of light from that row of clerestory windows." She stared up.

Sky bumped into her, and settled his hands around her waist. "It's a nice space. Cleaner than I expected."

Annie glanced back over her left shoulder and found herself staring at Sky's clean-shaven jaw. With his hands almost spanning her waist, she was reminded that he was a toucher. She wasn't.

Or at least she hadn't been. Now she thought she could be, because she liked the feeling of his body heat through her blouse. Not only did she find his warmth seductive, but she loved the woodsy scent of his soap or aftershave.

"What do you want measured?" he asked, his breath teasing her ear.

"Wha...at?"

Sky stepped around her and unclipped a metal tape from his belt. He wagged it in front of her face. "Measured...ah, didn't you need measurements for Sadie?" he asked, voice slightly gruff.

"Separated by a few feet, Annie felt her shaken senses coalesce, but her voice had deserted her. "I, uh. I, uh." She madly scanned the interior, hoping for a burst of brilliance that didn't come.

"I've never been in a teen center," Sky said, walking farther into the cavernous room. "Are they partitioned?"

At last her faculties returned, and Annie dug her notebook out of her bag. She managed to say, "Chantal Culver wants room to dance. That area needs to be as open as possible so staff can monitor it. My original thought was to create separate spaces for Ping-Pong, and basketball, and...what's that table game boys like—the one with plastic people on sticks?"

"Foosball? We big boys like that, too." Sky grinned.

"That's it." She rolled her eyes. "Males are so shallow."

"Ha! Why, because we choose to be active rather than sit around gossiping about friends who aren't there?"

"Right." She rolled her eyes. "You also sit around gobbling chips, drinking beer and shouting at teams on TV."

"Teens do that, too. However, even if you install a flat-screen TV, I'm sure you won't be supplying beer."

"No, but snacks and soft drinks...so a large fridge. A flat screen's a good idea." She wrote in her notebook, then looked up. "Bathrooms. We need two to meet code. If this building hasn't got plumbing that works, that's a deal-breaker."

"I think you're in luck," Sky said, stabbing a finger toward the far end of the room. "I see a door in each corner of the wall."

Annie hiked back there and called out, "You're right, and thank heaven both look fairly decent. This place couldn't be more ideal. And it's selling for a song."

"That may be, but all the stuff you mentioned adds up to a pretty penny. Not to mention staffing... I know you said your grandmother left you money, but this seems riskier than furnishing paint and decorative iron for residents."

"By riskier you mean if a teen gets hurt on the premises?"

"Insurance. I hadn't even got to that yet. I've mentally added up costs for the building—putting in interior walls, even half ones, sports equipment, a TV, a kitchen…well, the list goes on." He handed her a scrap of paper. "Take a good look at that list. Surely you aren't thinking of footing the bill for staff salaries."

"I've done quite a bit of research since Chantal gave me the idea. The place where I worked in L.A. had cubicles with movable half walls separating counselors. The sections snapped together with metal clips. I'd buy the building and partitions, and give it to the city. They'd be responsible for insurance. I've applied for grants to cover staff salaries. A number of teachers have had their salaries slashed, and I'll bet some of them would love to supplement their incomes running the center during the afternoons and on weekends."

As Sky continued to frown doubtfully, Annie added, "No new venture is ever risk-free. If I succeed with this, can you think of a better way for me to invest Gran Ida's money than in Briar Run's youth?"

"I sure could. Buy a sailboat and sail around the world. Or pick up a beachside condo in the Bahamas. But not you. You see this town through rose-tinted glasses. Like I said, I can buy into your reno project. But I'm not convinced by this idea. You're ready to bankroll sticky-fingered kids, some of 'em dopers, some dealers. We suspect that part of our teen population are already gangbangers. Don't you think they'll bring in drugs and liquor, and trash this building?"

"That's a cop talking, Sky. The home owner in you, the *dad,* should want to save kids like Deshawn and Chantal and their friends—for selfish reasons, among others."

"Selfish how?"

"So your family caseworker can look at the improvements here and tell the judge that Zack will be as safe living half-time with you as he is on the farm with his mother."

Sky set his hands on his hips above the laden belt, and lifted his eyes toward the ceiling. "I realize Corrine will never approve of Zack living in Briar Run. I have résumés out with police departments in safer small towns. I did some fix-ups inside my house. Painting it with your help will up its appeal. Should it sell before I find a new job, I'll probably rent in Koot and Sadie's area until something comes through."

Annie blinked at Sky. "I see," she said, but she didn't. She didn't want to see. She felt light-headed again, as though she might pass out. All the feelings he'd brought to life in her shriveled like dead grapes on a vine.

"Stop looking at me like I kicked your cat." He frowned, but was the first to drop his gaze.

"I don't have a cat."

"You know what I mean," he said defensively. "Nothing in the world means more to me than Zack. One of his mom's main objections to shared custody is this town and its bad reputation. You can't apply enough cosmetics to counter that in the eyes of Corrine, Archibald and their high-powered attorney. It is what it is, Annie."

Annie tucked the paper with his numbers and measurements in her notebook, and returned it to her bag. "I think we're finished here. I need to get back to my paint crew, and you're still on the city's clock…until you get a new job offer, of course."

"I can hear criticism in your voice, Annie. You act like I planned to deceive you. When have I not been frank about my feelings toward your more grandiose projects?"

Annie wanted to shout at him, to say he ought to be ashamed of—of what? *Of leading her on with his casual touching and his sincerity and his charm*. But those were her shortcomings, not Sky's. She'd begun to relax her guard around him. She'd always had a strong resistance to trusting men. Men made women fall in love with them, and then they died, or left their wives or lovers to raise their kids alone. Pain and betrayal came with the territory, as she'd learned from her own life and her work with single moms in L.A.

Without another word, Annie led the way to the door and stepped aside to let Sky pass.

"My plans needn't impact yours, Annie. As long as I'm chief of police, I'll worry about the Stingers—although I'm not sure I need to. I was on the receiving end of your martial arts expertise, remember. Are you hiding the fact that you're also a crack shot?" Sky knew he was trying too hard to relieve the tension he'd felt swirling around them from the minute he'd divulged his plans.

"I hate guns," Annie said, leveling a scowl at him after she'd locked the warehouse door. "It's too easy for criminals to lay their hands on guns."

"You won't get an argument out of me. Listen, I know when I'm beaten, and when you can't beat 'em, join 'em. So, here's an idea for your teen center. Have you considered teaching a beginner's class in judo?"

"I don't do judo, I do tae kwon do," she said stiffly as she padlocked the gate.

"I could take a class of boys, if you handle the girls. The training I got at the police academy doesn't have a fancy name, and the army called it close-order combat. But it all boiled down to martial arts."

"Really? You never told me you had hand-to-hand training," she said, gawking at him as he opened the passenger door for her.

"Yeah, well it's taken me a while to get over the embarrassment of you flipping me like a pancake."

She laughed at that, dissolving the tension that had grown up between them.

"You caught me totally off guard," he muttered, motioning for her to get in so he could shut the door.

She sat and swung her legs inside. "I must have." She kept gazing at him with new awe even after he'd slid behind the wheel. "You know, that's a great idea you just had. Girls and women feel empowered once they receive martial arts lessons. And boys like Deshawn, who are a little on the skinny side, yet have the good sense to be afraid of older bullies, would benefit from a few techniques. Although I'd prefer that we not call our classes combat lessons.

Real martial arts teach respect for opponents as a number-one rule."

Sky made a face, but started the car before drawling, "Whatever you say. But these opponents don't deserve respect."

"It's all about discipline, Sky. I don't want these kids to go out looking for fights. I'd teach a class in order to build character and confidence."

"I'll have to think about whether or not I can teach that way. Where I learned, we didn't stop to bow to our opponents or we chanced getting a knife in the gut."

She shuddered. "War is so terrible, so vicious."

"I'm talking about breaking up a plain old street fight. Or school knife fights."

"I think Gran Ida sheltered me growing up. I don't recall more than the occasional playground tussle. I wouldn't call them fights compared to the way kids kill other kids today."

He studied her. "That's a sign of getting old, Annie, when you start saying your generation was saner, smarter, all around better, than the current one."

"Hmm." Once again her thoughts drifted to the countdown of her biological clock. Sky couldn't be much older than she was, yet he'd gone to war, been married and divorced and had a child. Maybe life *was* passing her by. Maybe she ought to make more of an effort to get out and meet men her age. She'd barely gotten used to calling Briar Run her permanent home. And Sky Cordova, who'd lit a fire in her belly, had made it plain that he was moving on.

"What new plan are you cooking up in that brain of yours now?" Sky asked, giving her a sleepy-eyed smile.

"New plan?" She jerked up straight, then sank back, afraid her face might betray where her thoughts had wandered.

"Yeah, it's the way your eyes get distant and then you pop up with some new scheme."

He did have her pegged, so Annie was thankful they'd arrived at the Dodds'. The crew she'd left earlier was gone. Nor were they working next door at the Mickelsons'. That house was all painted except for the trim. "What time is it?" Annie checked her watch. "After five! I had no idea we'd stayed at the warehouse so long."

"My shift's over now. Listen, do you want to get something to eat? I skipped lunch and I'm starved."

"Me, too. But I'll just eat at home. If you let me out here, I can walk back to my house. We've both had a long day, and I'm still in my paint clothes."

"True, but you look fine. Restaurants around here aren't fancy. Besides, I'd like to celebrate tonight. You had a hand in today's outcome." At her puzzled glance, Sky elaborated. "Remember, in court I won extra time with Zack, partly because I took your advice and didn't mouth off to Corrine's lawyer in front of the judge."

"You did tell me that." Everything in Annie argued against any kind of personal relationship with Sky when he had made it very obvious that it was a dead end. On the other hand, he'd never indicated he wanted a relationship. That might all be in her head. "Sure. Okay. But we'll go Dutch."

"You're a hard woman. However, if you're so inclined, you can buy my dinner. I am, after all, a lowly public servant."

Unsure if he was teasing, and still debating whether she could handle the volcanic feelings he aroused in her without even trying, Annie eyed him apprehensively.

He threw back his head and laughed. "I'm kidding. Don't ever play poker, Annie. All your thoughts are reflected in your eyes."

"I hope not." And she meant it.

CHAPTER TEN

"HOLD ON A minute, Sky. I have another favor to ask you before we go eat." Annie stayed him with a hand on his arm. "I told Rita and Homer Gonzales and the two men you referred to me that I'd pay them something at the end of each workday. Rita and Homer live next door to the Dodds." She pointed. "I can run do it now. I trust you know where Roger lives?"

"Do you need to go back to your house for your checkbook?"

"I've been giving folks grocery store gift cards. Tonight I'll just pay them in cash. It's not much—little more than gas money."

"I swear, Annie, it's crazy to carry cash around. A druggie will kill for the price of a joint."

She put a hand to her head. "Please, I'm too tired and hungry for lectures."

Saying nothing, Sky put his cruiser in reverse and backed up to park in front of the Gonzales house.

Hopping out of the car, Annie pried a wad

of cash out of her jeans pocket and peeled off a few bills before she rang the doorbell. "Hi, Rita, I got back late from an afternoon appointment. The work you guys did looks fantastic. I stopped by to give you this to thank you for your labor today."

"Annie, heavens, you bought the paint for our house and we saw the wrought iron you ordered. Yesterday you gave everyone grocery gift cards. Girl, your grandma, who pinched pennies until Lincoln squealed, would turn in her grave to think you're out squandering your hard-earned money."

"Rita, I appreciate your concern, but painting homes on Rose Arbor is the just the tip of the iceberg. I want the help of people all over town if they have the time to pick up a sander, roller or brush. They say Rome wasn't built in a day, but it wasn't built for free, either. The little I'm giving you for helping is merely a token."

"Well, thank you. Homer took a huge cut in pay when the glove factory closed. He did find another job, mind you, doing maintenance at the racetrack. A lot of folks weren't so lucky."

"What was Homer's job at the factory?" Annie asked.

"He was a product inspector. No bad gloves

were ever shipped. So, the factory didn't shut down because of poor-quality merchandise."

"I've heard that from several former employees. I have to run. Will I see you at the Mickelson house tomorrow?"

"I'll be there. Is that our handsome chief of police waiting for you at the curb?" The older woman's eyes twinkled. "Uh-huh, what did I tell you...that he'd keep coming around, right? He's not just doing his duty when it comes to you, Annie."

Annie's eyes shifted toward the street. She almost gave away Sky's plan to leave his job for greener pastures. But it wasn't in her to be mean-spirited. "It's nothing like that, Rita. He helped me on another project. Neither of us got any lunch, so we're going now to grab something to eat, that's all." Annie scampered away rather than hear more of Rita's romantic predictions—her off-base predictions.

"If you take that long at Roger's place and Charlie's, I may die of starvation," Sky said.

"Rita's a talker. I did offer to let you off the hook, remember?"

"See, hunger's making you cranky." Sky gunned the cruiser.

"No, Rita's insistence that you and I should get romantically involved made me cranky.

She's persisting in this, even though I've tried to squelch her speculation. I did warn you people would gossip about us." Annie adjusted her seat belt. "From now on, you need to help stamp out the gossip."

His thumbs did a drumbeat on the steering wheel. "I haven't heard any speculation or gossip."

She shrugged and turned her face toward her side window.

Sky glanced at her reflection in the darkening glass. There was enough light from the sinking sun to profile the soft curve of her cheek, and to highlight a few dark curls that had managed to stray from under the odd triangle scarf she still wore to control her long, wild hair. Sky had a thing for her hair. It had been what first caught his attention. Now he found a lot more to like about the total package—although there was plenty that drove him crazy, too. "There, the house with the yard lights belongs to Roger and Loretta McBride."

"Oh, the McBrides live adjacent to the park. Is that why they have perimeter lights? You were right about the park being a disaster, by the way. It's a crying shame. Gran Ida took care of weeding the flower beds, and trimming the roses. Now the birdbath is broken, swings are torn down and the roses are dead. Restoring the park will be my final tribute to Gran," she said as she got out of the cruiser.

Sky shook his head, watching her hurry up the walkway. How could she possibly find more hours in the day to work on the park?

Annie wasn't gone long. She ran back to the car and flung herself into the passenger seat. "That was lucky. Charlie was at Roger's house. They were just sitting down to eat. It smelled so good and I'm about to pass out from hunger."

"We can't have that." Sky made a U-turn in the street.

"Wasn't that illegal?"

Sky flashed her a guilty grin.

"That's what I thought."

"It's shorter taking this direction to the restaurant I have in mind."

"Well, then, by all means, it's okay to break the law getting there." Annie gave him the old evil eye.

"Hey, I don't want you fainting away from hunger." He made two more left turns and merged with the highway that headed toward bluegrass country.

Annie scarcely had time to read a couple of road signs lit by his headlights when Sky pulled off the road and into the parking lot of a restaurant called Ye Olde Irish Pub. "It says they feature forty kinds of lagers and twenty ales," Annie said. "And you're in uniform, Chief."

"I got drinking out of my system a long time ago, Annie. Before I became a cop, when I saw how drinking can get out of hand, and the results." Sky cracked his car door ajar and sniffed the air. "Mmm, smell that grill."

"Race you to the door, Cordova. I'm ready to taste whatever smells so good."

Annie did beat him, but not by much. Sky reached around her, opened the heavy outer door and ushered her in. The interior was cavernous, but lit by small lanterns in the center of each round table. A bar stretched the length of the room down one wall. Booths lined the other three. It was to one of the booths that a hostess led them.

Again Sky guided Annie's steps with his broad hand nestled in the curve of her back. His casual touch felt more intimate to her in this setting. Trying not to think that they looked like a couple, Annie concentrated on checking the food on other diners' plates as she passed by. Even before the smiling hostess placed a menu in her hands, Annie knew what she wanted.

When the waiter came, she requested sweet tea with plenty of ice. "It'll save time if we order now," she said, glancing across the table at Sky, who'd asked for coffee, black.

"I'm afraid I don't know anything about their salad selections, but our waiter will, so you go ahead and order."

Annie frowned at him. Closing her menu she said, "I'll have a T-bone steak medium rare, fries and a double order of mixed vegetables."

Sky gaped at her as he managed to stammer out his order. "Give me an eight-ounce sirloin, fries and corn on the cob." After the waiter left and someone else whizzed past, dropping off a basket filled with steaming dark bread, Sky watched bemusedly as Annie pulled off two slices and slathered them with honey-butter. She moved her plate aside to let the waiter deliver drinks.

"I guess you plan to take half your meal home," Sky said.

She opened her eyes, because she'd closed them to savor her first bite of the heavy brown bread dripping with its sweet topping. "I intend to eat every morsel. Oh, I didn't mean to hog all the bread." She pushed the basket to his side of the table.

He helped himself. "I meant their T-bone is big enough for two."

They ate their bread in silence and when it

was gone, Annie asked, "Are you one of those guys who thinks a woman should nibble like a mouse?"

"Most do, don't they?"

A heated discussion ensued on that topic. Annie broke off and smiled at the waiter who carried their steaming plates to the table. "Mmm."

"These are piping hot, so be careful," he warned. The metal plates he set before them sizzled. "Can I get either of you anything else?"

"Ketchup," Sky said at the same time Annie asked for steak sauce.

Both appeared like magic.

They dived into cutting and eating their steaks. For a time, talk fell by the wayside. Sky spoke first as he buttered his corn. "This is my favorite vegetable. I wish it was easier to eat in public."

Annie blotted her lips with her napkin. "Everyone here seems too busy eating to pay attention to you, Sky. Me included."

He scanned the room. "You're right," he said as he unbuttoned the sleeves on his uniform shirt and rolled them up to his elbows. "I'm self-conscious, I guess. One time in Maryland at one of Corrine's horsey banquets, I ordered lobster and corn on the cob. Melted butter dripped down the backs of my hands onto the cuffs of my dress shirt. She ranted all week about how I'd humiliated her. Anytime we went out after that she'd remind me. I pretty much stopped eating corn until I found this restaurant."

Annie cut another slice of meat off her T-bone. "The messiest things to eat taste the best. If those things were on your banquet menu, I doubt you were the only one dripping butter."

"I was the only one at our table," he said, biting into his corn.

"Food is meant to be enjoyed." Annie dipped one of her fat golden fries into a pile of ketchup and grinned. "This place was a great choice. I feel like I'll never be hungry again."

Sky dispatched his corn, then wiped his face and fingers. "Skinny as you are, I don't know where you put all that food."

"I'm not skinny."

He held up his hands, fingertips touching. "I could circle your waist with my hands."

She started to say he had big hands, but the waiter came with the check and she snatched it.

"I was joking when I suggested you buy me dinner, Annie. Come on, give me the bill. I eat so many meals alone, tonight was a treat."

"You know, it was nice for me, too." She

looked up with real surprise at that discovery as she tucked cash inside the folder.

Sky's cell phone rang, cutting short the dance of slow-dawning comprehension their eyes had engaged in. He frowned down at his phone's readout. "It's my lawyer," he murmured, and his expression turned to one of apprehension. "Lyle? Sky here. Is something wrong?"

Annie handed the waiter the check folder and told him to keep the change while Sky listened intently to his caller. "Okay, that's good. To-morrow's pretty short notice, but I agree that we should take what we can get. Do I need to give her advance notice of my plans? Maybe we'll take in a movie, or hang out at my place watching TV. Do I ask what *she* does with Zack, Lyle? Do I ask her how often she goes riding and leaves him in the care of Archibald's teen-age daughters?"

Indicating with gestures that she was going to the restroom, Annie slid out of the booth and headed for the ladies' lounge.

By the time she came back, Sky was off the phone. He rose as soon as he saw her. "Are you ready to leave?"

"Trouble?" she asked, collecting the bag she always carried.

"No, but apparently one of my new visitation

days is going to be tomorrow—or not at all this week. Corrine knows it's a hardship on me to switch duty on such short notice. I'm reasonably sure Koot will trade with me, but it's hard when we're both on most days. Corrine knows that, too. She chose tomorrow out of spite."

"Maybe not, Sky," Annie said quietly as they moved toward the door. "Why don't you pick up the phone and discuss things with her directly?"

He let out a jagged laugh. "We communicate through our lawyers."

"Since she's happily remarried, I should think the two of you—or even all three of you, if she wants to include Zack's stepfather—could sit down over coffee and arrange a plan that covers six months or a year."

"The only plan that will suit Corrine is to cut me out of Zachary's life completely," Sky said grimly. "She's not a reasonable person like you are, Annie."

"Perhaps that's because you immediately get defensive or hostile," she said as he unlocked her door.

"You're darned right I do." He slammed her door after she got in, and stomped around the car, throwing himself into his seat.

"I'm not the enemy, Sky. I'm just saying you and your ex face coparenting for at least thirteen more years, or beyond if your son gets married and you share a grandchild or grandchildren."

"You just ruined a perfectly good meal," he muttered as he started the car.

Annie knew that tone, that closed look. She'd encountered this attitude numerous times in counseling divorced couples. She wasn't Sky's counselor, but where *was* his? she wondered. "Divorce doesn't have to be contentious," she ventured, hoping she could make Sky see that his life and his son's would be happier if the people who loved Zack got along. "Even if you don't agree on everything, it's infinitely better if you're not always at war. I can tell you, having worked with older kids from divided homes, that they have more trouble if the parents fight."

"Take it from me, *she's* made our divorce contentious. And if she thinks I'll go away quietly and not fight for more time with Zachary, she's mistaken. This last judge increased my visitations to once a week, but there's still the matter of holidays. Corrine's demanded she have him for birthdays and Christmas. When I first got back from military duty, I mailed him his gifts. Anytime I asked how Zachary liked them, she claimed they hadn't arrived. I put a tracker on one, and then she changed her story—said the box got smashed in the mail. So now, I make sure I hand him his gifts in person. I have to do it on one of my visits, which never coincide with his birthday. And heaven forbid I'd get to see him Christmas Eve or Christmas Day. Archibald's family *always* spends the holidays at their mountain cabin."

Annie faced him. "Holidays and vacations should be evenly split," she said matter-of-factly. "You need to keep plugging away through the courts, Sky."

"I need to win a lottery," he said. "Keeping a lawyer on retainer isn't cheap. As Corrine is well aware."

"Doesn't her husband shell out alimony or child support for *his* children?"

"They're older and they live with him—I mean, them. Anyway, his wife died. Lyle Baker, my lawyer, found out by nosing around the horse community that Archibald's wife operated a riding school and Corrine took riding lessons from her for years. According to a couple of Corrine's friends, she heard Archibald needed someone to live in and take care of his kids after his wife's death. I was gone, Zack was a baby. Corrine knew Archibald and his girls. She lived in, all right. I got divorce papers handed to me at an army camp in Afghanistan, with bullets raining all around. Next thing I hear, she's on a honeymoon in Bahrain where her new hubby went to buy a racehorse."

As she listened to Sky rant, something occurred to Annie. "Do you still love Corrine?"

"Love her? Are you kidding? Would you love someone who treated you the way she treats me?"

"Well, I've seen kids who love abusive parents. At times, it seemed as if the worse a child was treated by his mom or dad, the more he stuck up for them, or wanted to go back and live with them. Those cases taught me that love isn't always logical."

"It is for me," Sky said emphatically.

"Mmm-hmm. Do you hate her?" Annie thought that would be telling. Hate could render people incapable of moving on with their lives.

Sky had pulled up in front of Annie's house. He reached down and turned off the engine, but not before he studied her in the glow of the dashboard lights. "You should've been a lawyer, Annie, the way you cross-examine. Hate…it's a strong term. Hate does terrible things to people. I witnessed hatred in two war-torn countries— often blind hatred. So my short answer to your question is no, I don't hate Corrine. The question I wrestle with most is did I ever love her? Did I love her enough? The answer comes back to two things. I cared enough once to marry her. And our marriage, however brief, resulted in a son I wouldn't give up for anything in the world."

Moved by his from-the-heart statements, Annie stretched across the console and squeezed his hand. Her fingers felt the slight roughness of a big hand that identified Sky as all male. She felt his pulse quicken and she drew back. "It's getting late. I'd better go in. I want to play around on the computer with some ideas for the teen center. And morning comes earlier these days as we move into summer."

Sky tried to catch her hand, and sighed loudly when she eluded him. "I should get home, too," he said. "I'll probably have a message telling me what time I can pick Zack up. I still have to clear trading shifts with Koot." He opened his door. "I'll walk you to your door," he said as the dome light spilled over them.

"There's no need. I'm quite capable of making it from the curb to my door."

"Capable, no doubt. But…you didn't leave your porch light on. What kind of cop would let a woman march into darkness that might be full of boogeymen?" he teased.

"It was daylight when we left," Annie mumbled, deciding, however, that it was useless to try and dissuade him.

Sky let her go a step ahead of him, but as usual, he placed a hand lightly on her waist. "Got your house key?"

She stumbled on a raised corner of sidewalk as she dug in the front pocket of her jeans. "I took it out of my bag so I'd have it within easy reach."

Sky grabbed her waist with both hands, and they both laughed as she dangled the key in front of his nose. His touch always rattled Annie's nerves, and he never seemed to be in any rush to break the connection. She reached the porch first and pulled free to skip lightly up the steps.

Neither of them was prepared for two flying bodies to separate from the shadows on the dark porch, both slamming into Annie, knocking her off her feet, and then into Sky. His quick reflexes were all that saved him from falling, too, as her bag and house key flew into the garden.

Annie pulled herself together quickly. Lifting her feet from her position on the ground, she wrapped her ankles around the thigh of one assailant. He went down with a thud, tumbling backward into the porch steps with a grunt.

The second intruder didn't give Sky time to

check on Annie. A wiry guy dressed in black butted him in the stomach. Sky fought to keep his breath. His ears rang and his head snapped back. It was a miracle that he maintained his footing. There was no time to get his Glock from his holster before the guy struck a blow to his shoulder with a fist.

A cloud drifted across the moon and plunged the struggling quartet into blackness. Just before that, Sky saw Annie in a crouch. She sprang up, kicking out at her attacker, who'd gotten up to charge her again. Sky knew that the force of her kick, with her whole body weight behind it, would send the guy reeling.

It felt as though the fight went on and on. And yet, in real time, it was over fast. Sky and Annie ended up back to back, winded, but with prone assailants lying at their feet.

Sky unhooked handcuffs from his belt. Bending, he secured the man he'd struggled with. "If you'd left your porch light on, we could see these jokers."

An involuntary laugh bubbled from Annie's throat. "I know it's not funny, but if the light had been on, they couldn't have hidden on my dark porch. Since I took out all the foliage around the foundation, they wouldn't have had any place to lie in wait."

"True. Do you have rope somewhere so I can tie up the dude you took down? Then I'll call Teddy and have him bring a second pair of cuffs so I can transport these yahoos."

"I dropped my house key and bag in the scuffle. I'll sit on this guy while you phone for backup. When Ted arrives, I'll get a flashlight from your car and search for my stuff. I doubt my key flew too far."

Sky knew she was capable of handling the perp. He hauled out his phone and called Ted. The two talked briefly. The man Sky had knocked down began moving. He cursed and wheezed and wobbled to his knees. Sky shoved him back. "You're already in a mountain of trouble," he said, sounding tough. "What's your name, fella?"

The guy on the ground curled into a ball, but remained mute.

The clouds that had occluded the moon blew past. Sky saw Annie pull the shoelaces out of her sneakers and tie them together. She rolled the guy Sky had told her to watch onto his back. After giving the laces a yank, she looped them around the man's wrists and secured them to his belt. He was stirring, too, and attempted to get up. Failing, he made rude accusations to his friend as he flopped around the walkway on his belly.

"Where did you learn to use shoelaces as makeshift handcuffs?" Sky sounded surprised —and approving. "Is that something they teach in tae kwon do?"

"It's a trick I learned from a retired LAPD cop who gave our staff a workshop on self-defense."

"I've used a perp's belt to bind his hands, or feet, but I never thought of using shoelaces. And neither of these guys is wearing a belt."

"Shoelaces are effective," she said, leaning over the guy on the ground. "If you wiggle too much, they pull tighter and either cut off your circulation or slice through your wrist. Get it?"

The man on the ground swore again, but stopped moving.

They heard a siren down the block. Annie straightened and joined Sky. "Oh, I couldn't see it before, but your nose is bloody."

Sky gingerly wiped under his nose. "I knew he landed a punch to my face."

"There's my key," Annie said, spotting a flash of silver peeking out from under the leg of her trussed-up attacker. Looking around, she found her bag and pulled out a tissue. "Here. I'll run inside and fix you an ice compress."

"Don't. It's no big deal. Can you turn on your porch light so we can get a better look at these guys?"

Annie turned and charged up the steps.

Lights mounted on both sides of her front door soon blazed to life, illuminating a large section of the porch and the base of the steps.

Teddy Saunders shut off his cruiser's siren and bolted from the car, waving a big flashlight. "What have we got here, boss? Wait... isn't this where Koot's wife got hit during a recent drive-by?"

"It's one and the same," Annie replied, descending the steps again. "And I'm getting mighty tired of fending off these idiots. How old are you two?" she demanded, using the toe of her sneaker to nudge the smaller guy, the one Sky had tangled with.

Ted lifted the youth by the scruff of his black, long-sleeved T-shirt and sat him upright. "The lady asked you a question," he said, repeating the process with the second offender.

"They're schoolboys, too," Annie said in disgust.

"I'm not," the bigger one said, glaring at her. "School is stupid," he added belligerently.

"Right," Sky shot back in a withering voice.

"You were so smart tonight, lying in wait to take down a woman."

"It's a good thing you didn't call her a defenseless woman," the scrawnier kid said around a cackle. "She done whipped your butt, Roy Dell."

"Look who's talking like a big shot."

"At least I got taken down by a cop," the smaller of the pair bragged.

"Cut the crap," Sky ordered. "Roy Dell, is your last name Carter?"

"What's it to you?" the older kid responded sullenly.

"I did some digging after someone coerced a middle schooler into trying to torch Ms. Emerson's home. I came out with two names, Roy Dell Carter and Heywood Brown. I should've run you in for questioning sooner," he muttered.

The second kid stiffened. "We didn't do nothin' but talk to a dumb kid," the boy Sky had pegged as Heywood whined. "Somebody else, we don't know who, left gas and matches here. Ain't that right, Roy Dell?"

The older boy had clammed up again. But Heywood wasn't finished spilling his guts. "We didn't even get paid for hustling the kid. We were promised fifty bucks each."

"How much did you get paid for tonight?" Annie asked.

"Uh, fifty each for roughing you up and warning you to leave town and quit getting townsfolk fired up against the Stingers. I bet we don't get any money for this screwup," he lamented.

"Not getting paid for risky jobs twice ought to tell you this isn't your line of work," Annie said, arms crossed. "Maybe you should ask if I can offer you a better deal."

"Sure," Roy Dell sneered, "like we want everyone to see us painting with a bunch of old geezers."

"Cool it," Sky said. "Speak to Ms. Emerson with respect or don't speak at all. And, Annie, you're interrogating my collars again."

Roy Dell dropped his chin.

"No, wait a minute, Sky." Annie caught his arm. "I was going to bring up the teen center. Once it's operating, all the kids will want to go there to shoot hoops, dance, maybe take a few lessons in martial arts," she said, jostling Sky with her elbow. "The rules will be strict. Any teens I pay to help get the center set up will have to attend school every day, or be in classes to get a GED."

Sky threw up his hands. "If I have any say,

they'll have to prove they aren't drinking or taking drugs. And every kid involved cuts all ties with the Stingers." Sky eyed Annie first, then the teens as he let his words sink in.

Teddy's head swiveled from Sky to Annie and back to Sky. "So, are we turning them loose or what?"

"No! You're taking them in." Sky swiped at the blood below his nose. "Heywood, at least, can be charged with assaulting an officer. I'll come to the station shortly to write up charges. You go ahead and notify their parents, Ted."

"I didn't mean to assault no cop," Heywood said in a shaky voice.

"You meant to beat up a woman," Sky accused, jerking the young man to his feet. "Two against one, no less."

Heywood looked contrite. Not Roy Dell.

Ted Saunders latched onto both boys and dragged them to his cruiser.

"Are you sure you're okay, Annie?" Sky asked, seeing her sag against the railing.

"I'm fine. I always get weak-kneed after an adrenaline rush. You don't look so hot. Do you think your nose is broken?"

"Nah. It's stopped bleeding. Listen, I need to follow Teddy to the station. I'm getting the feeling you don't want to press charges."

"I should." She hesitated. "But I hate to. I believe we'll make more headway fighting the gang if we convert some of their members. We need to leak the story that they got their tails whipped tonight, though," she said.

"*We?* Have you joined my police force? This is their second offense that I know of. How can you trust them?"

"I don't trust them. They don't trust authority figures, either." Annie shrugged. "You speak for the law, Sky. Do whatever you think is best."

"I will. Before I go I'll take a turn around your house, inside and out, to be sure they didn't set any traps."

"They couldn't have gotten inside with my new wrought-iron security bars. You'll need a flashlight to have a look around the perimeter. I'll go get you one."

Bending, Sky scooped up the light Ted had left behind. "I have Ted's. You go inside. I'll be in touch tomorrow. I'm off, remember. See if you can avoid trouble for one full day."

Annie smiled. "With luck I'll buy the warehouse, wind down painting the Mickelson home and start on the Culvers' at the end of your block. Feel free to check on me. Hey, Zack begged you to let him paint. That might be something fun you could do together." She batted her eyelashes impishly.

"The wheels in your head never stop turning, do they?" Sky said, pointing her toward her door.

"Yeah, yeah! And bring back my shoelaces, okay?"

CHAPTER ELEVEN

Two full work crews showed up to finish painting the Mickelson home. After that, they all moved on to Davena Culver's, where Annie unloaded what she'd bought in Louisville—the paint and supplies necessary to begin beautifying the rambling, weathered three-story house. She set out a big pot of coffee and several dozen doughnuts as the workers gawked at the house, which could pass for haunted. "Consider this a bribe so no one looks at the size of the place and runs off screaming," Annie joked. "It's a big project, but it'll be so satisfying to see it brought back to life."

Roger McBride hitched up his overalls. "It's a good thing you told Loretta last night that I should bring a long ladder if I had one. Once this place is painted, it'll be like the mother ship."

"How so?" Peggy Gilroy asked around a mouth full of doughnut.

"You'll be able to see it from the end of the

block. Passersby will check it out and want their own houses made over."

A car pulled in and out jumped Sadie Talmage. She still wore a bandage on her arm, but otherwise appeared remarkably fit.

"Sadie, look at you." Annie rushed over to envelope her in a hug. "How did you find us?"

"I drove to your place. I can hardly believe how much work you all did in my absence. Your neighbor told me where to find you, Annie. She also told me she's pregnant and that she feels bad about not being able to help paint."

Rita Gonzales sipped her coffee. "I think we should start planning a baby shower for Missy Spurlock—now that she's telling the world. There's nothing like celebrating a new life to bring out the best in everyone."

Annie nodded. "And even her in-laws are happy."

"I'm so glad for her," Peggy said.

"If we didn't all know the Stingers are looking for opportunities to disrupt my work, I'd vote for a block party closer to her due date." Annie's remark was met with a chorus of agreement.

"Speaking of the gang… Did you have more trouble at your home last night?" Peggy asked, dusting sugar off her T-shirt. "George said at breakfast that he thought the cops came to your house again. If so, I slept through it. This physical exertion has let me get my best sleep in a long time."

"Tell George it was minor," Annie said, kicking herself for mentioning the gang. "Hey, I realize it must seem like I start you off painting and then I take off. I'm about to do it again." She told them about her plans for a teen center.

"I know that building," Charlie Fitzgerald said. "It's solid as a rock and in a great location for the kids."

"Exactly," Annie said.

Davena Culver emerged from her home, arms full of fabric. "Rita, here are your drapes," she called. "I love the material you chose from those bolts Peggy and I bought. The fabric was a dream to sew. Sadie! I didn't see you at first. Are you here to help make drapes?"

"Ooh," Rita squealed before Sadie had a chance to answer. "I'm dying to go home and hang these. Davena, thanks. I can't sew a stitch." Rita carried the bundle to her car. Others crowded around, exclaiming over the workmanship.

"We'd better get at this painting," Peggy reminded everyone. "Paint, drapes, wrought iron and now a teen center—they'll be the crown jewels in our town. All of this is guaranteed to put Briar Run in the running for most livable city in Kentucky."

"Don't be nominating us yet," Annie warned. "I haven't made an offer for the building , and even if I get it, there's staff to hire and a lot of work that needs to be done."

"Annie," Davena said, "don't discount our teen power. We have a lot of fine, talented kids who were forced out of circulation by a fringe group that got involved with the Stingers."

"I'm banking on them, Davena. Okay, break's over. See how much of this house you can prep and paint while I'm gone. Sadie, will you come with me? I'd like your design thoughts on the interior. Fingers crossed that I get the building!"

Davena followed Sadie to Annie's pickup. "I circulated the new paint chart along my street last week. My kids and I had such a hard time choosing colors. Do you think the sea-foam green with navy trim is tasteful enough?" she asked.

Annie blanched. "If you're having second thoughts, Davena, stop the crew now."

"It's just…the kids feel it's too stodgy. But Chantal wanted purple. Deshawn asked for yellow and black to match his school colors. Can you imagine what the neighbors would say if we looked like a giant bumblebee?"

Sadie laughed. "Kids have no taste."

"What is it about teen girls and purple?" Annie mused. "I remember wanting a purple bedroom so badly I pleaded with Gran Ida for weeks. What I got was off-white like the rest of the house. But she made me lavender curtains." Annie's reminiscence spilled out in a trickle of tears. "Sorry, that brought back memories."

Davena hugged her. "You're an angel, and so was your grandmama. I'll help you carry out her dream any way I can. You only have to ask. I guess I'll start on Jane Mickelson's drapes."

"I can help later," Sadie said.

"Thanks, but if you have other tasks, I'm keeping up, plus I'm having the time of my life," Davena said, grinning. "I still waitress three evenings a week, and I hope you don't think it's selfish of me to hope this stay-at-home sewing job lasts."

"I see it going well into next spring," Annie assured her.

Davena left wearing a happy smile. Sadie climbed into Annie's pickup, and as they drove off, she said, "I came today because Sky told Koot about last night's mess. Sky said you fought like a tiger, but he's still real worried about you."

"He is?" Annie darted Sadie a self-conscious smile. "They were just kids bent on mischief, and they took us by surprise. It *is* heartwarming to hear that Sky cares about my welfare."

"Koot said they were Stingers, and Sky blames himself for not picking them up when he found out they were involved in that attempt to torch your house. That's serious criminal activity, Annie. It goes way beyond mischief."

"Yeah, but to me they seemed…sort of reluctant criminals. They're the type of kids I told Sky I want to win back. Not solely by opening a teen center, but also by showing their folks that our town is worth saving."

"Koot and I used to have your kind of passion, Annie. The truth is we got worn out fighting the good fight."

Annie parked at the county records office. "You got worn out and Gran had a dream but no energy to implement it. Sadie, are you aware that Sky's only working here until he gets a job offer somewhere his ex considers safer? As chief of police, he's probably just worried because my determination to buck the Stingers has created issues with his ex and her lawyer."

"It's more than that, Annie. He wishes he had

enough staff to watch over you 24/7. He wishes
you weren't so visible. Okay, let's go see about
your building." Sadie shoved open her door.

Annie got out of the car, but all at once doubt
began to creep in. Was she being foolish? Gran
Ida's money had made everything she'd done so
far possible and would do so in the future. But…
she considered the money a down payment
of sorts. Gran had been counting on Annie's
ability to inject hope back into a community
that had fallen into hopelessness. People had
started to come out of their shells. Her shaky
will somewhat restored, Annie led the way into
the county recorder's office.

She handed the clerk an address. "I understand this building is in final foreclosure." She
named a price. "If that fee is right, and it's not
slated for the upcoming auction, I'm prepared
to buy the property and donate it to the city of
Briar Run for the purpose of housing a teen
center."

The clerk who wore a huge pair of round,
black-rimmed glasses blinked at Annie. Once
she realized that Annie wasn't joking, the process went smoothly.

The women left the office, with Annie clutch-
ing a copy of the transaction.

"Handing the property over to the town is

pretty gutsy, Annie, since Briar Run is in the biggest budget crunch ever."

"Well, if I held the deed, I'd owe taxes. City properties are tax-exempt. And we qualify for grants. I spent several nights filing volumes of online grant applications. Come on, I'll show you the building and a rough outline of the ideas Sky and I came up with."

"You're spending a lot of time with Sky. He won't admit to Koot that you're involved in a romance, but you can spill all to me." Sadie nudged Annie as she unlocked the pickup. "Just between us girls."

"He'll tell you I've involved him in a pack of trouble," Annie said, blowing out a sigh as she buckled herself in. "The truth is, Sadie, I got burned by a guy once. His family had a mile-long pedigree. I had zip, so end of relationship. I gather Sky grew up in a normal family. And he hates the impact his divorce is having on Zack."

Annie put the truck in gear and pulled into traffic. "His ex has tied him to a string of guilt that she yanks at will. When I'm with Sky, I do have romantic thoughts, but they're thoughts I need to curb. I'm back here to stay. And like I said, Sky clearly told me his sojourn in Briar Run is temporary. He's only here until he finds a job someplace more to Corrine's liking."

"If he loves you, his home will be where his heart is, Annie."

"Who said anything about love? I don't know if you could even classify us as friends."

"Take it from me, he's tapping at the door of love whether he knows it or not."

"What he also told me is that he doesn't want my death on his conscience. Does that sound like love?"

"Didn't you just pass the building you bought?"

"Oops, yes. See? Talking about Sky Cordova and love in the same breath messes with my mind." Annie circled the block and parked outside the chained gate. She handed Sadie a loose-leaf notebook. "You can look over my notes."

The women went inside and their chatter turned to serious talk on how to partition the big room into smaller, usable spaces.

"Annie, let me be in charge of this project." Sadie's dark eyes glowed. "Give me a budget and I'll stay within it. What you want done here is right up my alley. I know I said I'd sew drapes, but Davena can handle that." Sadie hugged the notebook. "This…is what I went to design school to do."

"It's all yours," Annie said. "And that's a relief. You're freeing me up to arrange programs and hire staff. We need parent and teen involvement. Davena said Briar Run has talented kids. If they help, and talk up the center among their peers, more of them will want to take part."

"I couldn't agree more. Give kids a vested interest from the get-go and it'll seem like their place. Are you going to have a counselor on staff, or is that a job you plan to take on?"

"My hope, and I discussed this with Sky the other day, is to enlist teachers and counselors from the schools around here. They know the kids, and teachers always need extra money, especially these days. Sky suggested he and I teach a class or two in marital arts." Annie wrinkled her nose and grinned. "I think he agreed not to call it combat training."

"I wish we'd had something like this to offer kids when I taught school in this district. Once the state slashed our budgets, after-school programs got dropped."

"I'm counting on school staff working with us, Sadie."

"I'm sure they will. Oh, how will you pay them? Shouldn't you have waited to see if your grants come through before you bought the building?"

Annie laughed. "I tend to put the cart before the horse. Don't worry, I'll have the funding. When you look for materials and equipment, get solid stuff that'll last. Look for bargains, but don't do it on the cheap."

"Okay, that's music to my ears. I'll head home and start working on plans after you drop me at Davena's to get my car."

"If you're not totally worn out, Sadie, I have a side trip I'd like to make. I want to look at the old factory."

"The glove factory? Don't tell me you've got an idea to turn *that* into something—like a basketball stadium?"

"No." Annie shook her head and locked up. "We'll put basketball hoops for scrimmages on the cement slab behind the center. The reason I'm wondering about the factory is that vacant buildings are more than an eyesore. They're a haven for unsavory activities."

"Ah, then you want the city to raze the factory?"

Annie gave a noncommittal response as they reached the property under discussion. "Darn, it's fenced off," Annie said, letting her pickup idle as she stared at the eight-foot fence with barbed wire at the top.

"That wire should deter vandals," Sadie noted. "But I still see graffiti on the walls."

"Who do you suppose owns the factory now?" Annie pushed her sunglasses up into her hair and studied the place as she drove slowly around the perimeter. "Roger McBride said the last conglomerate used the factory for a tax write-off. I don't think they can do that forever, do you?"

Sadie shrugged. "I have no idea. The city manager will know. You can ask Aaron when you surprise him with the building for the teen center."

"Uh…" Annie choked a little. "You sound as if it'll be an unpleasant surprise."

"Just saying. He's a tough bean counter who's sliced and diced city expenses since the day he was appointed by the governor to replace the mayor and city council."

"We've tangled a time or two already. I think I'll change out of my grubby painting clothes before I pay him a visit."

"Probably wise to be prepared to turn on some Southern charm."

"I'm not too good at that. Maybe I should send him an email."

Sadie didn't stop laughing until Annie parked at the Culvers', where the painting crew had attracted more helpers. They could see the face-lift taking shape.

Sadie drove home, and Annie spoke to the new recruits, all friends of Davena's. Annie had met some of them the day Sky took Deshawn to jail. Thanking them for participating, she pulled on gloves and grabbed a paintbrush.

Soon it was time for lunch. Annie was in the process of taking food orders from the crew when Sky unexpectedly appeared. He got out of his car and helped his son out, as well. Sky whistled through his teeth as he approached Annie. "I wouldn't have thought a partial coat of paint could have such an impact from the moment I turned onto my street."

"Daddy, can I paint?" Zack tugged at Sky's hand.

"We just stopped to see how everything's going. We're on our way to lunch, remember?"

"I'm going out to pick up grilled chicken or beef tacos, chips and drinks," Annie said. "I don't mind adding your order to mine."

"I want chicken and to paint." Zack flashed Annie a smile. "You're the nice lady who gave me orange soda. It was yummy, but I want a chocolate milk shake."

"Zachary," Sky chided. "Ms. Emerson buys lunch for her helpers."

"But I wanna help."

"I thought you wanted me to take you to Louisville to eat so you could spend time in the restaurant's playland."

The boy looked torn. Finally he said, "I get to go to the playland a lot. Mama never lets me paint."

Sky's expression was equally torn. "Okay. But we need to run over to my house to grab one of my old T-shirts so you don't get paint on your clothes." His eyes sought Annie's. "Do you mind bringing us back some food?" Sky pulled out his wallet.

"I've got you covered," Annie told him. "Do you want beef or chicken tacos, and do you also want a chocolate shake?"

"No shake. A beef taco and sweet iced tea if they have it. Since moving here I've become addicted to it."

"I'll be back in a jiffy." With that she tossed a box from another food run into the passenger seat, and started the Ram. She'd been shocked to see Sky, even though he'd joked about checking up on her. If she plied him with enough sweet tea, maybe she could talk him into taking her message to Aaron Loomis....

It took longer than she expected to fill the order. She usually tried to get in ahead of the regular lunch crowd but today she'd painted until the workers complained about hunger.

Driving back to the Culvers' with the food, she spotted Sky and Zack painting boards set across a pair of sawhorses. Her heart seized. Zack looked sweet covered from neck to toe in one of Sky's oversize T-shirts. Every so often, the boy adjusted the shirt, using the hand that held his paintbrush, and navy paint dripped on him. Annie wondered if Sky didn't realize paint would bleed through the soft cotton.

Between painting and hitching up his shirt, Zack's mouth appeared to be going a mile a minute, and his dad answered periodically. Annie had to force back a sudden yearning to be part of a family. A family like theirs...

She got out of her pickup and called for the nearest worker to carry the heavy box of drinks. Charlie Fitzgerald ran to her aid.

"Every day we get more people showing up on these jobs, Ms. Emerson. If you don't start turning some of them away, you'll go broke paying for lunches and giving out gift cards."

"The way I look at it is the more worker bees, the faster houses get painted, and the better our town looks to visitors or to anyone who might consider opening a business here." She grinned. "Guess what? Sadie Talmage volunteered to coordinate work on our new teen center. I want her to hire you and Roger to assemble interior walls. They'll be steel-banded prefab, bolted to steel runners."

"I know how those go together. The glove factory offices were partitioned using something similar. Roger and I did the initial work."

"Great. That's great. Hey," she called, "chow's here. Come and get it."

Painters set aside their cans and brushes. Annie handed around tacos based on the list of orders she'd taken. Charlie let everyone pick up their own drinks.

Sky and Zack were last in line. "I couldn't get him to quit painting," Sky said.

"His cheeks are pink, Sky. If you guys paint after lunch, find a shady spot."

"I found a shade tree where we can sit to eat. Join us?" he invited Annie as he juggled his and Zack's food and drinks.

"Don't mind if I do. Here, let me carry your tea."

"Can I carry my milk shake?" Zack stretched up both hands.

"Yes, but one sip now and the rest after you eat your taco," Sky said.

"Okay. I'm hungry." The boy rubbed his stomach.

"Painting works up an appetite," Annie said, smiling down at him.

"Yeah, and we painted lots and lots, didn't we, Daddy?"

"Indeed we did. Rita Gonzales mentioned that you'd just come back from a trip with Sadie. I didn't know she was out and about yet."

"She is." Annie sank cross-legged on the cool grass once Sky had settled Zack with his food. "I paid the foreclosure amount on the building, and had it deeded to the city. Sadie and I went to see it so she could take a look inside. The best news is that she wants to serve as design master and general contractor. All I have to do is interview and hire staff."

"And our city manager is on board?"

"Uh, not exactly." Annie bit off a chunk of her pork sandwich. "If I give you the deed and a rough-out of our plans, will you deliver it to him?" she mumbled.

Reality registered slowly because Nina Morino, Davena's friend, had cranked up hard rock on a portable iPod speaker. The noise cloaked Sky's resounding *no,* but Annie read his lips.

"I thought it was worth a try," she said with a shrug. "Okay, on a different subject, last night I hit on another fantastic idea to help people in the neighborhood."

Sky held up a hand. "You're dancing on two hot skillets and you want to jump on a third?

Before you lay it on me, just answer this—will it give me heartburn?"

"No. I don't know. Maybe."

"Daddy, I ate the meat out of my taco. Can I drink my milk shake now?"

Sky's eyes tilted toward Zack. "You don't like the shell?"

"It's got red stuff on it."

Reaching over, Sky inspected the taco shell. "Salsa. Sorry, I forgot to tell Annie you don't like salsa."

"It's okay. When Jenny takes me for tacos she forgets, too."

Turning back to her after handing Zack his shake, Sky explained, "Jenny is Zack's stepsister."

"She's sixteen," Zack said around a loud slurp. "She doesn't like taking me and Hayley places, 'cause Jenny thinks we're little brats."

"Uh, how old is Hayley?" Annie asked the boy.

"Eleven, but she's gonna be twelve before I'm six. Then she says I'll be the onliest little brat."

"Zack, there's no such word as *onliest*," Sky said. "And the girls shouldn't be calling anyone a brat. I'll mention that to your mother."

"Don't, Daddy! Mama says I'm not s'posed

to tell you anything about them or her, or the farm."

Sky shut his eyes briefly, then rubbed the back of his neck. "Gotcha. But you have my permission to tell them I don't want them calling you anything but Zachary or Zack. Now, where were we?" he asked, returning his gaze to Annie.

"It wasn't important."

"You sounded excited about a new idea. What is it?"

"I was thinking about the factory. It's sitting empty. I was told the corporation that bought it eventually used the operation as a tax write-off. When they passed the time frame during which they could legally write it off, my guess is that they fired the workers and walked away. I know they quit paying property taxes, no doubt hoping it'd go unnoticed since so many buildings are in foreclosure."

"I don't even want to know where this is leading. You want to buy it and turn it into a skating rink, a bowling alley or both?"

"No. But former employees who lost good-paying jobs could form a co-op and make gloves again. Our city manager would be within his rights to reclaim the property for Briar Run under a federal imminent domain law. If it's turned into a co-op, workers can earn decent wages again. I ran some hypothetical figures the other night, and set up a spreadsheet. Most former employees can walk to work or ride bikes, keeping some of their costs down. The upshot is they won't spend hours a day on a bus getting to low-paying jobs in Louisville or working two or three different jobs. No one I talked to said they hated making gloves. I bet if they could go back they'd leap on the chance."

"Imminent domain law?" Sky smacked his forehead with the heel of his hand. "And a social worker is an authority on this how?"

"I'm not an authority, but I researched it. Because folks like Roger, Charlie, Davena and Homer Gonzales, whose job pays half of what he made before, are good people. They lost their livelihoods and their personal dignity. Reopening is a win-win, Sky."

"Who'll buy the gloves if they make them?"

"Argentina," she said, peering at him over her straw as she drank her cola.

His eyes didn't shift to meet hers, but lingered on her lips still curved around the straw until, flustered, she glanced away. Annie felt his wanting as surely as if he'd kissed her. "Neither of us needs an entanglement," she blurted.

"I know. Believe me, I know." Sky shook his

head. "Daddy, the people all went back to work. Can I paint with Annie?"

Zack's observation and his question brought both Sky and Annie back to normalcy. She gathered up their garbage, leaped nimbly to her feet and left Sky to deal with his son's request.

"Zack wants to stay," Sky said, coming up behind Annie as she poured paint into a cardboard container. "But his mother asked me to have him back at the farm by three. They've got people coming to look at a horse. I guess it's important they all be home for a presentation or something, and I'm trying not to rock the boat. You said he's already had too much sun, so next time I'll be sure he has a hat."

"That's, um, good." Turning away from Sky, Annie said, "Zachary, thank you for the painting you did. Every bit helps. We have a lot of houses to paint."

"Will you paint fast and get to Daddy's place? I helped him pick colors. I wanted red," the boy said, but then wrinkled his nose. "He picked gold. I guess I like gold. Annie, do you think it'll look cool with this color?" He pulled out his T-shirt, directing Annie's attention to a big navy splotch.

"Well, you can paint a bit of each color on a

leftover board and see if you both like how they look side by side before we paint your dad's trim."

"Yeah, Daddy, that's what I wanna do next time I come." The boy ran over and hugged Annie, then ran back and slipped his hand in Sky's. She and Sky smiled at each other. Gone was any sign of their earlier strain.

"Bye, you guys," Annie said. "Zack, you're welcome anytime. You're a hard worker." She waved as he hopped backward to keep her in sight.

Feeling at loose ends after Sky had driven off, Annie wished she hadn't said something so dumb—so final—about not getting entangled when it wasn't how she felt at all. But his searing look had seemed so blatantly hungry, she'd let panic control her words. Once his car was out of sight, she returned to painting with vigor, all the while chastising herself for acting like a coward when she wasn't one in any other aspect of her life.

It was late but not yet dark when work wound to a close for the day. They'd made good progress on altering the appearance of the Culvers' home.

Annie, who'd once again bought grocery gift cards in lieu of cash, passed them around to everyone who'd worked that day. "I wish it could be more. Maybe tomorrow I'll get cards from one of the discount stores."

Peggy Gilroy, the eldest of the group, tucked the card in her pocket. "I think I speak for everyone, Annie. We've been in the dumps for so long that getting out in the sun, socializing with neighbors we'd lost touch with, is like a shot in the arm."

Roger McBride shuffled his feet. "I'll admit that when Loretta said you planned a meeting at the library to drum up interest in spiffing up the neighborhood, I laughed. Now I want more people to join us. I wish the rest of us had money to help buy paint." His speech drew mumbles of agreement from the others.

"Thanks, guys, but I feel guilty letting you give me all the credit. You know the expression *paying it forward?* That's what I'm doing. My grandmother gave me opportunities, and I'm trying to give opportunities to others. She wanted Briar Run to survive and thrive. So, same place, same time tomorrow?"

Annie heard Davena and her friends talking about the teen center as she threw a tarp over the paint cans in her pickup bed. What they'd done to date was a source of pride, she thought, driving home. Man, but she was beat. And before talk of the teen center reached the ears of Aaron Loomis, Annie needed to plan her speech.

IT WAS DARK. Way too late for a decent man to call on a woman. In fact, Annie's home was the only one on her block with lights ablaze. Neighbors on both sides of the street had obviously retired. It was close to midnight, and Sky sat in his car outside Annie's home, debating whether to leave.

He beat his thumbs rhythmically on his steering wheel, stopping when he recognized it for the nervous habit it was.

There was something he wanted to say to Annie. Something he'd chewed on all afternoon. *No guts, no glory.* The old military saying popped into his head.

He got out, shut his car door and strode up Annie's walkway. Memories of the last time he'd been here, also in the dark, loomed in his mind. He remembered how well he and Annie had operated as a team, taking down those kids sent to do her harm—sent by men who were content to hide behind children.

Tonight no one lurked on her porch. Still his heart sped up as he rapped at her door. He heard rustling inside, then Annie tentatively called, "Who's there?"

"Sky."

The door opened. She turned on her porch light and opened the security door with its wrought-iron scrolls. "This is a surprise. Have you apprehended more gang members?" She peered beyond him to the porch and then the street.

"I've been thinking about what you said while we were having lunch."

She refocused on him. "About the factory?"

"I dropped Zack off at Corrine's on the dot of three. She yelled at me for letting him get sunburned and getting paint on his shirt. I gave him my T-shirt," he said wryly, "but it wasn't too effective as a cover-up."

"Oh. I'm sorry."

"I was proud of Zack. He told his mom he'd had fun painting, and that next time he's going to help you paint my house."

"I'm afraid I can't give you a firm date on when that will be."

"That's not why I'm here." Sky tilted his head to one side and scratched his neck. "I, uh, came to clarify what you said about not getting entangled."

"Oh, that." Annie studied her bare toes.

Sky stepped forward, clasped her around the waist and pulled her tight him. Then he kissed her. Not a friendly peck as in *I want to be friends*. He put spark and sizzle into the kiss. After Annie's hands crept up his chest and clenched the fabric of his shirt, he slowly released her. "I came to say I lied. I don't want a new job somewhere else. And I want us to get tangled." Leaving his message hanging there, Sky withdrew and bounded down her porch steps, whistling on his way to his cruiser. He jumped in and with a low growl of the Crown Vic's engine, he drove off.

Barely around the block, he called himself an idiot and circled back, disappointed to see that she wasn't still standing in her doorway. What had he expected? Annie was the one who'd said she didn't want any romantic entanglements. He needed to give her time, let his message sink in.

CHAPTER TWELVE

ANNIE HALF THOUGHT she'd walk out the door in the morning and Sky would be sitting in his car. He wasn't. Nor did he come down the street from his house to the Culver work site. She expected him at noon for sure. But lunchtime came and went without his appearing or even calling. *So much for his big speech about wanting them to "get tangled."* But wow, his kiss! Annie's mind stalled every time she thought about it.

She had to learn from Sadie that the Louisville cops had apprehended their drive-by shooter. "Can you believe the idiot kept the gun rather than disposing of it?" Sadie said when she stopped by to give Annie her diagrams for the teen center. "Koot's covering Sky's shifts, because he's at the Louisville station, sitting in on the interrogations. The two guys in custody are believed to be pretty high up in the Stingers command."

"You make them sound like paramilitary instead of garden-variety thugs," Annie said.

"That's how they operate, according to Koot. I assume Sky told you Heywood got off with a promise to stay in school and do community service. Roy Dell had a prior run-in with the law, so the judge gave him a year's probation and ordered him to go to a local community college to take GED classes. Sky said you suggested that. Roy Dell also has to do community service. They're on my recruitment list for the center."

"Sky didn't tell me any of that last night." Annie frowned.

Davena Culver had joined them. "It must've slipped the chief's mind. He was probably preoccupied with his son. Chantal heard about Heywood and Roy Dell. She likes Heywood, and was disgusted that he let Roy Dell rope him in. She hopes this was a lesson for him. By the way, Chantal and some of her girlfriends can paint or do whatever needs to be done at the teen center after school lets out next week."

Annie, who'd reviewed Sadie's plans, rolled them up again. "You're moving so fast, I'd better have a heart-to-heart with the city manager today."

"Does that mean I shouldn't order the prefab room dividers or talk to Roger and Charlie about installing them yet?" Sadie raised an eyebrow at Annie.

"No, go ahead. I'll make myself presentable and pay Mr. Loomis a visit. I have more than the teen center to discuss with him. So, if you see fireworks exploding from his office, send the SWAT team to rescue me."

Sadie laughed. "No SWAT teams in Briar Run. We're down to four overworked cops."

The women split up and Annie went home to shower and rehearse her half of the conversation she needed to have with Aaron Loomis.

THE CITY MANAGER'S office—the former mayor's office—was next door to the police station. Annie looked for Sky's car, but apparently he wasn't back yet. In Briar Run's municipal offices, Aaron Loomis and a lone secretary sat at their respective desks. Annie gave her name to the secretary. "I'd like a word with Mr. Loomis if I may," she said.

The woman got up and spoke to the balding man ensconced behind a glass enclosure. Annie saw him don black-rimmed glasses, gaze at her and nod curtly.

"He can spare ten minutes, Ms. Emerson," the secretary said.

Annie picked up her briefcase and swept into

an office stacked with books, folders and piles of paper. She was glad she'd worn her most professional suit. Annie extended her hand and Loomis shook it. "Hello, I'm Annie Emerson. I don't know if you recall, but we've spoken before."

The man rocked back in his chair. "Yes...I keep track of newcomers," he said dryly. "Especially troublemakers."

"Ouch." It didn't slip past Annie that Loomis didn't offer her a seat. "I guess that means you're aware of how busy I've been with residential revitalization."

He grunted. "So far it looks okay," he said grudgingly.

"Glad it meets with your approval. I've taken time out from painting homes to bring you the deed for a new teen center I'm donating to the city." Annie opened her briefcase, took out a folder and set it in the center of his messy desk.

He snapped forward in his creaky chair. "Ms. Emerson, you can't give the city a teen center."

"I already did." Annie tapped the folder. "The building is free and clear. I'm exploring grants I hope will ultimately cover operating expenses. Until that's firm, I plan to cover the costs. If you're agreeable, I'd like to name it the Ida

Vance Teen Center after my late grandmother. She was one of Briar Run's earliest residents."

Aaron Loomis slicked both hands over his head several times. Annie wondered if that was why he was going bald at an early age.

"This is exceedingly unusual." He opened the folder. "Did the county clerk say this was legal? Who donates property to a city? Is it even wise? A center for teens? I know you understand that we have gang activity. Will this strain our already strained police force?"

Annie waited for him to wind down. But he continued to scowl at her. "There's more," she said in her most dulcet tones. "This may be trickier, and I'll need your assistance. Do you mind if I clear off a chair and pull it up to your desk?"

"I have a feeling it won't do any good to say no."

Removing piles of paper from a chair, Annie dragged it over. She took another folder from her briefcase. "If this idea works, it'll mean considerable business revenue for the city."

That got his attention as nothing had so far. Annie unfolded a plat map and put her finger on the defunct factory. She rushed through her plan to reopen the plant, her description almost identical to the way she'd explained it to Sky the previous day. Unlike Sky, Loomis had the benefit of her charts and graphs. He scanned one after the other.

"The corporation pulled the plug on the glove factory the day after I started this job," he said. "The demise of the city's largest employer hit city revenues hard. The result has been cutbacks in all services." He glanced up, engaged now. "What makes you think there are enough former employees around who'll be amenable to your plan? More important—exports to Argentina? That's global trade. If they're in the market for gloves, aren't they buying them now?"

Annie handed a sheaf of magazine and newspaper articles she'd printed out. "Their vast cattle companies and agricultural industries import a staggering number of cotton and leather gloves. These articles don't name their current supplier, but all the reports indicate displeasure with inferior products. Our first step would be to send samples to the people named in these articles. But to answer your first question... From casual conversations I've had with former employees who held major positions, I know there's interest. I gather tooling up would take weeks, not months. Of course, someone needs to find a source for raw material." She pulled out another paper. "I did some calculations. So, say we even had to import leather from Argentina and ship back the finished gloves, there's still a fair profit."

He studied her material a while longer. His secretary came to the door. "I'm going on break. You said ten minutes." She tapped the face of her watch.

Loomis waved her away. "I'm fine, Myrna. Ms. Emerson is almost finished. She's leaving me with a lot to think about." He rose, and Annie knew she was being dismissed. She got up and shut her briefcase.

"Thank you for your time. We're painting on Dusty Rose Street and will be there for several days. Or I may be at the teen center. I'll give you my cell number, since I think we should move on this ASAP," she said, jotting her number down.

She was almost out the door when Loomis called, "Somebody told me you're a social worker."

"I used to be. I'm more of a general contractor now."

"My older sister is a social worker. She's a know-it-all busybody, too." He smiled and his voice softened. "Our parents died when she was sixteen, and I was twelve. Her ability to juggle a lot of balls in the air at one time was what got me raised. I'll delve further into this idea of yours and be in touch."

At least he hadn't thrown her out, Annie told herself as she put on sunglasses. Again she checked for Sky's cruiser; it still wasn't in the lot. More disappointed than she cared to admit, she headed home to change back into her painting clothes. On the way she decided that since she was dressed professionally, this would be a good time to seek potential staff for the teen center. She'd come prepared with information and with applications she'd created the night before.

As it turned out, Sadie was at the center so Annie went in. "Sadie," she called into the cavernous room, "can I twist your arm to go to the schools with me? I want to have a word with the teachers, counselors and coaches about maybe working here."

"Hey, I'm your gal. I didn't see fireworks from the municipal building. I take it you won Aaron over? Oh, no wonder! You look like a million bucks."

Annie grimaced. "I don't know about 'won over.' He's concerned the center will add to an already heavy police workload. Is there a way we can keep a lid on who comes and goes?"

"If we post a one-time-infraction-and-you're-out rule and stick to it, yes."

At the school they found more interest from teachers than Annie had dared hope. Later, returning to the pickup, Sadie reached over and patted Annie's back. "It wouldn't have occurred to me to bring applications tailored to each position we need to fill. How do you manage to do everything you do, Annie?"

"I don't sleep," she quipped, except it was more true than not.

"It helps that you don't have a man demanding your time and attention. Although having a man in your life isn't all bad." Sadie winked.

The memory of Sky's kiss left Annie silent, and also wondering about his prolonged absence. "Do you worry a lot about the dangers associated with Koot's job?"

"Honey, he's been a cop all our married life. But who was the first in our family to get shot? Me! Hey, you sound like a woman who needs to know. Are you and Sky finally, uh, seeing each other?"

"The short answer is not really. Let's say there's interest, but he runs hot and cold, probably due to his past experience."

"What about you?" Sadie paused before exiting Annie's pickup.

"Yeah, me, too. I'm pretty independent."

"Do you like Sky's son?"

Annie's smile was quick and genuine. "He's darling. And smart. I feel bad for Sky that he doesn't have Zachary more."

"That's a good answer from someone who sounds as if she's contemplating a romance with a divorced dad."

"Contemplating isn't committed, Sadie."

"Give it time. Well, I can't do any more here today, so I think I'll go home. I ordered the walls, which is step one. Tomorrow's Saturday and Davena's bringing over a carload of teens. I'll get them to scrub floors. Oh, I almost forgot. Here's a list of the paint I need. If you can get it to me by Sunday, I'll be ready next week when the prefab stuff comes to put Roger and Charlie to work."

Annie took the list. "Sadie, I've decided to set up a bank account strictly for the center. I'll give you a debit card. That'll save us both time. I'll pay the salaries, yours included, out of a different account."

"You don't need to pay me! This project is keeping me from having a midlife crisis."

They both laughed, and Annie waited until Sadie got into her car before she left. Annie wondered whether it would be smart to install security alarms like the ones she saw at the schools, or whether arranging for an on-site security person might be better. She placed that on her list of questions to run past Sky. Maybe she should call him. *No! What would he think?*

She didn't see him that day or all weekend. Her paint crew doubled on Saturday. They finished Davena's house and were able to start on two adjacent homes, bringing them ever closer to Sky's.

Annie divided her time between painting and the teen center, always on the lookout for Sky's cruiser. By the end of Tuesday, with the two smaller homes done, she'd begun to think he was having second thoughts about his late-night visit to her home—or that it hadn't happened and she'd dreamed the whole thing. She had to admit she was baffled. Her list of things to discuss with him kept growing.

Wednesday, to her shock, he showed up at the painting project, which was two houses from his, acting as if he hadn't been away for five days. He had Zachary in tow. Annie was filled with so many doubts she didn't go to greet him; instead, she let him find her. Which he did by knocking on the aluminum ladder she stood on, painting an upper story.

"Hey, up there. My helper and I have a few hours. What can we do?"

Annie gazed down on a pair of upturned smiles so alike and so endearing her breath caught somewhere between her lungs and her throat. "Paint, uh, you can paint. The sanders are all in use by guys at the back of the house." She wanted to shout, *Where have you been?* In deference to Zack's excited hello, Annie calmly climbed down and acted as if Sky hadn't been MIA for five days.

"I wanted to paint Daddy's house today," Zack said, sounding disappointed.

"I'm sorry. I haven't bought his paint yet," Annie said. "He hasn't called to tell me what colors to get." She aimed small daggers at Sky, who seemed oblivious. "But, Zack, I bought a couple of things for you. They're in my pickup. Wait here, I'll get them." She climbed down and handed her dripping brush to Sky.

"You got something for me?" Zack skipped alongside her.

"I did." Annie opened her pickup and removed a sack. "First, I have a kid's version of what's called a carpenter apron. It ties in back and is made of plastic-covered fabric so paint can't soak through and ruin your shirt and pants." Annie helped him into the apron that hung a little past his knees. The pattern was masculine with pictures of pliers, wrenches and paint cans. "At the hardware store where I buy our paint, they had premade wooden birdhouses. You remember how you couldn't decide what colors you liked for your dad's house? Well, I bought three birdhouses, a packet of small brushes and sample cans of the paints you and your dad were debating. I'll put the birdhouses on newspapers under that tree. You can try different colors on each house and then you and your dad can go buy the ones you like best."

The boy flung his arms around Annie, who had bent to his level. He almost bowled her over—would have if Sky hadn't come up in time to catch her. "Whoa, Zack, don't knock Annie over. What have you got there? Hey, guy, that cover-up is neat. I hope you thanked Annie."

"I *was* thanking her, but I almost hugged her over."

Sky and Annie laughed, and Sky ruffled his son's sun-bleached hair. Slightly self-conscious now because Sky seemed so focused on her, Annie went through her explanation again about how Zack could paint the birdhouses.

"It was kind of you to think of him in the middle of everything you're doing. Aaron Loomis called me on Friday. You have him all worked up over the teen center. He asked if I thought my force could control unsavory interest in a place that caters to teens."

"What did you tell him? I'm almost ready to hire staff."

"I was honest. I said we'd see. Have you missed me?" He gave his sideways smile and ran his forefinger down her nose when she rose from spreading newspapers for Zack's paint project. "I think we may be close to cracking the upper echelons of the Stingers," he said excitedly. "That should make you happy."

"Close only counts in horseshoes." She opened a pack of brushes, gave Zack one and opened two small cans of paint. "Try this color on the bottom part of one birdhouse, and this color on the roof. Then you can see what it would look like if we painted your dad's house with these colors."

Sky arched an eyebrow at her before he knelt down. "Take your time, Zachary. We're not in a big rush today."

The boy nodded and sat cross-legged in front of the birdhouse.

Annie stepped a few feet away as Sky stood up; he seemed too close. "Uh, Sadie said the police in Louisville arrested the man they believe shot her. Frankly it surprised me not to hear the news from you."

"Yeah, well, I wanted them signed, sealed and headed to the big house before I said anything. That's taking time. The Louisville detectives invited me to sit in while they grilled those two, hoping to get to the higher-ups in the Stingers. For the past few days I left early and got home late. Koot and Teddy covered my shifts. Plus I was buried under a backlog of paperwork. Anyway…back to Loomis. Antsy as you made him over the teen center, you got him super worked up about the prospect of reopening the glove factory."

"Shh," Annie pressed a finger to his lips and cast a glance around to see who was nearby. "He hasn't agreed to let me go ahead with that yet. No one else knows."

"I didn't let on that I knew anything about that grand scheme of yours."

"Are you making fun of me, calling it a grand scheme?"

"Daddy, stop hurting Annie's feelings," Zack said, raising his voice. The adults whirled around and saw that Zack had paused in his painting and was frowning at them.

"We're just discussing something," Sky told

Zack. To Annie, he murmured, "We'll catch up on this later."

She nodded. "By the way, Chantal filled Davena in on what a judge ordered for Heywood and Roy Dell. Our teen center will run smoothly if we can get other former gang members on similar paths. I know we can beat this gang, Sky. If you nab the leaders, I'll redirect the kids."

"Those feats are difficult enough, Annie. And you want to add reopening the factory to what you're already planning to do?"

"Are we back to you thinking I'm being unrealistic? I thought we'd progressed beyond that, Sky."

He scooped up a paint pan and roller. "Sometimes it seems we have, other times not. I'm not sure how I fit into your life when you take on more and more projects."

"That's a good question," she said unhappily. "How *does* someone fit in who casually drops by after not showing up for days?" Annie wrested another ladder out of the back of her pickup and stomped off to the side of the house. If he felt left out of her life, well, too bad; she felt left out of his.

Annie didn't see Sky again until one of the painting crew brought lunch. She wondered if he'd even sit with her—except that Zack grabbed her hand and tugged her over to show her the birdhouse he'd finished.

"You did a great job, Zack." Annie admired his work from every angle. "Once they're all done and dry, I'll coat them with shellac so they'll hold up in every kind of weather. You and your dad can hang them from the branches of that big tree in his front yard."

"Can I take one to the farm? I have two homes, Annie. Three," he said, changing his mind. "I forgot Papa Archibald's vacation house in the Appa, Appa…some mountain. Daddy, what's that mountain called where Mama said we hafta go?"

"Appalachian," Sky filled in, not sounding pleased.

Annie assumed this was another bump in Sky's rocky road of shared custody. She aimed her question at Zack, but darted a quick look at Sky. "So, Zack, you're going on vacation soon?"

Sky took the last bite of his chicken. "His mother wants to spend the summer at Archibald's cabin. My attorney is looking into it now."

Nodding, Annie sat closer to Zack than Sky. "Well, Zack, if you don't get all three birdhouses painted today but you finish two of them, I'll run out and buy a can of shellac so you can take one to hang at the farm and the second to your cabin. The third one, for your dad's place, can wait till you're back. So we'll shellac the first two, and hot as it is today they'll dry in your dad's car trunk while he drives you home."

The boy sprang up and threw his arms around Annie's neck, exclaiming his pleasure.

She noticed that Sky, who sat on the opposite side of the blanket, had stiffened; she started to disengage Zack's arms. But Sky's eyes weren't trained on her. Rather he was watching a blue BMW that had double-parked at the curb.

An attractive blonde got out and, with little more than a sweeping glance around the work area, stalked straight up to the trio seated under the tree.

From Annie's perspective, the well-turned-out woman in spike-heeled sandals, sleek sundress and arms aglitter with gold bangles seemed out of place at a neighborhood paint party. The blonde raised her hand and waved a crushed paper in Sky's face. Annie felt her contempt as the woman—who could only be his ex—gave her a dirty look.

"Isn't *this* cozy," she snapped, tossing her champagne-streaked hair. "What you're asking for is totally impossible, Skylar. There's no way I can drive Zack down from the cabin once a week so you can bring him here to hang out with your paint-speckled girlfriend. You know we always spend every summer at the cabin."

"Mama," Zack cried, his arms still circling Annie's neck. "This is Annie. And look, she bought me birdhouses to paint. And I get to hang one in a tree at the farm."

The woman, who so far hadn't bothered to acknowledge her child, lowered her eyebrows in a perfect V over a dainty nose. "I guess you think it's clever, trying to buy my son's affection. You're wasting your time. If I have to hire a gaggle of Kentucky's best guardianship lawyers to ensure that Zack doesn't spend another hour in this…this dump of a town, I will." Sky bounded up to clasp the woman's arm and began hustling her toward the street.

"Apologize to Annie." His words grated like sandpaper.

Shaking her arm free, she accidentally kicked over the birdhouse Zack had just painted.

The boy ran to rescue it, sobbing for his mother to stop.

Annie figured Corrine had been too furious to see Zack's work, although he'd tried to direct her attention to it. Annie quietly helped Zack right the birdhouse and murmured, "It's okay.

Your mom didn't mean to kick over your project. See, no harm done."

As Sky urged her toward the street, the woman appeared confused, watching her son and Annie interact. As if realizing that the eyes of everyone seated around the partially painted house were glued to her, she said stiffly, "I'm sorry, Zachary honey. I didn't see it. You, uh... it's very nice." She blew him a kiss, then gave in to Sky's insistence that they leave the scene.

Peggy Gilroy sidled up to Annie, who'd managed to get Zack interested in eating again. "You okay, Annie?"

Touching a finger to her lips, Annie murmured, "I'm fine."

Several other women had joined them, staring out at the street where Sky stood, legs apart, arms crossed, and the blonde gestured wildly.

"That was some tantrum," Rita Gonzales put in.

"If everyone's through eating, we can get back to work," Annie said.

Taking the rather obvious hint, people tossed their garbage in a box, and went back to what they were doing prior to lunch.

Annie felt sorry for Sky. He would be on the receiving end of his neighbors' sympathetic— and maybe not so sympathetic—remarks. Com-

pelled, for Zack's sake, to ward them off in
advance, she raised the volume of the music
that had become part of their daily environment.
Visiting each volunteer, she requested discre-
tion and restraint. So the scene Sky returned to
was one of tranquility.

Without hesitation he climbed Annie's ladder and stood three rungs below her. "I'm not
making this up, Corrine asked me to apologize
for her."

"That's good, Sky. Thanks. I assume your
lawyer just won another round. Were you afraid
things would go in her favor? Is that why you
were so grouchy today?"

He winced. "Has anyone told you you're as
much of a shrink as a social worker?"

"You're shaking my ladder. It's dangerous to
have two on one ladder."

He stepped down, creating more of a sway.
Annie grabbed hold of the rain gutter and a section came loose. "Watch out below!" she yelled,
and panicked to see how close the broken gutter came to hitting Zack, who sat innocently
painting his second birdhouse. To her immense
relief, the heavy gutter was deflected by a tree
branch. It crossed Annie's mind that a work-
site was no place for a child as young as Zack.
Then noting the big smile he flashed his dad,

she shrugged off her concerns. Zack loved to putter around, and it was a cinch he didn't get to do that at his mother's.

AT THE END of the day, which included Annie's dashing out to buy a can of varnish at the nearest convenience store to spray the three birdhouses Zack had completed, Sky stopped her on the fly. "Hang on a minute. Zack wants to go out for pizza and we'd like you to come."

"Oh, Sky, won't that create more trouble for you on the home front?"

"Corrine can't order my life. She certainly didn't ask me to give the green light on Archibald. And after so many years of hassle, the new family court judge who's handling our case believes in equal custody. Her latest decree, the one that upset Corrine, says fifty-fifty means equal time, regardless of the season, for both of us. Up to now, Corrine has had it all her way."

"I'm glad, but court orders can't regulate what's in someone's head or heart. Zack's mother plainly doesn't want to share him. Seeing him hug me, a stranger, was like throwing gasoline on the fire. You should assure her that we don't have a relationship. That would start easing her mind. After you take a new job elsewhere, you and she really need to sit down and talk."

"I decided I don't want to move. And I told Corrine we *do* have a relationship. I thought we settled that the other night." Taking Annie's hands, Sky brushed a kiss over her chapped knuckles. Enveloped by the humidity of late afternoon, they let the moment drag.

"Daddy, Annie, aren't we gonna go for pizza?"

Her needs and desires overwhelmed by doubt, Annie detained Sky. "You say one thing and then another. I don't know what's truth and what's fiction anymore. I'm the kind of person who goes all in. I don't do anything halfway. And I expect the same thing from anyone I'm… involved with."

"That's been evident since the day we met. Look, I acted like a jerk this morning. Is there a possibility you'd be willing to give me a second chance?"

"A slim one," she said, letting him squirm—but not too long. "We all have flaws. Okay, I'll forgive yours if you'll forgive mine."

"Over pizza can you tell me what some of yours are."

"Are you kidding? And have you looking for them? You'd send them off to a lab to be analyzed."

Sky laughed from deep in his belly. Then he threaded his fingers through hers. They collected Zack and got in Sky's car.

At the pizza parlor on the outskirts of town, Sky asked Annie what she liked. When she told them Hawaiian, Zack bounced gleefully in his seat. "You like the kind me and Daddy like. Goody! Nobody at Papa Archibald's ever agrees. And Mama thinks we should only have vegetables on pizza. Ugh!"

"Vegetable toppings can be yummy. Have you ever tried it?" Annie asked.

Zack shook his head, and Annie let the subject drop.

After they ate and watched Zack play some of the kid games set up around the big, noisy room, Sky again took Annie's hand. "Instead of me dropping you off at your pickup, ride with us to the farm."

"As if one explosive encounter today wasn't enough?" Annie laughed.

"It's a pretty drive through bluegrass country. Doing the trip alone is boring. On the way back, you can tell me more about your plans for reopening the glove factory."

"Well, I should be home on the internet researching places that sell raw cotton and leather.

That's the piece of the proposal I don't have facts and figures on."

"Will an hour or so make a difference? The sun will set soon. You'll enjoy seeing the moon rise. And you'll like watching the thoroughbred horses in their pastures. You'll also see why they call it *bluegrass*."

"Sold. I lived here half my life, but horse farms weren't on Gran Ida's radar. Reading, sewing, gardening—those were our passions."

"You said she used to arrange work parties to care for the rose beds in the park. You come by your volunteer skills honestly," he said. "Aaron told me you want to name the teen center after your grandmother."

"And the park, once I have time to revive it. I've already sketched out the signs. Mr. Yost, who's doing the wrought iron, said his son can make them."

Zack's supply of quarters came to an end, and when he ran back to them, he was yawning. Sky boosted him up on his shoulders as they left the restaurant. "Annie's going to ride to the farm with us, Zack."

"Yay! Will you help me hang one of my birdhouses, Annie?"

"It'll be too dark when we get there," Sky said. "I'll help next time I pick you up."

"When will that be?" Annie asked. "We have your neighbor's house to paint, starting tomorrow, then yours. I can order the paint now that you've decided on the gold with dark blue trim."

"I wanna help," Zack said, buckling himself in. "But Mama said I hafta go to the cabin."

"We'll work it out," Sky promised.

Zack fell asleep almost before they got out of town. Annie turned to watch him and smiled. "Poor kid, painting tuckered him out. But he had fun."

"He doesn't seem to like the farm. As a kid I would've loved running wild in the country."

"Therein may lie the problem. I sense that there isn't a lot of running around, that his life's more structured."

"You're right." He sighed. "I need to follow as many of Corrine's rules as I can."

"True," Annie agreed. Then, because Sky asked again, she explained her plans for the glove factory. She also took in the beauty around her; the moon shining down on long, waving grass that indeed looked blue in the pale light.

At the farm, Sky got out, put two of the birdhouses on the porch, then carried his son to the house. From the car, Annie observed the exchange taking place at the door. A big man, older than Sky, came to stand behind Corrine.

He and Sky talked for a few minutes when Corrine carried Zack inside.

"Did everything go okay?" Annie searched for any sign that Sky was distressed as he got back in the car and turned it around.

"Archibald's going to hang a birdhouse here and one at the cabin. They agreed to let me have Zack for two days while we paint my house if I give them a week for their vacation."

"You're learning the art of compromise," Annie said, leaning over to squeeze his hand.

They rode in silence, hands still clasped, and were almost back at Briar Run when Sky's radio crackled to life. "Sky, it's Joe. Are you in radio range?"

Sky let go of Annie's hand and clicked on. "I'm just outside town after dropping Zack at the farm. What's up?"

"I'm on your street. A neighbor called. They caught two guys who were spray painting a couple of homes that Ms. Emerson's crew just painted on Dusty Rose Street. Folks are upset. Her pickup's still at the curb. Our perps slashed all four of her tires, but she's not around and they haven't been able to locate her."

"She's with me, Joe. We'll be there in ten minutes. The guys they caught? Local kids?"

"Nope, they're from Louisville, and both have

outstanding warrants. If I had to guess I'd say your neighbors, with the aid of shovels and brooms, landed us two upper-level Stingers."

"Hallelujah," Sky returned. "Call Morrissey's Garage and see if Don can tow Annie's pickup to his place."

Annie looked up from checking her phone, which she belatedly remembered shutting off at the restaurant. "Didn't I tell you the residents would take back their neighborhood once they were invested in it?"

"You did, smart lady." Sky held up his hand for a high five, and in spite of Joe's news about her vehicle and the graffiti, Annie high-fived back.

CHAPTER THIRTEEN

OVER HALF OF Annie's paint crew had gathered on the street where a tow truck was backed up to her pickup. She and Sky left his car and examined her slashed tires. "At least they didn't key the paint job," she said, and thanked him for arranging a tow. Leaving him with the driver, Annie began unloading paint from the back of her pickup. Roger McBride rushed over to help.

Once everything was out of the bed, Annie went with Davena to check on the extent of the graffiti. She still held a baseball bat in one hand and a flashlight in the other. "I swear, Annie, this was probably the only time I appreciated Remy Thacker being a nosy neighbor. She heard a noise, looked out and saw two guys messing with your truck, so she called the police. Before Joe Morales got here, Remy saw them start spraying the side of the Petermans' house. They're at a concert in Louisville, so Remy called me. I activated the phone tree Peggy Gilroy set up. It worked like a charm, except you didn't answer and we were worried."

"We went out to eat. I turned my phone off in the restaurant," Annie said. "Did you ask everyone to bring shovels and baseball bats?"

"No, I handed those out from my shed as they arrived. I had everyone park on Wild Rose and sneak in through my backyard so we didn't scare them off. We're all sick and tired of the Stingers intimidating us."

"You did good, Davena. Thanks to you, they didn't have time to paint a lot of graffiti. Covering it shouldn't take too long tomorrow morning."

"What about the Aaron Loomis 8:00 a.m. meeting?"

"I don't know about any meeting."

"Odd. He said he was phoning all the former glove factory personnel, and I'm sure he said you and he would explain why we were being asked to meet."

Annie dug out her phone again and saw that Loomis had left her a message to call him. She waffled. How late was too late to phone a city manager? It was now quarter to ten. He'd left his home number, so she decided to take the risk. "Excuse me, Davena. I'm going to step away and give him a call right now."

Loomis answered at once. "Ms. Emerson, I'm glad to hear from you. At your suggestion, I've looked into the idea of reopening the factory, and I feel we should move on it immediately. I did some fact-checking, including a call to an Argentine executive named in one of the articles you gave me. Believe it or not, they bought our gloves until the plant closed. He said he'd pave the way for volume purchases because the gloves they're importing now are inferior."

"Wow! Fantastic." The only problem was that Annie envisioned this putting a huge dent in her paint project, to say nothing of getting drapes sewn and completing the teen center. Most of her regular workers were former factory employees. "I'll do my best to make the meeting," she told Loomis. "A couple of Stingers slashed my pickup tires tonight. I'm having it towed as we speak."

"If you can't cadge a ride, take a cab— at town expense. It'll be worth it. This could breathe new life into Briar Run."

She signed off, seeing that Sky was hailing her. The tow truck was driving off with her pickup. "Davena, I guess I'll see you at Mr. Loomis's meeting. I'll ask Peggy to start a crew painting over the graffiti in the morning."

"So what's his big secret about?" Davena asked.

"He'll reveal that tomorrow. Sorry, Sky's my ride and he needs to leave."

When she reached his car, Sky opened the passenger door for her. "Joe took our lawbreakers to jail. I need to stop at the station and see that they're properly booked."

"Can you drop me at home first?"

Sky studied her for a moment. "You seem down. Was the graffiti worse than at your house?"

"No, but do you remember how you criticized me for taking on too many projects? Maybe I have."

"I didn't intend to sound critical, but what do you mean?"

She said that Loomis would be commandeering the former factory workers, many of whom she depended on for her projects. "It's a mixed blessing," she said with a sigh. "Jobs are *the* most important thing in this situation, and I gather we can get the factory under way pretty fast. But...the town's facelift is important, too."

"On Friday, school's out for the summer. I've been worried about a lack of jobs for our teens. Hire them to paint."

"I can't. Sadie asked quite a few of them to

help at the teen center, and I already agreed to fund them. The center is where their interest lies."

"Hmm. Maybe you'll have to put out another call for volunteers. With so many homes looking sharp, you shouldn't have a problem attracting more helpers. I hope not, anyway." He grinned. "I've got my own selfish reasons. Zack has his heart set on us painting my house. I already gave Corrine the date."

"You may have to adjust it, Sky."

"I can't, or it screws up their plans to go to their cabin. I know Corrine would have her lawyer jump on that."

Annie feared he was right. For the first time since she'd lost her grandmother and embarked on this hectic journey, she felt pressure of the type she'd left behind in L.A.

"You'll work it out," Sky said as he pulled into her driveway. "I've never met anyone who can juggle as many balls in the air at one time as you can." Leaning across the console, he kissed her, softly at first, then with more fervor. He drew back and ran a thumb over her lips. "Bad idea to start this. Joe's waiting at the station, but after what those yahoos did to your tires, I'm checking out your house."

Annie almost accused him of always kissing

and running, but the truth was that they both had things to do. She got out of his car feeling exhausted.

Her house was fine. Sky stole a last kiss when she walked him to the door. "Wait," he said, wrapping a strand of her hair around one finger. "How are you getting to Aaron's meeting? Morrissey has your truck." He frowned. "I can't promise to take you, until I get a time for our perps' bail hearing."

"I'll call a cab. Do you think they'll get bail?"

"The Stingers always have lawyers on tap, so they might. Don't worry, one of us is going to tail them—see if we can figure out who they report to." He paused. "I know I didn't believe in what you were doing at first, but thanks to you, Annie, we're whittling away at the gang."

"I guess it's good that they're cowards, not killers, the way they homed in on me."

"The fact that they sent their rank and file tonight instead of coercing Briar Run kids tells me two things. They're losing their grip here, and they don't like it."

"Davena was great tonight, wasn't she? If we had more mama bears like her, the Stingers would already be history. Hey, I hate to rush you, but I have to call Peggy Gilroy before she goes to bed. I need her to organize a paint brigade to deal with the graffiti."

"I'll be in touch." Sky brushed another kiss on her lips, then clattered down her steps.

She locked up feeling invigorated—feeling like Gran's dream would happen. Was already happening.

Flipping open her phone, she called Peggy, who wasn't happy about missing the excitement.

"Davena contacted the people who live closest to her street, Peggy. She and the others captured two Stingers, thanks to your phone tree. Don't worry, I'll get to the site tomorrow as soon as I can." Annie hung up, shaking her head, hoping she'd be as feisty at Peggy's age. But she didn't have time to worry about that right now; she had to bone up on the facts and figures Loomis wanted her to present in the morning.

SKY SHOWED UP unexpectedly the next day, just as Annie accessed the app on her smartphone to find a number for a local cab.

"The bail hearing isn't until eleven," Sky said, his right arm resting on her door casing. "Morrissey contacted me. He put four new tires on your pickup. I'll give you a lift to his shop and then you'll have your own wheels for the day."

"Great." She smiled. "What would I do without you looking out for me?"

He cocked his head. "Do you think you could get used to having me look out for you on a permanent basis?"

Annie froze in the middle of locking her house. "Didn't you want to get out of Briar Run as fast as possible?"

He let her finish locking up, then pulled her against him. "Yesterday, I told you no—and I meant it. You've gotten under my skin, Annie. Zack's crazy about you, too. You're good for both of us." He paused. "Are we good for you?"

She studied his features, and traced a finger over a laugh line bracketing his mouth. "Yes. Yes, you are. But I'm going to be late for a very important meeting, so your timing stinks. Can we talk later?"

He grinned and swept her down the steps and into his car. "No rush. No rush. We have plenty of time."

His unconventional approach to deepening their relationship shook her. Acting totally blasé, he dropped her off at the repair shop and drove on to work. He and Zack were on a path her heart had been traveling for weeks, and it felt right. But...

It took her less than half an hour to retrieve

her pickup and drive to the municipal offices, where she had trouble finding a parking space. Even then, once she stepped inside, she was stunned to see so many people. A few, like Roger, Charlie, Davena and Homer Gonzales, Annie knew. Others she'd heard of, like Lucy Portallis, once the glove factory accountant.

The minute Loomis caught sight of Annie, he called the meeting to order. His enthusiasm for reopening the factory as a worker-owned co-op stoked the excitement of everyone there. He'd obviously met with Lucy in advance, because she passed around a prospectus on proposed salaries, expected earnings and what was needed in individual investment.

Roger asked the first question. "All of this sounds fantastic, Lucy, but none of us have money for the initial investment to buy back the factory."

Loomis turned to Annie, and soon all eyes were pinned on her. She cleared her throat. "Since it was my bright idea, it seems fair that I invest in all of you."

"You already have," Homer said. "You kicked in plenty of cash to paint our houses. And the home renovations is something we all want to continue."

Davena spoke up. "Sadie Talmage told me

you bought the building to house the teen center, and you've agreed to furnish it and hire staff. Did you win a lottery in California?"

Annie took a deep breath. Time for the truth. "What I've done and anything I do going forward was made possible by my grandmother. Many of you knew Ida Vance as a woman with a generous heart. No one knew how generous. She left a trust. Through me, the town and people she loved are the beneficiaries. The projects I've tackled fulfill her last wishes for the neighborhood. I couldn't have accomplished any of it without your help, though."

The room was silent for a long moment. Annie hadn't seen Sky come in. He stepped up behind her, and set his hands possessively on her waist. "I hope I don't have to impress on all of you the need to remain quiet about the extent of Annie's financial involvement. No chatter in the café. No newspaper article lauding her—or not as long as we're still battling a criminal element focused on her. If you blab, it could place her in more danger. I have personal reasons for wanting to keep her safe." He smiled down at her, then glanced up again, saying, "But your reasons should be as obvious."

The grins everyone shared as they clustered around the pair turned into hugs interspersed with cheers. There was a general air of exhilaration at the town's new prospects, but the crowd's delight seemed to be as much for the fact that she and Sky were a couple now. Annie had difficulty breaking away. "Until the factory opens, we still have houses to paint. And our chief's home is scheduled for painting this week."

That prompted more questions. Someone called, "Are you getting married soon? Will you live in the chief's house or the one Annie inherited from Gran Ida?"

Sky smiled but ducked out without answering. Feeling her face heat, Annie stammered, "We've, uh, barely been on a date. We haven't discussed marriage. Sky has criminals to catch and I have plenty of homes to paint, plus I want to restore the park."

"And you've got a teen center to open," someone shouted.

Pulled aside by Loomis and Lucy Portallis, Annie listened to a suggestion to have workers pay into a fund that would eventually replace her seed money.

"I trust you two to figure out the start-up costs, and I'll give you a check." They left it at that, and Annie rushed out, expecting that Sky would be waiting to clarify their status. He was gone.

TWO DAYS PASSED, and except for a single gar-
bled message on Annie's cell phone saying he
was up to his eyeballs in work, Sky seemed to
fall off the face of the earth. At least, her earth.

One thing had changed. After the meeting
that established her as their golden goose and
underscored her as the primary target of the
Stingers, everyone else coddled her. It was as
if they were all suddenly afraid for her.

At her wits' end with having paint buckets
and ladders yanked out of her hands, escorts
following her around and being cautioned to be
careful for the thousandth time, Annie lost her
temper. "Look, I'm the same woman who drove
to Louisville for paint by myself and toted it all
the way here. I know you're well meaning, but
I feel smothered."

"She's right." Peggy Gilroy stepped up beside
Annie. "I watched her dig in her heels even after
the Stingers shot at her and ruined her paint
job with graffiti. The gang lost her one paint
supplier and she found another. Chief Cordova
thinks she's competent enough to be left to her
own devices. We should do the same."

Davena clapped her hands and shooed everyone back to work. Left with Peggy and Davena,
two of her staunchest allies, Annie muttered,
"I hate to sound like Pitiful Pearl, but where

is Sky? I wish he didn't think I was quite so competent. He implies that we're romantically, ah...you know, entangled." Annie remembered their conversation on this very subject. "Then he doesn't call or show up for *days?*"

Peggy chuckled. "Three days. And men don't think the way women do about romance."

Nodding, Davena agreed. "I heard from Margie Dumas, the night dispatcher, that the chief and Koot Talmage were called as expert witnesses for a couple of the gang members' trials. Oh, she said it's all hush-hush, 'cause those dudes got off before. This time they're going down. Nina said the moms who were losing their kids to the Stingers say the big leaders are pulling out altogether. The cops will get the credit, but we know it's all due to you, Annie."

Annie shrugged off the compliment. "So, you think the gang's really over?" She felt almost giddy with relief. "Sky and his force do deserve credit, Davena. Koot could've retired, and Sky could've gone to another job, leaving our neighborhood to the Stingers. They didn't."

"You're too modest," Davena said. "Deshawn told me how you stuck up for him when the chief would have charged him with a crime. Just the prospect of the teen center freed Chantal and her friends. I know you had a sign made to name it the Ida Vance Teen Center, but all the kids refer to it as Annie's Place. And they call Briar Run Annie's Neighborhood. We all do," she added.

"If your grandmother's looking down, she'd second that," Peggy said.

Annie held up a hand. "It's my neighborhood. I have a long way to go before it'll meet *my* approval. Once the factory reopens I'll lose my paint crew, so we need to paint faster. And tomorrow, whether or not Sky puts in an appearance, we'll start painting his house."

CHAPTER FOURTEEN

THEY WERE ALMOST set up to begin painting when Sky drove in, again with Zack. Sky carried a pink potted rose in full bloom. He walked straight up and presented it to Annie. "Zack helped me pick it out. It's called Bella Rosa, beautiful rose. That's how Zack and I see you, Annie." Leaning over the plant, he kissed her. "Sorry I've been AWOL, but I have news. The guys who shot out your window and one who slashed your tires are heading off to Kentucky State Penitentiary. And for all intents and purposes, the Stingers have folded."

"So I heard through the gossip mill. Is this rose for my house or yours?" Annie asked.

"Mine's still listed to sell. My Realtor has had some interest in it, I'm told. From an Argentine cowhide broker Aaron's apparently working with."

Annie gave a start. "So, you're still moving to a safer town?"

Sky looked confused. "This town *is* safe now.

And, uh, don't we have a...sort of understanding? I bought the rosebush for the park. For a garden like the one you said your grandmother tended."

"Oh, Sky, you make it hard to be mad at you." Annie inhaled the sweet scent, and everyone standing around relaxed. "Thanks. And, Zack, this is a wonderful gift."

"We love you, Annie," Zack piped up. "I brung my cover-up. Can I paint now?"

Annie smiled. "Would you like to paint the siding gold, or paint the porch railing blue?" she asked the boy.

"What's siding?"

"Those are the long boards on the house itself," Sky said as he helped Zack on with his painter's apron. "We'll do siding," he told Annie.

She set the rosebush in some shade, and returned to hear Zack say, "I wanna go up a ladder to paint like Annie."

In unison Annie and Sky said, "No!" Sky added, "Ladders are for adults only."

Leaving Sky to deal with his pouting child, Annie poured gold paint into a smaller cardboard carton, then set the main bucket beside it. She broke out new brushes and rollers and gave them to Sky. "Zack, you and your dad can paint next to each other, here at the front of the house.

You do the low boards while your dad paints the higher ones, okay? It'll be a huge help. When you use up all the paint in your bucket, your dad will give you more from his."

"Okay." Zachary took one brush from his dad. "Where are you going to paint, Annie?"

She hesitated. "Around the portholes."

Zack and Sky both glanced up to the top of the house. Sky frowned, so Annie scuttled away and clipped her half-full can to a ring on her belt.

Davena's friend Tanya Hall had rap blaring from an iPod as usual, giving the paint party a festive air. Annie climbed down once and moved her ladder to the right of a slightly shorter one on which Charlie Fitzgerald stood painting the midsection of the house. She noted that everyone was making good progress. A while later, Roger McBride announced that it was time for lunch. He loved to eat and always kept them on track for the noon meal.

"I don't have much to finish up here, Roger," Annie called. "I'll go for burgers when I'm done. Call an order in to Loretta, will you?"

"Sure, but I'll go pick it up."

Annie shot him a thumbs-up. "I'll pay you later."

Roger left. Soon after that, Sky stood below

Annie, squinting up at her. "There's a multiple car crash at the intersection of Mary Rose and Lavender," he shouted. "I'm closer than Teddy, who'd have to come from home. Koot needs help. Is it okay if Zack stays here and paints?"

Annie caught only some of what Sky said, but recognized the urgency in his voice. She nodded.

Watching Sky tear out in the cruiser, she hollered down to Rita Gonzales. "Rita, Sky's son is painting on the other side of the porch. I'll be done here in a jiffy. Keep an eye on him, will you?"

Rita, moving her body to the music, smiled and waved to Annie. The sun had shifted, and Annie saw two spots needing a second coat. She stretched as far as she could to touch up the areas. Feeling her ladder slip, she decided that what she'd done would suffice. As she stepped down a rung, her bucket caught and pulled her off balance. The ladder slid again. Standing completely still, she hailed the man below her on a shorter ladder. "Charlie, my bucket's caught on my ladder. If I unclip it, can I pass it to you before I climb down?"

Not getting an answer, she twisted around to find him. Her blood chilled. Charlie had abandoned his ladder. Zack was climbing up, trying to hold on to his brush and the small cardboard bucket.

"Zack, honey, don't climb any higher." Annie strove to sound calm when she wasn't. "Stay right there. I'll come and meet you and we'll climb down together."

"I want to paint where Charlie stopped," Zack said, and he crawled up two more rungs. Then he glanced down and must have seen how high off the ground he was. He started to cry.

She yanked on her stuck bucket, yelling now. "Someone! Anyone, please come help Zack." No response. Had they all gone to meet Roger, who'd returned with lunch? No one came. Giving her bucket a sharp wrench to free it, Annie felt her ladder give way, too. She crashed into Zack's and both of them and their ladders plummeted to the ground.

Annie couldn't stop her scream as she hurtled downward. Amid raining gold paint, she felt her leg slam against one of the cement porch steps. Her ankle took the brunt of the blow. Untangling herself from the ladder, needing to reach Zack, who lay there motionless, she saw others finally running toward them. "Call Sky," she panted. "Don't move Zack. Call an ambulance, or paramedics." Forgetting her injury, she scrambled toward Zack. Excruciating pain shot up her leg and the scene around her turned gray, then black.

When she came to, a paramedic she vaguely recalled from the night Sadie was shot was taking her pulse. "Zack," she said feebly. "How is Zack?"

Sky whirled around, his face dark with fury. "He probably has a concussion, or maybe a skull fracture," he shouted. "What were you thinking, Annie, letting him climb that ladder? I trusted you. I trusted you with my son. And you...and you..." He didn't finish his sentence, because a medic said that if he didn't hop aboard the aid car they'd go to the hospital without him.

The man working on Annie moved her foot a fraction, and her view of people hovering around got lost in a fog of pain. She had no idea how much time had passed when she surfaced again. Her sight remained fuzzy, but she was cognizant enough by then to realize she was in an aid car. A man spoke into her ear. "The E.R. doc said I could administer something for the pain, Ms. Emerson, but I need to know if you're allergic to anything."

Annie licked her lips. "Is Zachary all right?"

"It's you I'm worried about. You're gritting your teeth. I can alleviate your pain."

"I don't want anything. Is my ankle broken?"

"They'll x-ray it at the hospital," he said.

"It was a stupid, senseless accident."

"Most are," he murmured, taking her pulse again. "Let's look in your eyes. Did you hit your head?"

"No, only my leg."

The driver had pulled under the hospital portico and someone flung open the back doors. The paramedics couldn't help jarring her as they slid the gurney out and that had her fading again. She kept trying to find out about Zack, but the doctor prodded and poked her ankle and ordered her sent to X-ray. It was when the transporters left her alone in a hallway outside the X-ray room that she had another encounter she could have done without.

Sky's ex-wife burst out of a door marked Stairway. Spotting Annie, she shrieked, "You!" Annie was sure she said it with all the drama possible. "You ruined our vacation by letting my son fall off a ladder! It's your fault! You should have never let him climb it."

"How is Zack?" Annie's mouth felt dry and her tongue thick.

"You should ask! At least now Sky sees how irresponsible you are. He'll never let you near our son again." The blonde looked around. "There are no coffee machines here. I obviously exited on the wrong floor." She yanked open the same door and let it bang shut behind her. Even Annie's pain couldn't carry her away from self-recrimination. The accident *was* her fault. And it was her own fault that she'd lost something so right and good. Slowly, over time, love for Sky and Zack had sneaked into her heart. They were the family she wanted, but now could never have. Gran Ida used to say all things happened for a reason. It was true, or else why had Sky's ex stepped out on the wrong floor? Life all came down to fate.

When a tech came to wheel her into X-ray, Annie knew what she had to do.

HER ANKLE WASN'T broken, it turned out, but she had torn ligaments. "I'm going to truss you up almost as if it was a break," the doctor said. "It's a serious injury, Ms. Emerson. Don't bear weight on it for at least two weeks. If you don't have crutches, get a pair. No driving. I want you on pain meds."

"Please, before I go, will someone tell me how Zack Cordova is? A ladder I was on slipped and I caused him to fall several feet to the ground."

The doctor murmured a few noncommittal words as he breezed out of the room, but a nurse took pity on Annie. "I shouldn't share information about one patient with another, but you've been asking about him since you came in. Kids are resilient. He didn't break anything. He has a bruise on his head and a slight concussion. No skull fracture. I know you asked about that."

Annie felt only slightly relieved. Zack shouldn't have been on that ladder. And here she faced another dilemma. She wasn't sure how she'd get home. She could take a cab or call someone.... Weighing her options, she phoned Sadie Talmage. "Sadie...it's Annie. You heard about the accident at Sky's house? I'm in the E.R. I have a huge favor to ask. I need crutches and a ride home. You can say no if helping me will cause a rift between Koot and Sky."

"Why would it?"

"Sky is furious with me and he has every right. I failed to watch out for Zack."

"Don't you be fretting, Annie. Even carefully watched kids get hurt. With three of my own who all played sports, we have adjustable crutches. I'm at the teen center, but I'll have my daughter bring a set to the hospital. You hang tough, I'll be there ASAP."

And she was, or so it seemed to Annie, who'd been given a shot that made her drift in and out of sleep.

"Well, you don't look like you'll be swinging

from ladders any time soon," Sadie said cheerfully after she'd adjusted the crutches and had Annie test them.

"No, and maybe never again. Oh, Sadie, I ruined everything with Sky."

"He'll get over it. He hasn't had Zack often enough to know that curious boys can find trouble even if you're standing right next to them."

As they exited the hospital, Annie was glad Sadie had left her car in the patient loading zone. Using crutches wasn't easy.

Sadie helped Annie in, then pulled onto the street. "You're going to have to direct all of your projects from home for a while. One of the men can haul the paint and supplies. You've done enough business at the hardware store in Louisville that they should allow you a revolving account."

"If Sky and his ex don't sue me over this and wipe out Gran's fund, I'm going to hire Peggy Gilroy to oversee the painting. Aaron is heading up the factory co-op. You're handling the teen center, so everything's under control. I'm… going back to California, Sadie."

"What?" Sadie nearly ran off the road.

Annie nodded tiredly. "Sky accused me of not being trustworthy when he counted on me to watch Zack. It's true. I pressured myself to do more, faster. I hurt people I love. Your injury, Zack's, mine—it all proves that I'm a social worker, not a miracle worker. I let my plans get out of hand."

"No, you didn't. Like I said, Sky will get over it. He knows Briar Run is coming back to life because of you. And the Stingers left because of you."

"Sky's son is the most important thing in the world to him, which is as it should be. Through my negligence he could have lost Zack. Nothing is worth that."

"Sky bears some of the blame. Koot could have waited for Teddy."

Annie wasn't listening. Her mind was made up.

A LITTLE OVER a week after the incident, Sky called Koot into his office as soon as his lieutenant walked in. "Trouble?" Koot asked.

"What? Oh, no. Can you cover my shift tomorrow? Zack's been at their vacation cabin all week. He's scheduled for another X-ray tomorrow. Corrine's in a bind and can't bring him to town. Archibald took a horse to Sarasota to race, and Corrine forgot that his daughters promised their friends a sleepover at the cabin. She asked if I could pick Zack up tonight and take him for his X-ray tomorrow. She'll meet me at the farm in the evening when she brings the girls back. I so seldom get Zack overnight I jumped at the chance. Uh…things are going better with Corrine."

"I'll cover for you if you don't tell Sadie. She and half the town are mad at you for the way you're treating Annie."

"Annie let me down. Zack paid the price for her obsession with all of her renovations," Sky said stubbornly.

"It was an accident, bro. Annie was hurt, too. Should Charlie have laid his ladder down when he stopped painting? Yeah. Should Rita have quit bebopping to Jay-Z and listened to Annie, who asked her to watch Zack for a minute? Double yeah. But it's not Annie's fault her paint bucket got caught, or her ladder fell against the one you both told Zack not to climb."

"I don't need lectures from you, *bro*. Annie's injury hasn't slowed her down. She's still going on with all her pet projects. So, can you cover for me or not?"

"Yeah, yeah, I'll cover. Sadie and I thought you two were falling in love. We thought you'd both met your soul mates."

"I thought so, too," Sky said, glancing away. "Annie didn't care enough about us."

That ended the men's conversation, but Sky worried about a rift developing between him and Koot, and between him and Annie's supporters. With a sale now pending on his house, he wondered again about leaving Briar Run. It was a shock to realize he didn't want to go. But did anyone want him to stay? Everyone had sided with Annie—and darn it all, no one else knew how much he missed her.

WELL, ONE PERSON hadn't sided with Annie. When Sky arrived to get Zack, Corrine followed him to the car, and as he put the boy's overnight bag in the trunk, she said, "Zack keeps asking about that Annie person. I told him she's why he had to stay in the house instead of playing outside with the girls. I don't want Zack around her, Skylar. She's not still working on your house, is she? I know you may have a buyer, but—"

"Annie's crew finished my house," Sky snapped. "She was injured, too, Corrine. She hired a commercial painting firm out of Louisville to take over, I guess until she recovers. Although she'll probably need them to stay on after the glove factory reopens."

Corrine sniffed. "I read in the paper how she supposedly arranged that. The TV news made her look like a saint. We should tell the reporters that we know better."

Sky knew the news had broken once the Stingers disbanded. "Stay out of Annie's business, Corrine. She's done a lot for this town. And Zack's doing okay. There's no reason to wish Annie ill."

"Huh! You see to it my son doesn't get within a mile of her."

"You seem to be forgetting again that he's *my* son, too." Disliking the turn their conversation had taken—especially since relations with his ex had been better—Sky told her when he'd return Zack to the farm, then jumped in his car and roared off.

"Daddy, I want to see Annie."

Sky frowned at his son in the rearview mirror. "Did you hear your mom and me discussing Annie?"

Zack nodded. "Mama says Annie hurt me, but she didn't. Annie was gonna come help me get down the ladder. I climbed it after you said I shouldn't. Annie said I shouldn't, too. Annie's ladder fell. It was an *accident,* Daddy."

"Maybe so, but we're not seeing her. Hey, my house is all painted. I didn't hang your birdhouse yet. We can hang it together." That would distract Zack, and he could take it down when he sold the house.

"I want Annie to help," Zack insisted. "She bought it for me."

"Zack, we're going to have an uncomfortable visit if you keep asking to see Annie."

Sky noticed Zack had fallen silent. Another glance showed his son's jaw stubbornly set. It jarred Sky to be viewing a mini version of himself. But Zack didn't bring up Annie's name again.

THE NEXT MORNING Annie's paint crew set up across the street, and Zack climbed on a chair to watch. "I don't see Annie. Where is she? If she's painting over there, she can come help us hang my birdhouse."

"Zack, don't climb on that chair. I don't want you to fall again."

The boy jumped down. "I'm going over and ask Miz Gilroy where Annie is." Before Sky could grab him, Zack dashed out the door. Sky chased him across the street and felt a headache brewing when he saw Zack deep in conversation with Peggy Gilroy. She was gesturing and pointing down the street. Peggy was holding Annie's notebook, and Sky's stomach tumbled.

"I'm sorry Zack is bothering you," he said, finding his voice.

"He's not. It's good to see him looking chipper."

"Yes, well, he has another X-ray today to be sure the concussion is behind him."

"Annie got her ankle wrap off yesterday, but she still can't bear weight on it. She's packing all the same."

"Packing?" Zack and Sky spoke together.

"You didn't know she's moving back to L.A.? She's still footing the bills to beautify Briar Run, and I'm doing her job organizing the paint crews. Because *someone* stomped on her heart," Peggy said pointedly.

"Who?" Zack asked, all wide-eyed innocence.

Sky gripped his son's shoulder, turned him and crossed the street. Inside again, Zack kept pestering him to visit Annie, until Sky felt his frustration build. His frustration and his guilt. Peggy had planted that guilt, and Sky had always resented the feeling, even when he knew he was wrong.

"I'm going to take a shower," he said. "You watch TV. We'll have lunch out before your appointment."

"We haven't hanged my birdhouse."

"Hung, and we'll have time after your appointment."

"We gonna do it with Annie?"

Sky blew out a tense breath. "Just you and me." He stalked into the bathroom, and when he emerged fifteen minutes later, he felt a little better. "Zack, how about if we go to the café? You like their grilled cheese sandwiches." He got no response over the blaring TV. Assuming Zack was engrossed, Sky went into the living room. Zack wasn't there. Nor was he in the kitchen, or his bedroom or anywhere upstairs.

Frantic, Sky raced outside. That was when he noticed that the birdhouse no longer sat on the porch. His heart pounded like a jackhammer as he ran to the tree, terrified he'd find Zack trying to climb it. His fear only grew more intense because Zack wasn't there or anywhere in the yard.

Sky charged across the street. "Peggy, have you seen Zack?" Sky tried to keep the anxiety out of his voice.

"Not since he left here with you. Is he missing?" She set down her paintbrush.

"Yes." Overwrought, Sky spun one way, then the other. He raked a hand through his hair. "I left him watching TV while I showered. He's gone and so is his birdhouse."

"Kids get away fast, even when you think you know what they're doing. Oh, before you caught up to him earlier, he asked me where Annie lives. I didn't give him directions, but I said a couple of blocks over on Rose Arbor. Would he try to find her, even though you and Annie are on the outs?"

"Possibly." Sky tugged at his ear. "Thanks," he called back, dodging a car and digging out his keys as he ran to his cruiser. Peggy's words about how quickly a child could get away from an adult rang in Sky's head as he tried to keep to the residential speed limit, his whole body bathed in sweat. Joy rose up to clog his throat when he spotted Zack trudging across the intersection at Wild Rose and Rose Arbor. Sky would never have believed his five-year-old son could walk so far lugging a birdhouse.

He honked three times to get Zack's attention, and stabbed a finger toward the curb. He knew by the slump of Zack's shoulders that he felt trapped, which made Sky queasy. He loved his son with all his being. Didn't Zachary know that? Out of nowhere, it dawned on Sky, *He felt the same about Annie*. He couldn't let her leave town. He wanted her in his life—in their lives, he thought as he pulled up next to Zack.

Squealing to a stop, Sky jumped out. His son

stared at him, eyes narrowed as he squinted into the sun. His body language was something Sky understood. "I guess you're on your way to see Annie," he said.

The boy bobbed his head.

"Climb in. I'll take you."

"For real?"

"One thing you can always count on, Zack, I will never lie to you."

"But I love Annie, and you don't like her anymore."

"That's not true. I didn't think I did, but I do...lo-love her." Sky set the birdhouse next to Zack's booster. The way Sky's heart ached each time Annie's name surfaced told him all too clearly how wrongheaded he'd been. "I asked her to watch you and I felt she let me down, Zack. You have no idea how afraid I was, seeing you lying so still at the foot of that ladder."

"I 'splained what happened."

"I know, and I believe you. We have a couple of hours until your appointment. Maybe it's enough time for me to set things straight with Annie."

"You gotta 'pologize," Zack said earnestly, meeting his dad's eyes in the mirror.

"I will," Sky promised, and within minutes he'd stopped in her driveway.

ANNIE TOOK SOME time to answer the repeated knocking at her door. She balanced on crutches, aware that her face registered shock as she scrutinized her visitors through the wrought iron of her security door.

"I've come to apologize," Sky said without hesitation. "I was wrong to blame you for an accident."

Annie averted her eyes. "You were right to blame me. I'm going back to L.A."

"You can't go," Zack cried. "Me'n Daddy love you. He knows my hurt head wasn't your fault. I want us to be 'nother family, like Mama has Papa Archibald and his girls. Please."

Annie blinked away tears as she studied Zack. They dribbled down her face when her eyes met Sky's, so blue and steady. "I want to believe you," she whispered.

He made a fist with his right hand and tapped his heart. "It's true. You can't go. Please…forgive me. A while ago, I—I lost Zack. He…just vanished and I couldn't find him. I saw how easy it was to lose track of him. He…decided to walk here to ask for your help hanging his birdhouse. He could have been kidnapped or hit by a car on my watch, Annie."

"You have to know I would never have let him climb that ladder, Sky."

"I do. I hurt you and I'm sorry. You saved this town, and I'm so proud of you."

"But…I heard that you accepted an offer to sell your house."

"I'll rent until we settle…us. Annie, you can't let strangers finish what you started—finish our neighborhood. No one can do your plan justice but you. Stay, please, for me. Will you stay if I help you restore the park…so that next spring when the roses bloom, it'll be the perfect spot for a wedding? Our wedding…"

Annie saw remorse conflict with the love in his eyes. Love won. Fumbling amid her tears, she unlatched security door. Sky swept her into his arms and she dropped her crutches. The locks she'd clamped around her heart sprang open.

All her doubts disappeared by the time Sky boosted Zack into his arms and they all made a pact never to let any barriers come between them again.

EPILOGUE

SPRING ARRIVED IN Briar Run after a fall and winter punctuated by hard work. Young couples had begun to settle once again in a town filled with colorful homes. The newly restored park, with rosebushes ready to bloom, was another attraction, as were the teen center and, of course, the revitalized economy.

"Zack loves first grade," Sky said, slipping his arm around Annie's waist as they toured the park. "I miss having him during the week when school's in session, but I'm relieved that Corrine and I finally reached an equitable custody agreement."

"I'm glad, too. Glad Archibald figured out their lawyer was keeping Corrine stirred up so he could earn more money. Archibald is actually a pretty decent guy. Life's better for all of us." Annie leaned her head against Sky's shoulder as she paused to study the lifelike resin statue of her grandmother kneeling in a flower bed, one gloved hand holding a trowel. "How can I ever thank you enough for commissioning this likeness of Gran Ida? It brings me so much joy," Annie said.

As they admired the statue, a bird came and perched on Gran's shoulder and warbled a happy tune. Annie blinked back unbidden tears.

Gathering her close, Sky kissed them away. "I'm sorry she isn't here to see the park in all its glory," he murmured against Annie's sun-warmed hair.

"Don't mind me, Sky. These are happy tears. I feel Gran's presence every time I come here. You know, meeting your folks, and then you giving me your grandmother's engagement ring, was so special. But no gift will ever top the way you surprised me with this statue. It means my grandmother will attend our wedding this weekend."

"Are you nervous about the wedding? I remember Sadie saying you told her that you doubted you'd ever get married."

"Well, that was before you asked me. Before you and Zack filled my heart with love and I finally realized I have the capacity to love you back."

He kissed her lips and they both smiled through the kiss as a sparrow landed on one of Zack's hand-painted birdhouses. It was with reluctance that Sky finally lifted his head and leaned away. "Is everything ready for our important day? Aren't weddings usually frantic this close to countdown? At least it was when Corrine and I..." His voice faded away.

"If we were responsible for all the arrangements, I suppose it would be. With our friends in charge, all we had to do was supply a list of people to invite. Oh...and show up."

"Thank you again for agreeing to invite Archibald and Corrine and his girls."

"How could we not when Zack loves them?"

"I told Corrine not to buy him a suit—that it's casual."

"The invitations make that plain. I've lost count of how many times I told Davena and Sadie that I do *not* want them making me a frilly white dress."

Sky chuckled and they left the park hand in hand.

SATURDAY THE PARK teemed with people and laughter, and tables groaned with food. Residents who hadn't seen the restored park exclaimed over the statue and the roses, now a riot of color. Practically everybody who lived in Briar Run was there, including the Spurlocks with their new baby daughter, and Sky's parents, and two of Annie's former coworkers from L.A. Aaron Loomis came, too, even though his tenure at City Manager was at an end. Briar Run was on solid financial ground now, and the residents had been able to elect a mayor and town council to govern them again.

All at once the *Wedding March* rang out from speakers hidden among the roses. Talk stopped. People turned toward the park entrance.

The minister who had given the eulogy at Gran Ida's funeral went to stand in front of a gurgling fountain. He was joined by Sky, who beckoned to Zack. In black jeans and a light blue shirt, the boy was a carbon copy of his dad. "Where's Annie?" Zack whispered loudly.

A murmur rose from the crowd, and she appeared on the flagstone walkway on the arm of Koot Talmage, who was clearly bursting with pride.

"Oh, Annie's beautiful," Zachary exclaimed for all to hear.

His dad echoed a hushed, "She is, isn't she, son?" Words drowned out by a chorus of oohs and ahhs soared above the music as Annie slowly passed by.

Sky was suddenly deaf and blind to everything in the park except his soon-to-be bride. She floated toward him in her knee-length sundress made of simple white eyelet that fell over a pink lining made to match the baby roses twined in her hair. The roses were duplicated in a nosegay she carried in one trembling hand.

It was her smile that drew Sky. A smile that reached shining eyes, gazing at him with love. Love that humbled him, and he said so as he took her hand, and spoke the vows that bound them together as a family.

* * * * *

REQUEST YOUR FREE BOOKS!
2 FREE WHOLESOME ROMANCE NOVELS
IN LARGER PRINT
PLUS 2
FREE
MYSTERY GIFTS

✱✱✱✱✱✱✱✱✱✱✱✱✱✱✱✱✱✱✱✱✱✱✱✱

HEARTWARMING™

✱✱✱✱✱✱✱✱✱✱✱✱✱✱✱✱✱✱✱✱✱✱✱✱

Wholesome, tender romances

YES! Please send me 2 FREE Harlequin® Heartwarming Larger-Print novels and my 2 FREE mystery gifts (gifts worth about $10). After receiving them, if I don't wish to receive any more books, I can return the shipping statement marked "cancel." If I don't cancel, I will receive 4 brand-new larger-print novels every month and be billed just $4.99 per book in the U.S. or $5.74 per book in Canada. That's a savings of at least 23% off the cover price. It's quite a bargain! Shipping and handling is just 50¢ per book in the U.S. and 75¢ per book in Canada.* I understand that accepting the 2 free books and gifts places me under no obligation to buy anything. I can always return a shipment and cancel at any time. Even if I never buy another book, the two free books and gifts are mine to keep forever.

161/361 IDN F47N

Name _____ (PLEASE PRINT)

Address _____ Apt. #

City _____ State/Prov. _____ Zip/Postal Code

Signature (if under 18, a parent or guardian must sign)

Mail to the **Harlequin®** Reader Service:
IN U.S.A.: P.O. Box 1867, Buffalo, NY 14240-1867
IN CANADA: P.O. Box 609, Fort Erie, Ontario L2A 5X3

* Terms and prices subject to change without notice. Prices do not include applicable taxes. Sales tax applicable in N.Y. Canadian residents will be charged applicable taxes. Offer not valid in Quebec. This offer is limited to one order per household. Not valid for current subscribers to Harlequin Heartwarming larger-print books. All orders subject to credit approval. Credit or debit balances in a customer's account(s) may be offset by any other outstanding balance owed by or to the customer. Please allow 4 to 6 weeks for delivery. Offer available while quantities last.

Your Privacy—The Harlequin® Reader Service is committed to protecting your privacy. Our Privacy Policy is available online at www.ReaderService.com or upon request from the Harlequin Reader Service.

We make a portion of our mailing list available to reputable third parties that offer products we believe may interest you. If you prefer that we not exchange your name with third parties, or if you wish to clarify or modify your communication preferences, please visit us at www.ReaderService.com/consumerschoice or write to us at Harlequin Reader Service Preference Service, P.O. Box 9062, Buffalo, NY 14269. Include your complete name and address.

HWDIR13R

ReaderService.com

Manage your account online!
- Review your order history
- Manage your payments
- Update your address

*We've designed
the Harlequin® Reader Service
website just for you.*

Enjoy all the features!
- Reader excerpts from any series
- Respond to mailings and
  special monthly offers
- Discover new series available to you
- Browse the Bonus Bucks catalog
- Share your feedback

Visit us at:
ReaderService.com